## Her Hands Loosened from Their White-Knuckle Grip of His Shirt

Then, without thought to the consequences of her actions, Constance allowed them to slip beneath the hem of Gideon's shirt.

He sucked in a quick breath as she encountered the hardness of his stomach, the moist summer heat of his skin. Bit by bit, she allowed her fingertips to fan out so that she could explore further. His ribs, his back, his spine, then his chest again. His nipples.

"You don't know what you're doing, Constance," he whispered hoarsely, and she smiled, a slow, rich smile that made her feel beautiful and powerful.

"I think I do."

"You can't possibly want me to—"

"But I do, Gideon. I'm tired of being good. I want you to show me how to be very, very bad."

Then she was lifting on tiptoes and kissing him, allowing her own mouth the freedom he had displayed on so many occasions. She explored his lips, his cheeks, his jaw. She moved down to his Adam's apple, then dipped lower to nip at his collarbones. Then, when she drew back, she offered him the same look, the same smile Eve must have given Adam when she tempted him with the apple.

"Teach me," she whispered. "Teach me how to be wicked."

## SWEET DECADENCE

"A fast-paced, engrossing read destined to make readers wish there were more in this wonderful trilogy by the very talented Ms. Bingham."

—*Romantic Times*

## THE BENGAL RUBIES

"A delightful read with just the right touch of humor."

—*Romantic Times*

"Lisa Bingham demonstrates her versatile and incredible talent with her usual deft touch. . . . *The Bengal Rubies* is filled with all the necessary ingredients that make for a memorable reading experience."

—*Affaire de Coeur*

## SILKEN PROMISES

"Lisa Bingham at her talented best. . . . Filled with excitement, danger, and passion, *Silken Promises* captures perfectly the spirit of late nineteenth-century America."

—*Affaire de Coeur*

"The marvelously fast-paced, often funny, and yet tender romance is an ideal read for a cozy afternoon when you need to fill your heart with love and laughter."

—*Romantic Times*

## SILKEN DREAMS

"Simply wonderful! Lisa Bingham breathes life into your wildest fantasies."

—*Romantic Times*

"Bravo, Lisa Bingham! A real winner."

—*Rendezvous*

**Books by Lisa Bingham**

Silken Dreams
Eden Creek
Distant Thunder
The Bengal Rubies
Temptation's Kiss
Silken Promises
Sweet Dalliance
Sweet Defiance
Sweet Decadence
Wild Escapade
Wild Serenade
Wild Masquerade

Published by POCKET BOOKS

# LISA BINGHAM

# WILD MASQUERADE

**POCKET BOOKS**
New York   London   Toronto   Sydney

This book is a work of fiction. Names, characters, places and incidents are products of the author's imagination or are used fictitiously. Any resemblance to actual events or locales or persons, living or dead, is entirely coincidental.

An *Original* Publication of POCKET BOOKS

POCKET BOOKS, a division of Simon & Schuster Inc.
1230 Avenue of the Americas, New York, NY 10020

ISBN: 1-4165-0298-X
This Pocket Books paperback printing May 2004

10 9 8 7 6 5 4 3 2 1

POCKET and colophon are registered trademarks of Simon & Schuster Inc.

Cover art by Lina Levy

Printed in the U.S.A.

Dedicated to all those who
have helped me reach my dreams:
Mom, Dad, Nancy, and Elmont.


And especially Wade.

# WILD MASQUERADE

# Prologue

*New York*
*June 25, 1859*

Blackness cloaked the narrow street. A thick, heavy darkness that wafted from the alleys and tenement houses surrounding the elaborate theater district, bringing with it the smells of misery and desperation.

He knew this area well. He'd been born near here—inside one of those grubby buildings, in a two-room flat that smelled of boiled cabbage and decay. It was in that same building that he'd met Maura Kelly.

Dear, sweet heaven above, how he'd loved her. She'd been everything to him—his very reason for living. He had watched her grow, marveling at the manner in which she survived the torment heaped upon her by an alcoholic father and an invalid mother. Together, they had escaped the meanness of the world around them to sneak into the theaters and huddle in the darkness watching the actors rehearse.

He'd known from the beginning that Maura was destined to become one of those performers. Each year she became more talented and stunningly beautiful—and it was no exaggeration to think of Maura in that manner. The term *stunningly beautiful* was a statement of fact.

1

His lips tilted in a wry smile, and he began to walk through the darkened alleyways, his footfalls making barely any sound on the cobbled street. Tunneling his hands into the pockets of his coat, he tried to keep out the dampness caused by a drizzling rain.

Half closing his eyes, he could see Maura standing before him—as she'd been as a little girl, then later as a woman. Maura's features had been regal, almost haughty. Added to that were pale blue eyes and hair the color of gold. With such attributes, she'd been able to gain everything she'd ever longed to have.

Wealth.

Respect.

Adoration.

His steps slowed, then finally halted altogether in the thick shadows of a doorway. From this position, he had a perfect view of the Theatre Royale, the last place Maura had performed.

A sadness clutched his heart with a very real twinge of pain as he remembered how Maura had so quickly become one of the country's most beloved actresses—a position she had sought from the time she'd been thirteen and had taken a job as a seamstress with one of the local theaters. She'd slipped into auditions, worked in choruses, and flattered everyone in her path until she'd gained the attention she sought. She'd scrimped and saved to buy clothing and accessories to augment her prettiness so that someone would notice that she was destined for something far greater.

A tightness gripped his throat, and he fought the unmanly tears. Beautiful. So beautiful. But just when she'd begun to receive the accolades she so richly deserved, she had disappeared.

He wove slightly with the unbearable pain that inundated his body. Steadying himself against the gritty brick wall, he focused on one single thought to drive back the longing.

Maura had promised she would come back.

She'd promised.

Five years had passed, and he'd done his best to remain patient. He'd made a life for himself. No one would ever guess now that he'd once been from one of the poorest sections of New York. Maura would be so proud of him. She would laugh and toast him with her favorite brand of champagne. Then she would take his face in her hands and sweetly kiss him on the lips.

When she returned . . .

Surely, he didn't have much longer to wait.

Straightening, he drew his shoulders into a rigid, militant line.

Maura would be coming for him. He knew she would. So he had best prepare the way for her. Nothing could be left to chance.

Crossing the street, he reached into his pocket, removing the bottle of oil he'd already prepared. After igniting the wick, he calmly punched one of the lower windows with his elbow, then tossed the bottle through the shattered glass. Then, as the bottle broke and the fire began to spread rapidly over the hardwood floors, cotton runners, and heavy draperies, he hurried into the dense trees of the park farther up the block.

"For you, Maura," he whispered into the breeze, his nose already twitching from the scent of smoke. "For you . . ."

# *One*

Constance Pedigrue did not suffer fools gladly—
especially when the fool in question was intent on
delaying her.

Gathering her things, she stood from her seat on the
omnibus, her cheeks growing warm with impatience. She
didn't know why men often thought that women weren't
graced with the ability to use their brains. She'd been
perfectly aware that the driver of the crowded omnibus
had purposely driven a half block past her stop, then
climbed down from his seat to *personally* help her from
the conveyance. He must have thought he was being
overtly obliging—especially since he hadn't bothered
to help any of the previous passengers as they disem-
barked.

Constance offered him a withering stare nonetheless.
The fact that he was treading upon her privacy probably
hadn't occurred to him at all.

What was it about the opposite gender that led them to
press their attentions on females who had given every
indication of wishing to be left alone? What made them
think that any woman—especially one of Constance's
breeding and education—would be flattered by a wink

5

and a smile from some scruffy, ill-kempt, hadn't-seen-a-bath-in-the-better-part-of-a-week laborer?

Making her way through the chaos of skirts and walking sticks made by the other passengers, Constance planned her move carefully. If she tilted her chin just so, she could glare down at the driver in open dismissal, then climb to the ground on her own. There would be no tip for this gentleman—none whatsoever—even though Constance had made it a point to offer a penny to each and every person who had helped her along her ill-fated journey from Boston to New York City.

As she stepped into the doorway, the hot sun flowed over her body, and she was immediately suffused with the smells of dust, heat, and . . .

And this *man*.

Her nose wrinkled in distaste.

"Miss?"

He held out his hand, one covered in a sweat-stained glove.

Constance shuddered, cocking her head to an arrogant angle as she had planned. "Thank you, Mister . . . er . . ."

"Pepys. Just like that English writer."

Constance somehow doubted that this man was even distantly related to Samuel Pepys, but she didn't bother to refute the assumption. The sooner she was out of Mr. Pepys's company, the better.

"Thank you, Mr. Pepys, for your attention," she said, placing the basket in the aisle beside her feet so she could disembark with ease. "It really isn't necessary for you to—"

Her explanation was replaced by an involuntary squeal when the man grasped her waist and physically lifted her from the omnibus.

Horrified, Constance planted her hands against his coat and attempted to pry herself loose, but the man held her soundly. Offering her a wide grin, the driver carried her from the muddy street to the brick walkway on the corner, setting her down with the same delicacy he might offer a sack of potatoes.

Struggling to catch her breath and right her bonnet, Constance barely had the wits about her to gasp, "Mr. Pepys!"

She needn't have bothered. The man leaned close to press a card in her hand.

"Contact me. You won't regret it," he assured her, smiling.

Constance winced when she noted the chewing tobacco stuck to his gums and teeth.

He slogged through the mud to retrieve the basket she'd carried with her all the way from Boston and set it at her feet, offering her a wink as he did so. Then he was loping to the driver's seat and swinging aboard.

Constance swooped the basket into her arms and held it close to her body. "I think we're finally rid of him, Mr. Bentley," she muttered to the tabby cat ensconced inside the vessel.

The cat hissed, as if to add his own opinion on the matter.

To Constance's infinite displeasure, Mr. Pepys paused one last time to tip his hat in her direction. Then, flicking his whip at the double team hooked to the omnibus, he steered the coach into the main thoroughfare, splattering mud in all directions.

Too late, Constance held up an arm to protect her face. Despite her efforts, the gooey mess spotted her cheeks, her hands, and her skirts.

Constance huffed in disbelief. Since leaving Boston, she'd encountered nothing but trouble. What should have been a leisurely three-day journey had taken nearly a month—a month!

*If Papa weren't dead already, I would have thought he'd had a hand in the whole affair.*

The thought raced through her mind so quickly, Constance couldn't squelch it. Immediately, she was inundated with a wave of shame, then a tide of guilt.

How dare she think evil of the dead when her father was the very reason she was about to begin her adventure?

But that didn't change her feelings. She was more sorry that she'd unconsciously breached social etiquette than she was at her father's passing. She was glad the old goat was gone. But she would guard her inner feelings to her dying day so that no one else knew of her parental betrayal.

She spied a bench in front of a small store and sank wearily into its depths, needing a moment to recover from the heat and the pressing timetable she'd been competing with since dawn.

*Oh, Papa.* She inwardly sighed, as if by apologizing to herself she could apologize to him.

But why should *she* apologize? Her father had never loved her or Constance's two younger sisters. He'd rued the day they'd been born female, and, deprived of the sons he'd craved, he'd set out to make his daughters' lives a hell of his own creation.

*Stop it! You shouldn't even think such things.*

But she did. She'd thought them all her life— especially since Constance was the only Pedigrue sister old enough to remember the truth.

Her father had lied to them.

He'd lied to them all.

Constance had been only five at the time, but she clearly remembered the homestead where she and her sisters used to live with a *mother* and a father. Louise Pedigrue had been a beautiful woman, so filled with laughter and fun. But as the years passed and Alexander grew more fanatical about his work as a minister, the joy had dimmed. Louise had grown more careful—and she'd taught her daughters to choose every word and deed with utmost caution.

Even so, there had been times when the Pedigrue women had escaped the tyranny for a picnic in the meadow or playacting in the attic. To this day, Constance could hear her mother's sweet voice interpreting the classic roles of Cassandra, Ophelia, Lady Macbeth.

Sighing, Constance delved into her pocket for a cotton handkerchief and dabbed at the moisture dotting her brow and upper lip.

If only Constance had been more alert to the signs, perhaps she could have prevented what had happened. One evening, she'd awakened from her bed to hear her parents arguing. After tiptoeing to the common room, she'd seen her father strike Louise so hard she'd fallen to the floor. Then, kneeling, Louise had begged for his forgiveness.

Terrified by the scene, Constance had hurried back to her sisters lest she be caught eavesdropping. But she hadn't been able to sleep. Especially when her mother came to their bedroom, held each one of her daughters close, whispering over and over again, "I will do anything to protect you. Anything."

A trickle of moisture plunged down Constance's cheek, and she started in surprise, dashing it away.

Tears? At this late date? Hadn't she told herself often enough that there was no way a five-year-old child could have prevented the succeeding events? Her mother's disappearance the next morning. Her father's insistence that they pack up and leave immediately. His lies about Louise's having found younger, better-behaved children to love.

Only Constance had suspected a deeper, darker explanation that would necessitate the rush. For years, she'd been haunted by the doubts. Had her mother really abandoned them? Or had their father done far worse than slap her? Had he . . . killed her?

Jumping to her feet, Constance pushed the thought to the dark recesses of her soul—as she had already done a thousand times.

The past was in the past, she told herself firmly. Right now, she had the future to contend with—and a new life to begin.

Hefting Mr. Bentley over her arms, she marveled once again at the opportunities she'd been given since Alexander Pedigrue's death. Not only had she been liberated from a man she'd grown to hate, but the stipulations of his will had offered her a new beginning.

*New beginning.*

What a wonderful phrase. Until her father's death, Constance had thought she would spend her life inside the same bleak house generations of Pedigrue women had called their home. But a reading of Alexander's will had disclosed an astonishing twist of events. Her father had not been as poor as they had always believed. He'd been worth millions, having inherited a family fortune.

Her lips twisted. Naturally, her father hadn't seen fit to pass such an inheritance on to his daughters. No, the old coot had wished to test them beyond the grave. Evidently, years of servitude on his behalf weren't enough. Each of his daughters would have to "prove herself" by working a year in a position of his choosing. If they succeeded in their tasks and behaved as proper women should, he would award each of them a yearly stipend of five hundred dollars and permission to live in the Pedigrue home.

Blast his ornery hide, Constance thought as she re-pinned her bonnet. He'd been miserly to the end.

*But that's not quite true.*

Constance grimaced at her conscience's reminder. In one respect, their father actually had been kind. Rather than insisting that his daughters pursue missions in India or lives as caretakers in old-age homes or orphanages, he'd granted each of them a wish come true.

The whole situation still struck Constance as odd—and, indeed, she'd accused her younger sister, Patience, of tampering with the will, since she'd seen a copy of it mere months before Alexander's death. But her sister had denied such a charge. It had been their father who had sent Felicity to the "Wild West" to become a teacher. It had been their father who had allowed Patience to escape Boston as a governess. But more astonishing still, it had been their father who had instructed Constance to journey to New York City to work as a seamstress in a theater.

Would wonders never cease?

Resisting the urge to stretch her cramped muscles, Constance searched for a street sign to help her gain her bearings.

So far, her journey had not been a smooth one. The first train she'd taken had been delayed midway through its journey by a small explosion in the furnace. This had resulted in Constance's missing the rest of her connections.

She'd begun to think the whole trip was cursed—bad weather, broken machinery, misrouted correspondence, and mistakes in the transferring from her father's solicitors had delayed her for weeks.

After arriving in New York, Constance had hoped her luck would improve. But at the railway station, all but one of her trunks had been stolen sometime during their transfer from the baggage car to the claim area. Then the proprietor of the boardinghouse where she'd originally arranged to stay had become far too familiar—going so far as to take her hand and caress the exposed flesh beneath her glove. And now she'd been propositioned by a grimy no-gooder who had splashed her best traveling gown with mud.

Briefly closing her eyes, Constance bit her lip, calling upon the deep reserves of serenity and efficiency that she'd developed over years of caring for a cantankerous father. But the emotions didn't come. Instead, her anger burned brighter. This was the gateway to the nation, after all! Was it always so devoid of decorum?

"Hey, lady, get out of the way!"

Constance looked up in time to see a handcart filled with newspapers barreling her way. Flattening herself against a lamppost, she barely escaped injury.

A sustained yelp came from inside the basket, and the contents shifted.

"It's all right, Mr. Bentley," Constance crooned to the animal inside, but, judging by the resulting growl, the cat had not been reassured.

Knowing it would be best if they both made their way off the crowded walkway, Constance backtracked the extra half block the driver had taken, then glanced up at the crooked street sign bolted to the corner of the building at her left. When the number she found corresponded to the slip of paper she'd tucked inside the wrist of her glove, she nodded in satisfaction. At least that dolt of a driver hadn't taken her too far out of the way.

The thought was enough to remind her that she still held his card. Grimacing, she ripped it into tiny pieces and tossed the remains into a crate of garbage stacked next to the gutter.

"Good riddance," she muttered to herself.

Striding up the sun-dappled lane, Constance brushed ineffectively at the front of her gown. Rather than helping matters, the action merely caused the gooey mess to smear over the black wool, creating an even more noticeable problem.

"Drat and bother," she grumbled to herself. The last thing she wanted was to meet her new employer looking like this. Throughout the journey from Boston, Constance had taken great care of her appearance, knowing that first impressions were incredibly important. On trains, she'd barricaded herself in the leeward side of the car, leaving her window shut despite the heat. On the ferry, she'd remained belowdecks to avoid the salt spray. Even the omnibus had provided a challenge to avoid muddy shoes and satchels.

Only this morning, when she'd been forced to abandon her plans to stay at the boardinghouse, she'd found her way to a nearby hotel and closed herself in the ladies' lounge. There she'd taken a clean cloth and a clothes brush from her carpetbag to repair whatever damages had occurred to her wardrobe until she could see to a proper cleaning. She'd even paused to tidy her hair and fluff the ribbon of her bonnet. But now . . . *now* some dolt named Pepys had splattered her with dirt—and who knew what else—mere inches from her destination.

Constance's mood grew blacker still, and she paused in mid-stride, tugging at the strings of her reticule. After wriggling her fingers in the crocheted bag, she removed a small brass-encased writing tablet and a tiny pencil. She delicately touched the lead point to her tongue and opened the tablet to the spot where a neat list of names had been printed. Beside each entry was a plus or a minus sign, signifying what sort of acknowledgment letter that person should receive for the service rendered. Mr. Quiggly, the baker who had shyly presented her with sticky buns for her journey, had received a minus. Although it had been sweet of him to offer the repast for her trip, it had been highly improper for the widower to do so in such a public place as the main landing. It had been even more improper for him to have tried to kiss her cheek. Nevertheless, because he was an old family friend, he would receive a kind, if firm, thank you note. Then there was the first railway porter who had helped her stow her bags—a plus. He had been efficient and polite. The railroad café—a minus, since the food had been congealed upon its arrival. The railway offices—a minus for their poorly serviced equipment. The shipping line—a minus for their inefficiency. The clerk at the Richardson's Ladies Hotel and Boardinghouse—a definite minus. And the Franklin Omnibus Company . . .

She quickly placed a minus sign next to the establishment's name. Then, regarding the state of her skirts and the presumptuousness of the driver, she added another. The owner of that particular business deserved a stern letter of remonstration, to be sure.

Tucking the case into her bag again, Constance surveyed the crowded sidewalk, studying the facades of the ornate, gilt-encrusted buildings on either side. Despite her recent agitation, a shiver of anticipation coursed up her spine, and a tingling radiated through her body.

She was here.

She was actually here!

Lifting the basket she held a little higher, she whispered, "Soon, Mr. Bentley, we'll be right in the middle of all the excitement, just you wait and see. In a few weeks' time, no one will recognize either of us, we'll be so steeped in glamour."

A muted mewl of protest was her response. Poor Mr. Bentley. He had survived mile upon mile of travel, all of it closed in a stuffy wicker basket. Now that he had finally reached his new home, he was probably eager to find a niche of his own before escaping to examine his new surroundings. As soon as Constance had met her employer, explained the delay in her arrival, and arranged new lodgings, she and Mr. Bentley would relax for the rest of the day.

"Just a few minutes more," Constance encouraged close to the lid. Her actions were greeted by a few odd stares from passersby, but Constance didn't mind that they thought she was speaking to her shopping parcels. In no time at all, one of her most secret dreams would be granted.

For as long as she could remember, Constance had always been fascinated by the stage. It was a part of her character that her father had done his best to beat out of her. As far as he was concerned, only women of low morals would subject themselves to the indignities to be found in the theater.

But even when Constance had been forced to read her tomes of drama huddled near a low-burning candle, even though her love of costuming and make-believe and melodrama had been stifled for most of her life, she had never given up hope that one day she might pursue some sort of theatrical career.

And here she was, about to become a cutter and

seamstress for one of New York's finest dramatic establishments—a position her *father* had insisted in his will that she assume mere weeks after his death.

Constance sniffed. She still suspected the terms in the testament were the result of tampering rather than her father's true edicts. But Patience had sworn she'd never touched the will other than to deliver it to their father's solicitors. So if the instructions had been altered, Constance didn't know how—and she didn't care. After being granted her freedom from her father, all she wanted was a chance to live her own life. The fact that she would be allowed to do so while working for a New York theater had thrilled her beyond belief. When her year's probation was finished, she would collect her five hundred dollars, but she would never live in her father's house.

Never.

Constance gasped when she was roughly jostled by a group of newsies running to the corner with their bags of papers. Mr. Bentley howled in protest, and Constance huffed in indignation when she noted that the catch to the basket had been broken in the scuffle.

Despite the overwhelming weariness that clung to her limbs, Constance told herself to hurry. A clock chiming in the distance reminded her that the afternoon was waning, and she still had so much left to do. Her one remaining trunk had been left in storage at the station, and, with the basket damaged, she had best report to her employer as soon as possible so that she could begin searching for new habitation. There was no possibility that she would be returning to Richardson's Ladies Hotel and Boardinghouse, and Mr. Bentley would not be patient for much longer.

Glancing at the scrap of an address again, Constance scowled. Her solicitor's writing went beyond incomprehensible. The names of the theater and the person she was supposed to contact were mere swirls of ink. She was thankful that the numbering was a trifle better to read. One-eleven . . . and something that appeared to be "Kensington."

Heading down the appropriate side street, Constance gazed wide-eyed at the buildings stacked against one another like children's blocks. There were a good many theaters here. More than she would have believed possible. But in the glare of the noonday sun, the establishments appeared far less "magical" than she had imagined they would. In fact, there was something downright . . . *seedy* about the whole area.

Averting her eyes from a rough-looking fellow leaning against the wall and struggling to catch his breath as he fought a bout of hacking coughs, Constance increased her speed. The sooner she arrived at her destination, the better.

She was walking briskly now, her skirts swaying, the basket jouncing. She knew that it was an unseemly gait for a woman of quality, but she couldn't help it. Up ahead, the narrow street opened onto the green, jewellike colors of a park. Opposite the ornate iron gates was the elaborate facade of a building—its walls covered in white marble and gilt and oak.

Instantly, Constance surmised that the building was either being finished or was in the midst of renovation. A bevy of workers were running in and out of the massive front doors. As she drew nearer, she recognized carpenters and stonemasons, moving men, upholsterers, and decorators from the wares they carried with them.

Constance paused in her stride to allow four men to lift an enormous mirror from a crate and carry it up the shallow steps to the entrance. A gasp caught in her throat when they passed directly in front of her, allowing her a glimpse of her appearance.

Thunderation. Her cheeks were flushed, her hair mussed, and the damage to her skirts caused by the flying mud was more than she had imagined it to be.

Tugging at the strings to her bonnet, she swept it from

her head as she followed the men with the mirror inside the cavernous lobby of the theater. Stepping out of the path of the workers, she set the basket on the ground and took a handkerchief from her reticule. Dampening one corner with the small flask of toilet water she kept for just such occasions, she did her best to wipe the dirt from her cheeks and repair the damage to her coiffure. Then she donned her bonnet again and retied the bow at a jaunty angle. If she couldn't change her clothes before meeting her employer, she could at least tidy herself as best she could.

Twice she tried to catch the attention of a bustling workman so that she could ask who was in charge, but both times the men either didn't hear her or were too caught up in their own thoughts.

Then, just when she despaired of ever being noticed at all, a hush settled over the vaulted lobby. Glancing around her curiously, Constance saw that the work in the theater had stopped momentarily, and all attention had focused on the enormous mirror. Thick ropes were being wound around the shiny surface, before being attached to another rope which led to an elaborate pulley system.

Constance's eyes widened in amazement as she realized that the half-dozen men situated on the floor and upper balcony meant to heft the mirror up to the blank wall situated in the middle of a split staircase spiraling up to the first balcony level.

Despite her eagerness to find her employer and receive her orders, Constance watched the laborers with the same rapt attention as the people gathered around her. One worker in particular caused her to gaze his way in unconscious fascination.

He wore a coarse pair of trousers that clung to muscled thighs and narrow hips. Above that, he had donned a checked shirt that had been left unbuttoned nearly to the waist to expose a good expanse of sweat-dampened skin and his woolen underwear.

As he turned in her direction, the bright light from the

17

huge foyer windows flooded his face, and she was allowed to see him clearly for the first time. Her breath hitched, her mouth grew dry. Convulsively, she studied the dark, nearly black hair, the regal profile, the jutting jaw.

*Oh, my . . .* a voice whispered inside her head. Never, in all her life, had she seen such a beautiful man.

Never.

# Two

Constance tried averting her eyes, knowing she shouldn't be studying any stranger so openly, let alone a common laborer. But it was difficult to ignore the man. The longer she looked his way, the more she was affected.

He had a presence about him. A strength. An air of command. Raking narrow fingers through brown-black hair, he shouted orders to his men, gaining immediate obedience.

A strange frisson of excitement raced down Constance's spine. His voice was low and deep, seeming to come from some great well, its resonance settling in her chest and leaving an odd sort of ache.

Shaking herself free from the spell he had unwittingly cast, Constance did her best to look away. She focused on the patterned carpet, the silk-covered walls, the thump and shimmy of the basket as Mr. Bentley did his best to escape.

But such measures were temporary at best. As if drawn by an unseen force, she found herself scrutinizing the stranger who stood on the landing above her. When he vaulted onto the thick marble railing and balanced there, checking the rigging and the mountings on the wall, she could not account for the way she wanted to call out to him and warn him to be careful.

*Get a tight rein on yourself, Constance,* she railed inwardly. But the silent chiding had little effect.

"Lift!"

The stranger's voice boomed over the cacophony of the other workers. Immediately, the muscles of his arms strained against his rough cotton shirt, and he grimaced from the effort, his lips drawing back to show white, even teeth.

In front of Constance, the beveled mirror sparkled and flashed as it jerked upward. Thousands of droplets of sunshine were refracted onto the floor, dazzling her momentarily.

She lifted a hand to shield her eyes as the mirror dangled in place a good foot off the floor, but still far from its intended mark.

"Again!"

The men strained, their grunts of effort echoing in the hot air gathering in the lobby. Dragging her gaze away from the leader, Constance was riveted to her spot.

The mirror was more beautiful than she had first noted. The edges were faceted like a precious jewel. The outer surface had been etched with an elaborate design of twisted vines, leaves, and cabbage roses, while the top portion had been ornately decorated with plaster cherubs and tangled golden ribbons.

The sight was enough to divert Constance's attention from her own bedraggled coronet of braids and soiled traveling costume. It was even enough to cause her to ignore the basket at her feet, the lid bumping up and down, and Mr. Bentley's head poking out to . . .

Mr. Bentley.

*Mr. Bentley!*

Too late, Constance stooped to slam the lid shut. But by that time, Mr. Bentley had jumped free and was streaking toward the stairs.

"No!" she shouted without thinking, already running to retrieve the animal.

At the same instant, there was a deep *woof* from the shadows beneath the stairs, and a huge beast of a dog raced after the cat.

Constance gasped in horror, a sense of doom washing over her as the cat streaked beneath the mirror, heading toward the stairs. The dog, a Saint Bernard by the looks of it, followed, hitting the bottom of the mirror as he passed and causing it to sway ominously.

"Dammit! Hold the ropes steady!" the man shouted from above even as the frantic cries of the cat and the steady barking of the dog began to drown out his instructions.

Constance frantically called to Mr. Bentley, but the cat ignored her, streaking between the legs of one worker and causing him to stumble. The rope he held snaked free of its pulley. The mirror shimmied, then tipped alarmingly to one side.

"Dammit! Hold the blasted thing or—"

The man yelled his instructions, just as the cat jumped onto the balcony railing, stood poised between his legs, then launched into the air.

Horrified, Constance watched as the animal seemed to lunge in slow motion. She could see the danger, but, no matter how hard she tried, she couldn't move fast enough to stop the train of events.

The cat was falling, falling, straight onto the head of another worker who gripped a set of ropes below. The fellow screamed as Mr. Bentley steadied himself by digging his claws into his hair and shoulders. As the cat jumped down, the rope whizzed free. Heedless of the consequences, the dog on the landing above threw himself against the man precariously balanced on the railing, knocking him over the edge.

Constance screamed, but the man managed to cling to the rope. Rather than plummeting to his death, he swung wildly toward the horrified crowd, then back again.

Straight into the path of the mirror.

His feet hit the glass first, then his body. Ropes whizzed, flying from their pulleys as the beautiful mirror shattered into a dozen jagged pieces. Then the pieces themselves rained to the marble floor, where they broke again, disintegrating into glittering bits of rubble that bombarded its shocked audience.

Constance automatically covered her face as shards of gilt and plaster and glittering mirror rained about her. Then there was silence, absolute silence.

Dread filled her heart as she dared to open her eyes and lower her arms. Immediately, her gaze was drawn to the man who had been in charge. Slowly, he rolled to his feet, shaking his head to clear it. Then, brushing the glass from his clothing, he turned to glare at those who had crowded into the lobby to watch the proceedings.

"Who in hell let a damned cat inside?" he growled, the words measured and thick.

Looking at him, at his blazing eyes and rigid fists, Constance knew immediately who was in charge of this establishment—and not just the crew at the mirror.

This man had to be her employer.

*No,* a little voice whispered inside her head. *No. He couldn't possibly hold my future in his hands. Not that man.*

But even as her heart made such an assertion, she knew she was right to assume this was the owner of the establishment. His aura of command, his effortless sense of power, could not be feigned.

"Well?" he demanded, cut glass still tinkling to the floor around him. "Who let the damned thing loose?"

His dark eyes swept over the gathering, and Constance's heart sank. Briefly, she considered lying. She considered rushing outside and leaving Mr. Bentley to his own rewards. But even as she thought of such a solution, she knew she couldn't do it. Especially since Mr. Bentley had chosen that moment to twine around her skirts and purr.

The man planted his hands on his hips and glared her way, ignoring the dog who stood poised at the bottom of the steps and barked furiously in her direction.

"Who are you?"

Constance instantly bent her head, then opened her mouth, intent on answering, but her tongue had grown so dry that a mere croak escaped her lips.

The man prowled toward her, his body moving with a grace and deliberation that she had never seen in any human being before. Unfortunately, his movements reminded her far too much of the way Mr. Bentley stealthily slid through the tall grass at home, stalking small birds on the back lawn.

Knowing she must divert his attention until she could manage to regain her voice, she scooped the wriggling Mr. Bentley back into his basket, slammed the lid shut, then gripped the container in front of her as if it could ward off evil spirits.

Unfortunately, her action didn't ward off her employer at all. He was still striding toward her, his black eyes glittering, his jaw clenching in such a way, she knew he kept a tight rein on his temper.

"Well, Madam? Are you going to explain yourself or not?"

The words were so hot, so accusatory, that a trembling welled up inside her. He was angry, so incredibly angry. More furious than she'd ever seen a living soul—including her father.

Images welled in front of her. She could see her father striding toward her, a willow branch in his hand. She could feel the sting of his lashes against her skin.

This man would be no different. He meant to beat her. He meant to humiliate her for an accident that her carelessness had allowed to happen.

"No," she whispered, trying to back away from him. Automatically, she held out a hand. "No!"

But he was still advancing.

Knowing she had to do something to save herself,

Constance allowed her instincts to take over. A job was no longer important. Neither was a good first impression. Both elements had been lost forever. All that remained was to protect herself.

Whirling, she pushed past the workers closing around her. Rushing outside, she dodged down the front steps, hesitating in indecision before racing toward the park opposite the theater.

"Get back here!" a deep masculine voice shouted.

The order added speed to her steps. Soon she was running, running, through the front gates, down the footpath to a narrow bridge. Beyond that stood a grove of trees. If she could dodge into the rich shade, surely she could find a place to hide.

Her shoes rang against the boards of the bridge. Mr. Bentley howled in protest. Her lungs, unaccustomed to such a burst of exercise, burned, straining against the stays of her corset in an effort to draw breath.

*Just a little farther!*

She could hear the man closing the distance between them.

*Twenty yards! You'll be safe in twenty yards!*

But even as the thought raced through her head, a hand shot out to grasp her by the elbow and bring her to an abrupt stop.

The basket flew from her arms, and her bonnet tumbled backward to hang by its strings. Mr. Bentley shot free, racing over the grass to streak up a tree and hide in its leafy branches.

Then Constance was being forced to face the stranger.

He held her tightly. His chest heaved as he fought to calm himself enough to speak.

Knowing he would strike her now, Constance lifted her hands in front of her face in a purely reflexive gesture and squeezed her eyes closed.

*Do it,* she willed him silently. *Hit me now while I still have the strength to bear it.*

* * *

Gideon Payne was furious. No, he'd gone beyond a state of mere fury. He was enraged through and through and wanted nothing more than to find an outlet for his emotions.

But the moment the woman held up her arms as if she expected him to beat her, the emotions that had overtaken him seeped away, leaving him spent and irritated.

Exhausted.

"Put your hands down," he growled. "I'm not going to hit you."

She didn't move, and he offered a curt sigh. Damn it all to hell. Did he look like the sort who would strike a woman?

As soon as the thought entered his head, he was forced to admit that he probably did look like such a man. After all, he'd raced after the girl as if she'd committed murder.

But that didn't mean he intended to hurt her.

Even if she had brought a cat into his theater.

Even if she had been responsible for the destruction of a very expensive mirror which had been ordered more than a year ago from a manufacturer in France.

"Dammit, woman. Put your hands down, or I will give you cause to fear me."

That particular remark was enough to cause her arms to lower with aching slowness. Then her chin lifted and her eyes opened, and Gideon was offered his first clear look at her face.

"Dear God," he whispered, feeling as if he'd been slugged in the stomach.

Rich honey-gold hair had been combed savagely away from her brow and arranged in a crown of plaits around her head, framing a face that was heart-shaped, delicate, unforgettable.

Gideon's heart skipped a beat, then began knocking against his ribs in a sluggish tattoo. Even the eyes were the same. Crystal blue, such a light, silvery blue as to appear almost ghostly in the bright sunshine.

"Maura?" he whispered, even as he knew such a question was preposterous. Maura Kelly was dead. The resemblance between the actress and this woman was mere coincidence.

But the similarities were stunning. So much so that he found himself drawn to her, the old familiar lusts and urges bubbling to the fore—emotions that he hadn't felt in years. Emotions he hadn't *allowed* himself to feel. His hands tightened around her upper arms, and he automatically drew her against him, wanting to feel her hips grinding against his own, wanting her to ease the ache of his own loins. An ache that reminded him that it had been so long since he'd touched a woman.

Because none of them was Maura.

One of his hands slid to her buttocks, crushing her skirts and causing them to flatten between them. Only when she whimpered at the rough contact did his actions pierce the haze of wanting that had closed out all thought, all reason.

"Almighty hell," he whispered, more to himself than to her. Loosening his grip, he allowed her to back away, but only slightly. His brain might tell him that this was a stranger, but his body was doing its best to convince him that this stranger was really his wife.

Narrowing his eyes, he stared hard at the lady, cataloging her face, her form, analyzing the differences between her and the woman who could have been her twin. Unable to stop himself, he allowed his palms to slide up her body to her shoulders—such delicate shoulders, far too frail and slim. Frowning, he tested the arch of her neck and allowed his thumb to slip under her collar to graze the delicate sweep of her collarbone.

Familiar. Oh, so familiar. How could he ever forget?

Unable to help himself, he framed her face in his hands, forcing her to look up at him. Then he scowled at what he saw.

The emotions in this woman's eyes were not familiar to him at all. Maura had never regarded him with a shred of fear or hesitance. From the day he'd first touched her, she'd displayed an eagerness he'd never encountered in another woman. She'd returned each caress with passion and a wanton desire. She had only to look at him to set his blood raging.

The memories rose in him, heady and overpowering. He could not prevent himself from bending closer, inhaling the perfume that clung to her skin. For a split second, his senses were jarred at the faint whiff of lilac water—not an expensive Parisian perfume. But he didn't allow himself time to think about such things. Not now. Not when his blood surged through his veins, thick and hot and rich. His body was growing heavy with delight, his senses reeling.

"Just once," he whispered.

The woman's brow creased in obvious confusion, but he didn't allow himself to think about the reaction. He couldn't let her go. Not until he'd tasted her.

His head lowered until his lips grazed her cheek, her chin, the corner of her mouth. She trembled in his arms like a baby bird, and he offered her shushing sounds of reassurance. But he didn't stop. He couldn't stop.

Unable to wait any longer, he pressed his lips to hers, softly at first, then more insistently, hungrily, devouring her, filling himself with her sweetness. Immersing himself in a heady wave of passion. Her body felt so right, her lips so warm. His tongue bid entry, wanting to experience the rest of her, but to his infinite surprise her teeth remained firmly clamped, and she—

*Crack!*

Gideon reeled in confusion, automatically lifting his head. But it wasn't the noise that pierced the haze of carnal sensation that had invaded his brain, it was the sharp, stinging pain in his cheek.

Straightening, he touched the area at the same moment that his scattered wits acknowledged what had happened. The woman had slapped him—and, judging by her militant stance, she was more than willing to do so again. Her small hands had balled into fists, and her lips were tightly pursed.

Belatedly, he realized that his arms had snapped around her waist and he held her so tightly that not even a hairsbreadth separated them.

The woman must have become aware of the situation at about the same time, because she braced herself against him and pushed with all her might.

Gideon hissed when her efforts ground her hips more tightly against his arousal.

"Let me go," she whispered hoarsely. "If you don't, I'll scream."

Realizing she meant what she said, he gradually put some space between them, but without releasing her altogether.

"You don't need to make a fuss," he offered in his most placating tone.

"Fuss? Fuss!" She drew back her hand to slap him again, but he quickly caught her wrist. Forced to defend herself with her words, she hissed, "You should be ashamed of yourself for . . . for . . . attacking me in such a manner."

"I didn't attack you, I kissed you."

"There is no difference between the two in my mind."

"There's a great deal of difference in mine."

She clamped her jaw shut and glared at him. Gideon might have grinned in amusement if she weren't disarming him with her uncanny resemblance to his dead wife. He supposed that he should feel some sort of chagrin for his actions. After all, he'd accosted a total stranger. He'd taken incredible liberties—but he didn't feel sorry for what he'd done. Not in the least.

The woman wriggled free from his grasp, her fingers nervously touching her lips, and he felt surprisingly chilled without her.

"I suppose you want an apology," he said, his tone conveying that he did not intend to offer one.

"I-I don't want anything from you," she said, and he frowned at the thread of fear feathering her tone.

Damnation. She had no reason to be *afraid* of him.

Then again, maybe she did. His heart pounded in his chest as if he'd run a mile, not a few yards. His hands itched to touch her again, and his mouth . . .

He still wanted to kiss her. Over and over until they were both weak.

*Dammit. Get hold of yourself!*

Breathing deeply, Gideon schooled his features as best he could, hoping to allay her suspicions. The last thing he wanted was to frighten her. He would much rather—

What? What did he want from this woman? A person he'd encountered only minutes ago. An interloper who had caused havoc at his theater.

Knowing that he had at long last found a safer subject to focus upon, he said, "I think you owe me an explanation." To keep from pulling her toward him, he folded his arms across his chest, knowing that he would have to move quickly if she decided to make a second escape attempt.

*"I* owe *you* an explanation?" she sputtered in patent indignation.

"The mirror," he offered succinctly.

Her lips pursed in annoyance, and for the briefest moment her self-righteousness waned. He watched as her gaze dodged guiltily toward the tree.

The marmalade-colored cat glared malevolently at them both.

"I believe that beast belongs to you?" Gideon prompted.

"So what if he does?"

"If he does, then you would be the person responsible for the debacle that occurred in my theater."

She had the grace to flush. He watched with great delight as the delicate pink color flooded her cheeks. How long had it been since he'd been around a woman who still had the ability to blush? Maura had never blushed in his presence, but then, he supposed Maura had spent most of her time making others blush.

"Well? Is that animal yours?" he urged when she didn't speak.

"Yes, Mr. Bentley is mine," she admitted in a small voice. "So I suppose that his actions are also my responsibility. It was an error on my part not to watch him more carefully."

The woman was incredibly courageous, Gideon decided. She might look fragile and dainty, but she had a spine of iron. Not many of his men would have the temerity to offer him such a blatant look of pride when admitting to an error.

"Even so, Mister . . ."

"Payne, Gideon Payne."

Payne? That wasn't the name she'd been given by her father's solicitors. But then, her father's solicitors had not proven to be completely above fault in procuring her travel arrangements. Why should another error surprise her?

"Even so, Mr. Payne," she repeated, "I don't think that the destruction of your mirror entitles you to become so free with your . . . your . . ."

"My what?"

"With your kisses, Mr. Payne."

So she was as prim and proper as her attire suggested she might be.

Or was she? For the briefest moment, he thought he'd detected an answering spark of passion during their embrace. Right before her hand had planted itself into his jaw.

"I suppose that as far as the kiss is concerned, you are correct. Nevertheless, I will not be offering an apology, since I am far from repentant."

She looked away, her features twisting as if she'd had a taste of a particularly sour lemon, but she didn't reply.

"Now, if you would be so kind . . ." Gideon gestured behind him in the direction of the theater. "I believe we have some things to discuss."

She didn't budge.

"What sorts of things?"

Tarnation, the woman was obstinate.

"The mirror, for one."

The look she offered him spoke volumes. Obviously, she expected him to draw her into his private lair, then ravish her completely.

"I don't think I would care to join you," she said with artificial politeness.

"*I* don't think you have much of a choice." He snagged her elbow. "I want matters between us settled as soon as possible." When she continued to balk, he added, "I also believe that you came to the theater on some sort of errand. Otherwise, why would you have been there at all?"

She shifted uncomfortably, and he knew that he'd stumbled upon the one reason she might be tempted to brave his company.

"Am I correct?"

She stared at a far-off spot for some time, then curtly nodded.

"Come along."

She sniffed. "I am not a child to be spoken to so patronizingly."

Gideon resisted the urge to lift her bodily and carry her back to his office. Never in his life had he encountered a woman so set on driving him completely around the bend. She was completely pig-headed, ornery, and sanctimonious. He should turn her loose, forget the mirror, and count himself fortunate for escaping a maddening afternoon.

But with each second that ticked past, Gideon felt more drawn to her. He needed to know who she was, why she had come to his theater.

More than that, he needed to know if her resemblance to Maura was somehow intended to rouse his own emotional ghosts.

"Miss . . ."

"Pedigrue."

"Do you have a first name?"

"You are being patronizing again, Mr. Payne."

His lips twitched, but he forcibly kept them from breaking into a smile. Such spirit. Such pious displeasure. She was a joy to watch.

"You are right, Miss Pedigrue. But I would genuinely like to know your name. Your whole name."

She scrutinized him, measuring his sincerity, then offered, "Constance Pedigrue."

Miss Constance Pedigrue waited expectantly, and Gideon surmised that she had expected some sort of reaction on his part. But try as he might, he could not remember having heard such a name before. Could Maura have mentioned her? Could she have made some offhanded remark about a woman who bore a resemblance to her?

No. Maura would have been furious if she'd discovered she wasn't "one of a kind."

Knowing he had to move now, while he still could, while he still had the wherewithal to resist risking another slap in the face, Gideon released his hold of her elbow.

"Come with me, Miss Pedigrue." He turned, striding back in the direction he'd come from, fully expecting her to follow him. When he didn't hear her answering footfalls, he glared over his shoulder.

"Well?"

She was clasping her hands. Her bonnet hung from its ribbons, making her appear as young as a schoolgirl.

"I can't leave without my cat."

Her cat.

Gideon sighed. As far as he was concerned, he'd seen enough of the beast. The last thing he wanted to do was bring it back to the theater, where Willoby could bark and chase the feline into even more mischief.

But it was obvious from the set of Constance's shoulders that she didn't intend to take a step until her precious pet had been coaxed from the tree.

Resisting the urge to swear—something he'd done far too many times since meeting this woman—he marched to the tree, swinging onto the lowest branch.

The cat hissed, backing deeper into the dense leaves, but Gideon didn't allow it to retreat much farther. Snatching the animal by the nape, he cursed again when the tabby scratched the back of his hand.

"Don't hurt him!" Constance called from below.

"I think you should offer the mangy animal the same set of instructions," Gideon muttered to himself. Then, knowing his grasp on the cat was tenuous at best, he jumped to the ground and handed Mr. Bentley to Constance.

She immediately stuffed the cat into the basket—a situation to which Mr. Bentley vociferously objected.

Gideon didn't allow her to comfort the feline.

"My office," he snapped, wiping the blood from his hand onto his trousers. "Now."

# Three

Constance wasn't completely sure that she should follow Gideon Payne back to the theater. After all, there was nothing to prevent this man from exacting some sort of horrible revenge for the current state of his mirror.

Not for the first time since leaving Boston, Constance wished that she had insisted a traveling companion be hired to accompany her to New York. But she had assumed her journey would take a few days at most and that she would be working as soon as she arrived.

As her spirits sank to their lowest point yet, Constance heartily wished that she had never come to this place—never come to this city. Since leaving home, she had been beset with trouble, and the scattered trail of calamities didn't bode well for whatever ills the future still held in store.

But as she trailed behind the man who had kissed her—passionately, thoroughly, in a way that made her toes curl in her shoes—she also realized that she had no real choice. Not until she'd made an attempt at salvaging her current means of employment and offering recompense for the broken mirror. If she behaved civilly, maybe Gideon Payne would give her another chance.

Perhaps he would allow her to take the costuming position her father's solicitors had originally procured. After all, his mood had lightened considerably since their kiss.

*That kiss.*

The memory of it caused her knees to grow weak and her limbs to tremble. No man had ever touched her like that before—no man had ever really touched her at all until she'd taken this ill-fated journey. Even so, the bumbling attempts of the baker in Boston, the blatant forwardness of the boardinghouse clerk, and the all-out gall of Mr. Pepys had in no way equaled Gideon Payne's masterful possession. When his lips had covered hers, the world had fallen away, and she'd been forced to cling to him to keep from shattering into a thousand incoherent pieces. She'd had to summon every ounce of self-control she'd ever owned to lash out at him, to stop him in the only way she knew how, with a vicious slap to the cheek.

Constance cringed when she remembered the stinging contact of her hand against his jaw and the vivid impression her fingers had made on his skin. She'd never struck another human being in her entire life—yet in this man's presence she'd been reduced to the same violence she had always despised in her father.

But she'd been right to defend herself.

Hadn't she?

Gideon was first to step into the lobby of the theater. His workers had returned to their tasks, but their attention was clearly divided between their assignments and the man and woman crossing the threshold.

Seeing the ruin caused by the mirror, Gideon sighed.

"I've got one or two things to attend to here." He waved in the general direction of a long, twisted corridor. "Go to my office. I'll expect to see you there, ready to talk, once the cleanup has begun."

Constance wasn't at all sure where the man's office might be. But she wasn't overly willing to ask for directions—especially since he'd mentioned cleaning up the littered remains of his beautiful mirror.

Wincing, she ignored the crunch of broken glass beneath her shoes and the half-dozen pairs of eyes that turned in her direction. She would find her way to this man's inner sanctum if she had to search every nook and cranny of the building.

To her relief, such extreme measures didn't prove necessary. After shouting orders to his men, Gideon rejoined her partway down the corridor. Taking her elbow, he pulled her through a curtained archway. From there, he led her down a narrow corridor to a small, airless office at the opposite end of the building.

"Gideon! We've got a problem!" someone shouted from another portion of the theater.

She heard Gideon swear under his breath.

Opening the door, he all but tossed her inside. "Ten minutes. I'll be back. Wait for me here."

Huffing in irritation, she whirled to offer a quick complaint, but the moment she scowled in his direction, he slammed the door.

His footsteps moved away, paused, then returned. Waiting, she held her breath, sure that he meant to throw another order her way. To her complete astonishment, she heard the distinct click of a lock being turned.

Rushing to the panels, she banged on them with her palms. "Let me out of here!" When she received no response, she demanded, "I order you to unlock this door. *Right . . . now!"*

Despite her steely tone and barely checked fury, the door remained firmly locked, and, judging by the silence on the other side, the man had long since disappeared.

She set Mr. Bentley's basket on the floor, then perched on the edge of an ornate leather chair. Lacing her fingers in her lap, she kept her spine stiff and her features as emotionless as possible, knowing that if she allowed her composure to wilt even slightly, Gideon Payne would choose that moment to return.

After several minutes, however, she could not prevent the way her toe tapped an impatient tattoo on the floor. Huffing, she vainly watched the hands on the wall clock inch their way through ten minutes. Fifteen. Twenty. Forty-five.

But there were no sounds of footfalls, no bellowing orders from her employer.

The muscles of her back and shoulders were beginning to tremble from the rigid posture, and bit by bit her stance faltered. Weakened. The weariness she'd fought all day pulled at her limbs like a weight.

The clock rasped and ticked and began to keep track of the next hour.

Suddenly far more understanding of Mr. Bentley's plight, she opened the basket and allowed the cantankerous feline to spring free. Immediately, he began to sniff his way around the room, regarding each new book and chair with infinite suspicion and distaste. Then he offered a low, piteous yowl.

"I know just how you feel, Mr. Bentley," Constance whispered through a throat that was thick with rising tears. "We've made a mess of this whole trip, haven't we?"

The cat sprang onto the desk and tipped his head as if to deny any responsibility for their current state.

Her misery doubled. "I suppose you can't be blamed for all our misadventures, can you?" Constance searched through her reticule for her handkerchief, then searched her pockets and, finding it missing, sobbed out loud at the latest misfortune.

Since leaving Boston, she'd been dogged by disaster. Now she was responsible for the destruction of a beautiful mirror—and she was sure that Gideon Payne would demand some sort of recompense.

The tightness in her chest grew more and more unbearable, until Constance could no longer contain her disappointment. Sobbing, she threw herself onto the couch, her tears falling like rain.

How could this have happened? How? The mirror cost a fortune, she was sure. As soon as Gideon Payne discovered she had no money to repay him, his anger would return full force. She wouldn't be surprised if he threw her in jail for her foolhardiness.

She wept even louder, searching vainly for something, anything, to use as a handkerchief. Finally locating a scrap of velvet, she wiped at her eyes and blew her nose, all to no avail. Her woe could not be contained. Such a sequence of catastrophes was completely foreign to her, and she wasn't sure what to do next. Such misadventures were generally reserved for her siblings. Her younger sister, Felicity, was always jumping headlong into trouble, and Patience had a temper that could make a bishop swear. But Constance . . .

She was the "constant" sister. A rock of composure. She was good and polite and kind even when she felt the urge to knock heads together.

If her sisters were here, they might have some idea of how to extricate themselves from the situation. But, alas, neither of them was in a position to come to her aid. Any pleas for help would have to be made through their father's solicitors, since Constance had no permanent addresses for her siblings as yet.

So what was she going to do?

Swiping at her tears again, she forced herself to think. Somehow she had to find a way to reimburse him. If she paid for the damages, he would have no reason to quibble with her about the accident.

But she didn't have any money! Her solicitors had offered her a small allowance for the journey and two new dresses to augment her wardrobe. The pittance would in no way cover her current debt.

Constance gripped her hands together to still their trembling, gazing wildly about her as if there were some sort of escape. Instead, she was greeted with the sight of an untidy desk, a barred window, row upon row of crowded bookcases, and a dozen packing crates still awaiting someone's attention.

Standing, Constance did her best to control her tears. In an effort to divert her black thoughts, she bent to investigate the titles of the books. Seeing that they were dramatic tomes that had been categorized on the different bookcases by genre and period, she automatically began lifting them from their packing containers and arranging them neatly on the shelf. Perhaps if she made herself useful during her wait, her employer wouldn't be so angry when he returned. Maybe she would even be able to arrange to reimburse him for Mr. Bentley's actions by paying a portion of her weekly salary to him—say, fifty cents a week.

*For the rest of her life.*

No. She wouldn't think about such long-term obligations. Not yet.

Stuffing the scrap of velvet into her pocket, she rushed to complete the task she'd assigned herself. If she hurried, she might have a half-dozen shelves filled before Gideon's return. Then she would point out her efficiency and demand an opportunity to repay him for Mr. Bentley's folly.

The hour had grown late by the time Gideon was able to untangle himself from the minor emergencies that continued to crop up throughout the evening. As he strode to his office door, he realized that night had fallen, and someone had already lit the gas lamps to ward off the thick shadows.

Hesitating outside the door, he admitted to himself that he wasn't really sure why he'd made Constance Pedigrue a virtual prisoner—or why he'd avoided coming to her aid until now. He supposed that most of his reasoning lay in the fact that he had been confronted with Maura's double, and he didn't mean to let her go without more information concerning her intentions.

Even so, a part of him also admitted that his motives weren't all so clear-cut. Constance's appearance had startled him, yes, but that did not account for the fact that he had been unable to tamp down the more carnal images that sprang unbidden into his mind's eye. Visions of undressing this woman, touching her, caressing her, to see just how far her similarities to his late wife might extend.

Shaking his head to relieve it of such thoughts, Gideon slid a key into the lock and opened the door as quietly as he could, hoping to take Miss Pedigrue unawares. She had a sharp tongue and a keen wit, and for once he would like to employ the element of surprise himself.

Especially since she might smack him again for ignoring her so long.

But when the panels swung wide on well-oiled hinges, he frowned.

The woman was nowhere in sight.

Striding into the room, he made his way to the window, wondering if she'd somehow made her way through the bars. But outside the night was inky black. Still.

Turning, he raked his fingers through his hair, wondering if he'd imagined the woman. But in the same instant, he noticed a slender shape curled up on his sofa. Maura.

No, not Maura.

Constance Pedigrue.

Of their own accord, his eyes studied her frame, noting her flushed cheeks and patches of what could only have been dried tears. A pang of guilt shot through his chest as he saw the way she'd drawn her knees to her chest and clutched her arms around her waist as if chilled.

Asleep. Constance Pedigrue had fallen asleep.

His remorse intensified as he glanced at the clock and realized that he'd left her alone in this room for several hours. He really hadn't meant to abandon her to her own devices for so long, but a new mirror had needed to be ordered, paintings had arrived requiring his inspection, and the wood-carver had encountered problems with a section of molding. The hours had sifted through his fingers without his being aware of it. And the entire time, Constance Pedigrue had been locked in his office, forced to wait for his return.

Sighing, he realized he generally wouldn't treat Willoby in such a fashion, let alone someone of the gentler sex. Yet he had behaved abominably with this woman.

*A woman who ruined my mirror.*

That wasn't her fault. It was the cat's.

*A cat that belongs to her.*

Gideon shoved such arguments aside. What was done was done. He could only control the future.

So what should he do next? If he woke her, Constance would demand some sort of retribution for his tardiness. She would insist that their long-awaited conversation commence. They would determine a way to settle their differences, then she would be gone—chasing after whatever errand had mistakenly brought her to his theater in the first place.

*No.*

Gideon couldn't account for the panic that settled into his bones at the mere possibility. He couldn't allow this woman to walk away so quickly.

So what did he intend to do?

Gideon planted his hands on his hips and studied her intently. Somehow, he had to find a way to keep her near him for a few more days. By then, he would have tired of the novelty of encountering Maura's double, and he would be able to handle the whole situation impassively.

So how did he intend to buy himself some time?

He thought for several long minutes, reviewing each moment of their confrontation. As he did so, he realized that he knew very little about this stranger except her name and the fact that she was beholden to him. He wasn't even sure why she'd stumbled into his theater.

So her indebtedness would have to be his main bargaining tool. He would have to insist that she stay with him until matters had been arranged to his satisfaction.

Even so, she'd already shown a tendency to willfulness. He had no guarantees that the expense of the mirror would keep her here. If he really wanted to cure himself of her strange effect on him, he would have to keep her near him. Night and day.

But how? Gideon had spent the past month living in a converted storeroom on the third floor. He couldn't expect any woman to agree to such an arrangement.

Which meant that his only other alternative would be to order that the town house be opened.

Maura's town house.

The home he'd given to her on their wedding day.

His fingers curled into fists at the mere thought of entering that building again—but unless he rented a hotel suite, he could see no alternative. Especially since Constance Pedigrue appeared to have more moral starch in her drawers than the women he usually encountered.

That meant the town house was his best hope for success, but since Gideon hadn't wanted to darken its door, the house hadn't been inhabited by anything more than a skeleton crew of servants in more than two years. He would need to ensure that the building was fit for habitation before he took a woman there.

So what should he do about tonight?

Gazing around him as he deliberated the question, Gideon noted that Constance had not been idle during the time she'd waited. To his surprise, the packing crates of books had been emptied and pushed out of the way. A quick perusal of the shelves lining the walls informed him that she'd organized the titles by genre and author—something the man he'd asked to perform the same task hadn't been able to master.

*Evidently, she has a sharp mind to go with that tart voice of hers.*

Feeling suddenly weary, Gideon sank into the chair

behind his desk and set his feet on the blotter. From this vantage point, he saw Constance more clearly, since a weak wash of lamplight spilled into the room from the hall and over her features. Without the sass and vinegar he had seen reflected in her features, he thought the fragility of her bones and the pallor of her skin gave her a little-girl-lost air.

No, not a little girl, he decided as his gaze strayed to the plump shape of her breasts, the tiny waist, the swell of her hips. If Maura had lived, would she still look like this stranger? Or would the years have made her even harder, more aggressive?

Gideon's memories washed over him like a wave, but he resolutely pushed them away. He didn't have time to grow sentimental. The fact remained that he needed to find a believable reason to keep Miss Pedigrue firmly chained to his side. Otherwise, he was sure that she would devise some means to escape him.

Glumly, he realized that his options were limited. He could offer her a job, seduce her, or lock her up again.

Since he was sure that both of the latter ideas would not be wise, he focused on the first. A job.

He supposed he would have to find her "respectable" work. She could assume a position as a maid in the town house, he supposed, but the moment the idea occurred to him, Gideon abandoned it. No. Somehow, he sensed that by installing her as a servant in his household, he would create even more emotional barriers between them.

He needed something else, something that would cause her to be in contact with him during the day as well as the evening. But here at the theater, there was a distinct lack of "respectable" positions. His performers generally supplied their own costumes, cleaned their own dressing rooms, and saw to the intricacies of their own performances.

There had to be something this woman could do here. Against his will, his mind formed an image of Maura parading across the stage. She had been so regal, so entrancing. If she desired to perform, this woman would be that way, too—perhaps more so. There was an innocence to her nature that Maura couldn't have duplicated no matter how hard she might try. Maura had always had an old soul—whereas if this woman were to adopt the same routines . . .

Constance Pedigrue? Perform in front of an audience?

What was he thinking? Constance Pedigrue would never take the stage. She wouldn't allow such indecencies. Especially not in a burlesque house.

His lips spread in a slow grin. He was quite sure that Constance was not aware that she'd stumbled into a burlesque theater. If she were, he was sure he would have received a tongue lashing. Her outraged morals would have insisted on it.

No, if he was going to keep her near his side, he was going to have to . . .

*By his side.*

He straightened, his eyes narrowing as he peered at the woman on his settee. That's it! He would offer her a position as his assistant. A sort of glorified clerking job. She wouldn't dare to find fault with such an occupation.

Standing, he moved to her side, intent on waking her now that he had made up his mind. But as soon as he crouched beside her, he hesitated.

Deep lines of weariness etched the corners of her mouth and fanned out from her eyes. His gaze fell to the basket with its broken hinge, and he noted the stub of a train identification label. Tipping it to the light with his finger, he saw that the origination of the journey was Boston, the destination New York. The date on the stub was nearly a month old. How could such a simple journey take so long?

Again, he felt a tug of guilt. This woman had probably been traveling for some time. Looking at her, at the way she slept with her hands tucked beneath her cheek, he doubted she'd rested at all since leaving Massachusetts—although what she'd been doing since arriving in New York he hadn't a clue.

Sighing, he stood, staring at her as if she could help him to determine the best course of action.

In the end, he did nothing.

Moving as stealthily as he could, he crossed the corridor to one of the prop rooms. After rummaging through the contents of a steamer trunk, he removed a flowing velvet cape and a rabbit fur muff. Both items should prove an adequate substitute for a blanket and pillow.

Gideon was about to close the door again, when his gaze latched onto the huge shape of a portrait leaning against one wall. The surface had been covered with a dust cloth, but he knew immediately who the subject of the painting would prove to be.

An unseen force seemed to pull him closer and closer. Grimacing at his own folly, he whipped back the cover and found himself face to face with Maura's image.

There were slight differences between Maura and the woman in the other room, he had already determined as much, but the portrait made such discrepancies even more blatant. Maura's figure was more voluptuous, her hair a brighter shade of gold—but there was still an amazing likeness. Enough to cause Gideon's stomach to clench.

After all these years, after all that had happened, he shouldn't feel a thing for Maura Kelly Payne.

But he did.

And he hated himself for the fact.

Against his will, he reached out to trace the painted, life-sized rendering. He remembered a time when he had touched the woman herself. Her skin had been soft and fragrant. Her body lithe and womanly.

He'd met her at a theater in Chicago—a theater owned by an old childhood friend, Luther Hayes. From the moment Gideon had seen Maura beneath the glow of the oil lamps, he'd been spellbound. She'd worn a glittering golden costume mimicking something out of *The Arabian Nights*. Rather than music, she'd chosen an accompaniment of drums, providing a pagan, primitive mood for her performance. When she'd begun to remove her clothing, layer by layer, Gideon had known he must have her as his own.

Gideon had expected some sort of resistance from Maura—after all, he'd sensed that Luther had been trying his best to court the woman's favors as well. Luckily for Gideon, Maura had immediately returned his attentions. Within days after they'd met, she'd wound him around her little finger; within weeks, she'd moved her things into his hotel room—and he hadn't minded one bit. He'd felt a surge of power each time she'd strutted across the stage and begun to remove her clothing—because *he* would be the man to take her home. *He* would be the one to bring her to an inferno of passion.

Less than a month had passed before Gideon decided to make the arrangement permanent. By that time, he'd gained a fortune by erecting legitimate theaters in several states. But the moralistic productions had a limited audience appeal, and he'd longed to diversify into the world of burlesque. Maura would prove to be an asset to the expansion of his businesses. Her name and reputation would provide immediate interest.

From the beginning, their life together had been tempestuous and glorious and sweet—marriage had seemed but a mere formality for the relationship. Their desire for each other had known no bounds. In Maura he'd found a mate who had been a mistress, a wanton, and a maiden in distress—a powerful combination for any man's ego. Gideon had adored her completely.

Until she'd betrayed him.

Slept with his best friend.

Luther Hayes.

The thoughts raced through his head with the power of a gunshot, and he automatically recoiled, disgusted with the way he'd been wallowing in the past. From the moment Maura's casket had been lowered into the earth, he'd vowed that he would never think of this woman again, never recall the last night he'd seen her.

In another man's arms.

Turning resolutely away, Gideon shut the door behind him. Maura was dead. He'd best remember that fact.

But when he returned to his office, he was forced to admit that such reminders would not be so easy to heed. Not when he'd been confronted with Maura's double.

He wasn't sure why Constance Pedigrue had come to his theater. He wasn't sure if he wanted to know all the real reasons. Right now, his only concern was to confront the mélange of emotions she'd brought with her.

The time had come, once and for all, to rid himself of Maura's spell. If this woman could help him do that, he would be indebted to her for far more than the price of a mirror.

Bending, he placed the velvet cape around her shoulders, then slid the muff beneath her head as a makeshift pillow.

Constance sighed, settling more firmly into sleep. As she made soft, incoherent sounds of pleasure, the liquid shadows of the night flowed around him, warm and redolent with might-have-beens.

Knowing he must keep some distance between them to prevent himself from lifting her in his arms and carrying her up the steps to his hidden lodgings, Gideon stood and returned to his chair. Sinking into its depths, he told himself he, too, should try to get some sleep. Morning would come soon enough, and with it would come the complications that hung around this woman like pale ghosts.

But try as he might, he couldn't rest.

He could only stare at her.

And wonder.

# Four

Louise Chevalier gripped Etienne Renoir's hand as the train they rode ground to a stop. The trip they'd taken had not been a long one. Baltimore to Washington, D.C. Nevertheless, she was feeling the strain from the journey—from so many journeys. In the past month she'd crisscrossed the country from Massachusetts to Missouri, then home again.

Sighing, she gazed at her reflection in the gilt mirror that hung on the opposite wall of her private car. Standing, she studied her reflection, using a finger to sweep a single lock of blond hair into place.

Did she look as old as she felt right now? Did she look like the mother of three grown women?

The thought would have been depressing if it hadn't taken her so long to locate her daughters' whereabouts. They'd been mere babies when her late husband, Alexander Pedigrue, had stolen them and disappeared.

Closing her eyes, she remembered the last dreadful argument she'd had with her husband—the night before he'd left her.

Always a jealous man, he'd become a zealot in the last few years of their marriage. He'd begun to suspect that the past Louise had invented for his benefit had been untrue.

Pressing a hand to her lips, Louise shuddered. For years, she had berated herself for the mistakes she'd made. She'd been but a girl when her parents— performers in a traveling carnival—had been killed. Forced to fend for herself, Louise had sought refuge at a church.

It was there that she had been introduced to Alexander Pedigrue. Although the man was reported to be heir to one of the largest mining fortunes in the country, he'd been practicing as a minister. Louise had instantly been drawn to his self-assurance, his peace, his belief that God could provide miracles for his devoted children.

When such an important man had begun to seek her attentions, Louise had known instinctively that he would not approve of her former life. Hadn't he railed against the "ungodly who tramped the stages, taking upon themselves the lies of Satan"?

In retrospect, Louise knew she shouldn't have lied to him—indeed, she should have fled such a man. But Alexander had wooed her, married her, and taken her with him to his new parish.

There she'd begun to see pieces of the real man. His cruelty. His self-righteousness. His fanaticism. But by the time she'd garnered enough courage to leave him, she'd been pregnant with the first of her three children. And she'd known that Alexander would track her to wherever she chose to hide.

Taking a deep breath, Louise tried to turn her attention to her appearance again. Instead, she saw Alexander as he'd been that last night. Backhanding her, he'd accused her of having an affair, of lying about her life and the parentage of her children.

Abandoning her pride, she'd begged him to remember that she'd been a virgin when they married. She'd sworn on peril of her soul that no other man had touched her. Foolishly, she'd thought she'd appeased him. The following morning, he'd encouraged her to attend a charity quilting bee in town—and she'd gone in an effort to please him.

But when she'd returned, she'd found their home empty and her children gone.

A sob rose in her throat, but she held it back through sheer force of will. For nearly twenty years, she had searched for her daughters. She'd hired countless detectives to seek them out. But Alexander had eluded her.

Until two months ago, when one of her detectives had discovered the obituary of Alexander Pedigrue in a Boston newspaper.

Immediately, Louise had rushed to reunite with her daughters. She'd mourned the fact that their childhoods had passed without her, but the future still remained.

Looking back, she supposed she'd been naive to think that reentering her daughters' lives would be so easy. She hadn't counted on Alexander having filled her daughters' heads with lies, poisoning them against her should she ever find them. After interviewing a servant who had once worked with the Pedigrues, Louise had discovered her girls had grown up thinking she'd abandoned them in favor of a lover and other children.

*Damn Alexander to hell and beyond.*

A hand touched her shoulder, squeezing gently.

"Don't fret, *ma cherie.*"

She squeezed Etienne's fingers with her own.

"I can't help but fret. With all the trouble we've encountered already, I feel sure that something horrible has happened to Constance as well."

After arriving in Boston, Louise had found herself unable to approach them, but she'd been determined to help them. Fully aware of her husband's pettiness, she and Etienne had bribed one of the law clerks who worked with Alexander's solicitors into letting her see the will before it was read. When Louise had discovered that her husband meant to send Felicity on a mission to India, Patience to serve as a companion at an old-age home, and Constance to become a seamstress for an orphanage, she'd taken matters into her own hands.

Using the signet ring her husband had given her on their wedding day, she'd made an alternative document—one granting each of her daughters a wish for an adventure—and pressed the family crest into the sealing wax.

A chill feathered down her spine at the recollection of how Alexander had meant to treat his flesh and blood. The man hadn't been satisfied with subjugating his daughters to his every whim, to withdrawing them from society and virtually enslaving them. No, he'd wanted to continue his domination from beyond the grave.

As soon as the alternative will had been returned to the solicitors' office, Louise had waited patiently, knowing that once her daughters had tasted independence they would be easier to approach.

Unfortunately, upon arriving in St. Joseph, where she'd been sent to teach, Felicity had unknowingly become embroiled in the Underground Railroad—a fact that had very nearly cost Felicity her life.

Next, Patience—who had found a job as a governess on a small island near Nantucket—had impulsively married her mysterious employer.

It had taken weeks for Louise to ensure that her daughters were safe and happy. Such efforts had brought about two of the reunions Louise had craved for years. And she was blissfully aware that her two youngest children had grown to accept and love her.

But one more reunion remained. The one Louise worried about most.

Constance.

Constance had been old enough to remember their life as a family. Had she believed that Louise had abandoned her? Had she grown to hate the mother she'd once known?

"She's *fine,* Louise," Etienne insisted gently, and she grimaced.

"I suppose that after so many years not knowing where my girls were or how they fared, I feel compelled to worry about them all at once."

"We know that Constance's journey was plagued with delays, but you received a telegram this morning from the man I sent to watch over her. She should have arrived in New York yesterday afternoon."

"I can't help thinking something will go wrong—just as with the other girls."

"Something has already gone wrong. Her three-day voyage took nearly a month. So cease all this superstitious nonsense. Of all your children, Constance is the least likely to land in trouble."

"True."

In their conversations with their mother, Felicity and Patience had reaffirmed that Constance had not changed. She was still the "constant" Pedigrue sister, prone to good deeds, prudishness, and a willingness to please.

Etienne slipped one arm around her waist, drawing her close. As always, his nearness caused a rush of sensation to spill through her body.

Poor Etienne. He had been her bodyguard for more than a dozen years. From the first, there had been a bond between them. Etienne had always been willing to offer her his advice, or a shoulder to cry on—and over time the relationship had deepened even more. They'd become friends. Confidants.

Nevertheless, there had always been an imaginary line that Louise had been afraid to cross. In searching for her daughters, she had never considered divorcing her husband or having an affair. She'd been adamant that no hint of scandal should ever touch her name. She would not give Alexander Pedigrue ammunition to fight her in the courts.

So Etienne had waited.

Waited for her to be free.

But she knew he would not wait much longer.

"You know I love you, Louise."

She sighed. Once again, he'd read her thoughts. Sometimes it seemed as if they were two halves of a whole, completely in tune with each other and bereft if alone.

"And I love you, Etienne."

His body stiffened. It was the first time she had dared to say the words aloud.

Louise knew her reticence bordered on the same superstitiousness that made her worry for Constance. But she'd been so sure that if she declared her feelings something horrible would happen to drive them apart.

Etienne turned her in his arms, his head lowering, his lips covering hers in a kiss that was as powerful as it was tender, as passionate as it was reverent.

When he drew away, they were both breathing hard.

"This isn't the time," he murmured.

She shook her head, unable to summon a verbal response.

"Tonight," he whispered, taking her hands and pressing his lips to them. "Tonight we will make plans for our own future."

Louise nodded, knowing exactly what he referred to. Since Etienne came from a very religious family, there would be no half-hearted gestures to seal their relationship. He wanted marriage. Perhaps even children.

The thought should have frightened her to the core. After all, her last attempt at motherhood had been horribly thwarted. But Louise found herself wanting to hold a child, wanting to watch it grow.

Etienne's child.

He kissed her again as if to seal the bargain. Then, stepping in front of the mirror again, Louise schooled her features into the professional mask she adopted whenever she mingled with her public. No one must ever know that she and her bodyguard were on the verge of becoming more than mere lovers. Her theater fans wouldn't understand. The other actors and actresses in the company wouldn't refrain from gossiping. So the relationship would have to be kept a secret for a little while longer. Just as so many elements of her life had been kept a secret.

Taking her bonnet from the tufted chaise of her private car, she pinned it carefully to her head.

"As soon as you've seen me to the theater, I want you to send word immediately to the Royale and check on Constance's progress. She should have arrived by mid-afternoon. Make sure that she's checked in with the manager of the theater and that she's found a suitable place to stay."

Etienne grasped her hand when she would have brushed past him. Pulling her to him, he framed her face in his palms, forcing her to acknowledge his open adoration.

"How long, Louise?" he blurted. "How long before we can be wed?"

She smiled in delight at his impatience, feeling a girlish impatience that she hadn't experienced in years.

Marriage.

To Etienne Renoir.

After so many years of waiting, her anticipation was as heady as Etienne's.

"I thought you meant to wait until tonight to make our plans."

"Tell me now."

She pretended to frown, to dally, to consider, then in a rush said, "If all is well with Constance, why don't we plan for the middle of July?"

"So long?"

"It's barely two weeks away!"

He kissed her again, grinning. "Yes, and that's an eternity."

He stroked her cheek, his adoration plain and beautiful to behold, especially in a man normally so fierce and forbidding.

Leaning into his caress, she whispered, "The time will pass quickly."

"I will hold you to that, *ma petite,*" he whispered as he kissed her knuckles.

Then, releasing her, he assumed his customary grim mien, opened the door, and ushered her into the crowd of waiting people.

Hildegard Potts hugged the stair rail, pausing at the top of the third floor of the theater, where she tried to catch her breath. Her stays were pinching her ribs unmercifully, but until this moment she hadn't dared pause in the quick trot she had adopted since Gideon Payne had sent a carriage to fetch her. Mere minutes ago, the conveyance had arrived unannounced at the town house where she, Roberta Merriweather, Hiram Birch, a chambermaid, and two stable masters had worked since Master Payne had given the town house to his bride, Maura Kelly.

Poor Miss Maura. She'd been gone two years now.

Potts automatically genuflected, and she whispered, "God rest her soul." In the time since Maura's death, no word had come to them from the master himself until this morning. He sent them their pay the first of each month, come rain or shine, but he hadn't visited his own home since the funeral, not that Potts blamed him. Those had been terrible times. Terrible times, indeed, and the man had a right to mourn any way he pleased.

Especially if by staying away he kept himself from burning the house down to the foundations.

Potts crossed herself again, remembering that awful night when Miss Maura had died and the master in his grief had set the draperies surrounding her portrait ablaze. If it hadn't been for Birch, who had doused the flames and dragged their employer from the room . . .

Potts shuddered. She didn't want to think of such things. The past should be left in the past. Even after all these years, Master Payne, the servants, and a few of his close friends were the only people to know what had really occurred that night. The only story to be released to the public at large was that Maura Kelly Payne had died after a tragic fall.

Having regained some semblance of calm, Potts waddled toward the fly garret at the end of the landing, where she had been told she could find Master Payne. The door was partially open, allowing her a glimpse of the monstrous backdrops, ropes, pulleys, and catwalks that lined the upper floors of the stage.

Not wishing to put herself so high in the air with only a rough railing between her and three levels of space, Potts rapped the doorway with her knuckles and waited.

"Over here!"

The response came not from the fly gallery but from a storage compartment across the hall.

Mrs. Potts hurried toward the sound, a joy flooding her matronly frame at the familiar voice. For the short time Gideon Payne had lived at the town house, she'd grown accustomed to doting on him—sometimes thinking that he could have been her own son.

Stepping inside, she frowned at the dimly lit, cramped cubicle that obviously served as Master Payne's temporary living quarters. She sniffed in disdain, happy beyond measure that he'd finally sent word for the town house to be prepared and his belongings moved. Even so, she couldn't help wondering what had spurred him into changing his mind.

A figure stepped from behind a changing screen. Tall, lean, and rugged—and clad in little more than a towel slung around his hips and another which he'd been using to dry his hair.

"Hello, Potts," he offered cheerfully, allowing the cloth he'd been using to drape over his shoulders.

Potts could not prevent the happiness that blossomed in her bosom at the familiar greeting.

"You're looking well, sir," she commented—glad that she hadn't been forced to lie. He *did* look well, if a trifle tired and underfed. His hair was as she remembered—

too long and wavy but infinitely attractive. His eyes sparkled with intelligence and a hidden current of mischief. His body was trim and heartbreakingly attractive. And his voice . . .

He could melt butter with that voice. Even an old woman such as herself wasn't immune to the effect.

"Come give me a hug."

He held his arms wide, and Potts giggled and blushed like a maiden. Touching the scorching heat of her cheeks with her palms, she refused the offer of a quick embrace.

"You rascal," she scolded. Then, falling into a routine as familiar as breathing, she said, "You haven't been eating your greens."

"I have."

"Doubt it. By the looks of that scrawny hide, you haven't been eating enough of anything."

He offered her a bark of laughter, then closed the distance between them and grasped her hand, quickly kissing her knuckles.

As she tittered and cooed in embarrassment, he winked at her and said, "And you are as lovely as ever."

To her relief, he moved away, walking to a converted steamer trunk that served as a bureau. Patting her bosom, she willed her heart to still its furious beating.

Slipping a shirt from the hanger, Gideon shrugged into the sleeves.

"How is Merriweather?"

"As scatterbrained as ever—but she's in full feather since you sent word to us at the house that you would be living there for a time. I think she's already cooked enough for an army, and it's not yet ten o'clock."

Needing something to do with her hands, Potts took a brush from a nearby crate and stood on tiptoe, smoothing the errant locks that tumbled from Gideon's head as he buttoned his shirt.

"I hope she's made some of those rum raisin cookies."

"She was on her second batch when I left," Potts said,

somewhat distracted. At this close vantage point, it was much easier to see that a portion of Gideon's boisterousness was an act. Lines fanned out from his eyes, and when he wasn't looking her way, there was a hardness to his features that hadn't been there the last time she'd seen him.

Becoming aware of her scrutiny, Gideon met her gaze, and Potts knew in an instant that she should ignore the changes for the time being.

"How long will it take for the town house to be ready for habitation?" he asked as he took a pair of trousers from a hanger, then disappeared behind the changing screen.

Pleased that he had respected her delicate sensibilities for once, she hastened to assure him, "The house is ready now, sir. Merriweather and I have ensured that the rooms were always kept up should you return suddenly."

"Good."

Gideon stepped from behind the screen and took a ring of keys from the end of his bed. Removing an elaborate brass affair, he extended it to her.

"This is to the Gold Room. See that it is readied as well."

Potts licked her lips, a hand flying to her throat. "The Gold Room?" she whispered, sure she couldn't have heard correctly. She and Merriweather had been forbidden to enter the Gold Room under any circumstances.

The mistress's room.

Since her death, it had never been touched.

"Yes. I want it completely restored."

The Gold Room. Miss Maura's room. The place where he'd tried to start a fire so long ago.

"Did you hear me, Potts?"

She cleared her throat. "Yes, sir."

"Will you see to it, then?"

"Of course."

"Good."

Reluctantly, she took the key, the metal cold as the grave against her flesh.

Gideon sat on the side of his bed and began to pull on his socks. "I also have an errand I need you to do for me before you return."

"I'd be happy to do anything I can to help," she said, then pushed the key into the pocket of her skirts in order to squelch her uneasiness.

The Gold Room had been firmly locked up since the funeral, and only Master Payne had a key. The fact that he had surrendered it now warned her that many more changes were in store for all the residents of the town house. She could only wonder why, since it wasn't her place to ask.

Gideon gestured to a tray that had been left on his bed. "An acquaintance of mine spent the evening in my office last night."

"Your office?" she repeated in confusion.

"Yes. I believe that my friend succumbed to the exhaustion of traveling. Take this downstairs, tell her to drink some tea and help herself to the rest."

*Her.* The acquaintance was a woman.

Potts brightened. Had Master Payne found a new love?

The fact that he'd probably entered into a liaison with the woman didn't bother Potts's sensibilities as much as it should have. She was happy to hear that Gideon's heart was on the mend.

She peered at him carefully, then sighed to herself.

No. From the looks of him, his heart wasn't involved. Much more likely, the man had found himself a mistress to warm his nights.

Pity. Potts would have given anything if Gideon had found himself a new wife.

"Tell Miss Pedigrue that I'll be down in a moment to begin our negotiations."

Negotiations? Surely he wasn't being asked to pay for

the woman's services. What woman in her right mind would *negotiate* the opportunity to spend time in this man's bed?

A fierce heat flooded her cheeks again, and Potts chastised herself for such thoughts. If Master Payne was calling the unknown guest *Miss* Pedigrue, then their association must be beyond reproach. After all, a man would not call a future consort or a barroom hussy *Miss* anything. Until Potts knew the exact circumstances of the arrangement, she knew she would do well to treat the stranger with utmost respect and courtesy.

"Is there anything else, Master Payne?" she asked as she gathered the tray.

"Not yet, but stay close at hand. I'll need you to assist Miss Pedigrue as soon as our discussion is finished."

"Very good, sir," Potts said as she backed from the room.

But as she made her way downstairs, Potts wondered just how she would be expected to *assist* the mysterious Miss Pedigrue.

Constance stretched, wincing when a stab of pain shot from her neck to her shoulder blades. Blast it all, she needed a decent night's sleep. First the train, then the succession of pitiful hotels, then . . .

Her eyes flew open, and she regarded her surroundings in confusion. She was lying on a leather couch, a red velvet cape wound around her torso and a furry muff resting beneath her head.

Something dropped beside her, and she started, automatically recoiling until she heard a familiar purring and felt a wriggling feline making its way beneath the folds of the cape until it came in contact with her hand and nudged for her to scratch its ears.

"Mr. Bentley," she sighed, all of the memories rushing back. The omnibus driver. The broken mirror. This room.

And Gideon Payne.

She shot into a sitting position, and Mr. Bentley rolled onto the cushions, peering at her from beneath the red velvet, his green eyes displaying an irritation that could not be denied.

Automatically, she reached to scratch him again, her gaze leaping to the door. It was tightly closed, just as it had been the night before, but she wondered if it would be locked. Someone had obviously come in to offer her the cape.

Someone?

Or Gideon?

Footsteps sounded outside her door. She hurriedly stood, automatically sweeping her hands over her hair and tucking the stray strands behind her ears. She wished she had a mirror or, better yet, a washbasin. But there was no time for regrets as the noises grew nearer.

Praying she didn't look too much like a beggar from the streets, Constance positioned herself next to the window and laced her fingers together in what she hoped was a demure pose.

Gideon Payne was probably furious with her. Not only had she incurred a monstrous debt, but she'd freely rearranged his office, then had fallen asleep on his couch. She bit her lip in consternation. He might not send her to jail after all. He might send her straight to an asylum.

No. She had no choice but to wait for his return.

Vainly, she fluffed her skirts and pinched her cheeks. She was hoping she could blunt the man's anger by appearing as feminine as possible.

The key jiggled in the lock. Constance held her breath in indecision, her mind whirling. There had to be something more she could do to help argue her case. After the kiss in the park, she knew the man found her somewhat pleasing.

Hesitating only a moment more, Constance released the top three buttons of her jacket to reveal a sliver of delicate batiste from the shirtwaist beneath.

The door swung open.

Constance stiffened, then forced herself to relax.

*Be at ease with him.*

But it wasn't her employer who entered. No, it was a rotund woman who wore a lace cap over the tight bunch of curls arranged about her head.

"The master will be here soon enough," she said. "He stated you weren't feeling well last evening, so he sent for me to fetch you."

*Master.* The word didn't settle well with Constance's nerves.

"He said to bring his breakfast in here. You're to help yourself to a cup of tea and then . . ."

The woman's eyes met Constance's, and she stiffened, the blood seeping from her rosy cheeks.

Constance glanced over her shoulder, peering out the window, sure that some sort of phantasm had materialized behind her, but there was nothing to be seen except the brick wall of the building across the alley. "What's wrong? I don't see—"

Constance wasn't even allowed to finish her statement. As soon as she regarded the old woman again, the lady gasped, dropping the tray onto the floor with a clatter. Shrieking, she genuflected, then raced from the room, slamming the door behind her.

It took several seconds for Constance to absorb what had occurred. Then, mumbling under her breath, she bent to scoop up the food and broken crockery from the floor.

Too late, when her hands were filled and her guard down, she heard the door open and a pair of heavy footsteps enter the room.

"Tell me, Constance," drawled the dark-haired gentleman who filled the threshold with his wide shoulders. "Do you always have such a startling effect on people?"

# Five

Constance tried to swallow the lump that gathered in her throat, but she found it thickened all the more when she met the man's eyes. Brown-black eyes as hard as flint.

"I . . ."

Whatever she'd been about to say died long before it could be formed into words.

Offering an impatient sigh, the man strode to a metal wastebasket, extending it in her direction.

Constance quickly dumped the crockery inside, then sprang to her feet, moving to the safety to be found behind the desk. As she did so, she felt the warm light of the sun strike her face.

The man's hissing inhalation could not be ignored. Staring at him, she saw that his eyes had narrowed, and he was gazing at her with the same sort of hungry disbelief he'd displayed in the park.

"Why do you keep staring at me?" she asked quickly, wondering why both he and the elderly woman had lost their composure once they garnered a good look at her face.

The man ignored her, setting the waste bin on the desk

and closing the distance between them. Grasping her chin, he held her cheeks up to the light.

"Did Luther Hayes send you here?" The demand rasped from his throat. "Are you in his employ?"

"I-I don't know anyone by that name. I was instructed to come here by my solicitors. E-evidently they arranged employment for me with someone at this theater."

She drew free when a blatant anger flared in his eyes, then a weary acceptance. "You intend to perform?"

The mere idea caused her to blush. She might have become somewhat daring since leaving her father's house, but that did not extend so far as to contemplate acting.

"No! I was to take a position as a **costu**ming seamstress and cutter."

When the man continued to gaze at her with patent disbelief, she scrambled to find the scrap of paper she'd stuffed into her pocket.

"Here's a copy of the information I was given before boarding the train."

The man scowled, studying the scribbled instructions. He gazed at her one more time, looked at the paper, then tucked the scrap into his shirt pocket. Sinking into the chair behind the desk, he swung his feet onto the blotter and surveyed her over steepled fingers. His suspicion was still clearly reflected in his narrowed gaze.

"I'm afraid you've made a mistake in coming to this particular theater for work."

Constance's stomach sank. She should have known that working in a theater was too good to be real. Her father would never have allowed such a thing. Never in his lifetime or in hers—although how such arrangements could be made without his knowledge, she didn't know.

"I have no need for a seamstress," he continued.

"Oh." The sound seeped from her nerveless lips, and her knees began to tremble. Despite the early hour, the office became hot and airless, and she regretted the vanity that had insisted that she lace her corset so tightly before embarking upon New York's streets.

She had to sit down. Now. Before she swooned.

Moving blindly, she made her way to the leather couch, wincing when more china crunched beneath the soles of her shoes.

"You see, Constance"—there was no denying the mocking edge to his tone—"according to the scrap of paper you gave me, you were to join a theater located at One-eleven Kensington."

She nodded.

"This is One-seventeen. You have come to the wrong establishment."

Her heart began to thump against her ribs, and a chill settled into her fingers. "Oh, no." Constance could not prevent the response. Nor could she prevent the way it sounded very small and meek. Everything that had occurred to her in the last twenty-four hours had been the result of a mistake. A horrible mistake.

"The address you seek is located in the next block," Gideon informed her, deepening her humiliation. The mirror, the kiss, her imprisonment in this room had all been caused by her inability to read her solicitor's handwriting.

"It was a very beautiful theater, actually. I was tempted to buy the place and refurbish it before buying this property."

For the first time, Constance was struck by the fact that Gideon Payne was using the past tense. She'd been about to rise from her place when she inquired casually, "Was?"

"It burned down two weeks ago."

Just after the will had been read. Just after plans had been made, her sisters had departed, and Constance had been forced to wait for her own transportation tickets to be delivered.

Her eyes flickered shut, and she bowed her head, pressing her fingertips against her temples.

*Think. Think,* her mind commanded, but she had a difficult time concentrating. Instead, she was flooded with a host of problems all at once.

What was she going to do? She had no means of employment, no one to turn to for help. She had very little money at her disposal—certainly not enough to pay for the damages Mr. Bentley had incurred. It would take at least a day to contact her father's solicitors and inquire what she was supposed to do to gain her inheritance now. In the meantime, she could end up living on the streets.

*No, no, no.*

"I'm afraid that you are out of a job, Miss Pedigrue," Gideon reminded her with needless efficiency. "After the fire, all of the Royale's performers and employees moved on."

Which would mean that if she was intent on finding some other job as a seamstress, she would have to compete with Theatre Royale's displaced workers.

A silent sigh of regret escaped her lips. *Will my misadventures never end?* she thought as she realized the extent of her predicament. Not only was she without the means to support herself, but, according to the requirements stipulated in her father's will, she could not receive her inheritance until she had worked at the theater he'd chosen for one full year. Without that money, she would have no future dividends to depend upon unless her father had made some sort of backup plan.

When she opened her eyes again, it was to find Gideon staring at her quite openly. She shivered at what she saw in his expression. A blatant cynicism, curiosity, and a strange sort of wariness.

Dropping his feet to the floor, he set his hands on the desk, his voice growing low and harsh. "Why don't you dispense with the acting, Miss Pedigrue?"

"Acting?"

"I think that we've passed the time for you to be coy."

"Coy?" she parroted, wondering why this man seemed to enjoy talking in riddles.

"Tell me why you're really here. The fact that you look the way you do can't have been an accident."

Her head shook from side to side in confusion. "I don't understand. I told you how I came to be in this theater. I can assure you I made an honest mistake."

"So you've said. But if there's more to your story, I want the truth now."

The fact that he thought she'd held something back in her narrative was disturbing. What more could he possibly expect her to tell him?

"Mr. Payne . . ." Her rejoinder was quelled before it could be uttered when she realized he was watching her intently. Too intently. Making her abruptly conscious of the fact that this man had touched her, had kissed her—but even after such intimacies, he thought her less than honest.

His brow arched mockingly as if he'd read her thoughts, and a sticky silence flowed into the room.

"Is it possible that we have already met?" he murmured.

His tone held a dangerous silken thread. One she did not entirely trust.

"No. Never."

"You're sure?"

Sure? She was positive. She would have remembered this man and the obsidian color of his eyes. She would have recalled the way his nearness caused her pulse to flutter alarmingly and her innate sense of decorum to falter.

"Yes, Mr. Payne," she said through clenched teeth. "I am very sure."

"You may call me Gideon."

Her lips pursed. If he thought she meant to call him by his first name—a total stranger—he had another think coming. She wouldn't dream of becoming so familiar.

Familiar? She'd kissed him. She'd felt his breath

caress her cheek. What did it matter if she called him by his first name?

It mattered. It mattered a great deal. She must see to it that she escaped from this situation with some sense of dignity. That would never occur if she ignored propriety at this late date.

"Were you an acquaintance of my late wife, perhaps?"

*He had a wife?*

No. He'd asked if she'd known his *late* wife.

"No."

"And you're sure that Hayes didn't send you?"

"I don't know a soul by that name."

He pondered her responses with more energy than she thought necessary.

"Mr. Payne . . ."

"Yes, Miss Pedigrue?" he inserted smoothly, mockingly, making sport of her own formal title.

"I can assure you with every breath in my body that you and I have never met. Nor have I encountered your wife, or anyone else in New York. I have never been to this city before my arrival yesterday."

"Then perhaps you will enlighten me as to whether we have any mutual acquaintances elsewhere."

She wasn't sure why he would ask such a thing. What did it matter if they might share common friends? Moreover, since she'd rarely been let out of her father's sight, she doubted very much that she'd ever met anyone from this man's milieu—even if he had no way of knowing such a thing.

But even as she was tempted to ask him, she ignored the urge. Her only real objective was to escape this meeting as soon as possible.

"Well, Miss Pedigrue? Am I to assume from your silence that we have mutual acquaintances or not?"

"We definitely do not, Mr. Payne. As I told you before, I am from Boston—"

"I know people in Boston."

"Perhaps. But unless you knew my father, Alexander Pedigrue, then I doubt our paths ever crossed."

"Why would you say that?"

"Because, Mr. Payne," she said tightly, summoning as much patience as she could muster, "my father rarely let us out of the house, let alone allowed us to mingle with the city's society."

Too late, she realized how much she'd revealed in such a hasty statement—the fact that her father had kept Constance and her sisters prisoner, that they were not of the "blue blood" set, that she didn't entirely regret Alexander Pedigrue's passing.

But if he noted any such information, Gideon gave no indication. Instead, he focused on a single word.

"Us?"

"I have two sisters."

"Where are they?"

"In various parts of the country fulfilling their own employment requirements." Not wanting him to inquire further, she said, "Mr. Payne, let me disabuse you of the slightest notion that I came here on some nefarious errand."

His eyes narrowed, and he studied her so intently that she began to feel as if he were an inspector and she were a counterfeit painting. Finally, he took a deep breath, broke eye contact, and allowed her time to breathe.

"I apologize for my skepticism concerning your character, Miss Pedigrue."

She wasn't completely sure what crime he'd thought she'd committed, but she found herself miffed that he felt it had been his right to forgive her.

"Mr. Payne, I don't know what you think I have or have not done, whom I know or do not know. I made a mistake in coming to this theater—a very honest one, as I have explained. I was so distracted by the activity outside your building yesterday that I didn't double-check the address. If I had, you can rest assured that I wouldn't have darkened your door with my presence."

Adding a prim sniff as punctuation to her pronouncement, she gathered her reticule from the cushion of the couch and tugged her gloves over her fingers, continuing, "As it is, I think it would be best if I left you to your own devices, gathered up my cat, and made my way to some sort of boardinghouse until I can contact my father's solicitors for further instructions."

Scooping Mr. Bentley from his perch on the bookcase, she shoved him into the basket, ignoring his hisses of displeasure. Then, after rescuing her bonnet from a packing crate, she marched to the door.

Her hand closed around the cool porcelain at the precise moment the man at the desk said, "We haven't finished our business, Miss Pedigrue."

She shot him an irritated glance. "Since we had no 'business' to begin with, Mr. Payne, I don't see—"

"There's the small matter of the mirror."

Her lips pursed in annoyance. Botheration, she'd forgotten the mirror.

"I believe it was your cat—Mr. Bentley, did you say?—who was responsible for the damage?"

This couldn't be happening to her. Such messy situations never occurred to Constance Pedigrue. She prided herself on being the soul of propriety and gentility. A lady through and through. Women of quality didn't get themselves into such scrapes—and if they did, there was always some sort of knight in shining armor to save them.

Constance opened her mouth to deny the charges, then changed her mind. They both knew that such protestations would be a waste of breath. She was buried up to her neck in this unfortunate predicament—and there would be no knight to save her. She would have to depend on her own wits.

"I can pay you back," she said, but her voice sounded weak.

"How?"

She licked her lips. *How?*

"As soon as I've begun working . . ."

"I've already explained to you that the likelihood of your being employed at the theater at One-eleven Kensington is all but nil."

*Think, Constance, think!*

"I suppose I could . . ."

*You could what? Obtain a loan? Raise the necessary cash to pay for a ten-foot mirror edged in gilt? Not likely.*

"Mr. Payne," she began again, setting her things down. Mr. Bentley immediately bounced out of the basket and ran beneath the couch. "I'm a woman of my word. If I give you a promise, I *will* repay you. In fact, if you will direct me to the nearest telegraph office, I will wire my father's solicitors for funds." Whether the money would be sent or not was, unfortunately, another matter, but she bravely added, "I swear to you that I will return within the hour."

He shook his head. "I'm so sorry, but your word isn't good enough, Miss Pedigrue. After all, I don't know you from Eve. For all I know you could be a very consummate liar."

True.

"I don't know what else I can do to convince you, Mr. Payne," she whispered, knowing that she was going to be thrown in jail for sure. He would have her arrested and sent to the salt mines.

Her eyes filled with a damning moisture at the mere thought of what her sisters would say once they received the news. Blast it all. *Blast!* What had made her bring a cat to New York, anyhow? It had been a stupid, foolish thing to do.

Tugging at her reticule, she struggled to open it so that she could retrieve the lace-edged handkerchief, then remembered she'd lost it sometime the day before. Delving into her pocket, she retrieved the scrap of velvet and wiped her nose.

Even with her head bent and her eyes furiously blinking away the tears, she felt Gideon rise from his desk and move toward her.

He took the scrap of velvet from her hands. Then, as it unfolded, she realized she hadn't found a patch of fabric as she'd assumed. A sizzling heat flooded her cheeks. Even from a distance, she knew that what he held was a narrow boudoir corset—the kind she'd sometimes seen in magazines made for rich pampered women or circus performers.

"A very . . . ingenious choice of accessories, Miss Pedigrue."

"I can assure you that it isn't mine! I merely—"

He waved aside her protestations. "I'm sure it doesn't matter how or where you came by such an . . . extravagant piece of frippery."

She stammered, hoping to salvage the situation, but he continued, undaunted. "No, Miss Pedigrue, I think the major issue we should focus on is your financial situation. If you would care to dictate a telegram, I will have one of the stagehands deliver it to the telegraph office. In the meantime, I see no other way out of the situation than for you to accept my conditions."

She choked back a sob.

". . . than for you to come work for me rather than my theater."

*Work for me . . .*

The words shuddered in the room, and Constance forgot about her faux pas with the corset as she gazed up at the man who towered over her.

"Work for you?" she echoed blankly, sure that she'd heard him incorrectly.

He nodded.

"You need some sewing done in your home?"

"No."

Her heart thumped against her ribs in disappointment. She was going to be forced to serve as some sort of cleaning woman, she was sure, to take over the same kinds of jobs that she had only recently abandoned at her father's house. She regretted the fact, regretted the recent dashing of her dreams of a theater life, but she could not complain. Not when her future was about to be salvaged.

Gideon closed the distance between them. When he reached out to tip her chin up to the light, she had to force herself not to blink or tremble or fall at his feet in gratitude.

"As a matter of fact, if you complete the assignment in a competent way, I might even consider making the arrangement permanent. You could even advance to a managing position," he murmured, his voice so low and rich that her stomach quivered in response.

"What do you mean?" The words escaped from her lips in a breathy whisper that she despised but could not prevent.

Gideon shook his head. "I'll explain your duties more fully once you've had a chance to freshen up. As it is, I'll need to mull over the possibility of a promotion. I'm not sure my people would appreciate working for a woman."

"But you said—"

"I'll still give you plenty to do in the meantime. You'll have a very respectable position as my personal assistant."

"Your assistant?" Constance breathed.

Gideon sighed, planting his hands on his hips. "Tell me, Miss Pedigrue. Am I going to be treated to a constant parroting of my own words?"

"Your own . . ." She snapped her jaw shut and yanked free from his hold, hastily gathering her wits. "Oh, no, sir. It's just that . . . I thought you said you wanted me to work as your assistant until some other position becomes available."

He huffed in indignation. "I did say that."

"But . . . you hardly know me."

"I don't know you at all, if the truth be told." He pivoted on the ball of his foot and returned to his desk. "So what would possess you to hire *me* for such an important task? I would think you'd want someone you know. Someone with a great deal of experience."

The moment the words left her mouth, Constance realized she should have kept her questions to herself. After all, this man was giving her employment—a very proper and ladylike position—as his personal assistant. Considering the debt she owed him, she shouldn't allow him to dwell on second thoughts.

But since the query had been uttered, there was no unsaying it.

"I am willing to employ you—on probation, mind you"—he stabbed a finger in the air—"because you seem to know your business."

He waved a negligent hand toward the shelves. "The last man I asked to put those books away took three days to unload a single crate. You, on the other hand, completed the entire assignment in a few hours."

Constance didn't completely understand the warmth that flowed through her body at his offhanded compliment.

"I've got other such jobs I need someone to do— organizing, dictating, scheduling—provided that you've got a mind for them."

Her chin tilted ever so slightly at the intimation that she might not be smart enough to handle the work he would send her way. Then, catching his intense regard, she entertained some of her own suspicions.

"Before I agree to anything, I think you should outline a few more of the . . . *tasks* you intend to assign to me." There was no ignoring the emphasis she employed.

"No surprises, hmm?" he drawled.

"I would prefer to avoid them." She arched her brows. "After all that has occurred to me since my arrival in New York, I'm sure you understand."

He laughed, and the sound caused a frisson of unfamiliar emotions to skitter down her spine. There was something altogether sensual, altogether . . . knowing about the sound.

"Have you really had such a terrible time of things, Constance?"

He stepped closer, causing her pulse to knock at her temples with an anxious pressure.

"Surely not all of your experiences have been bad."

The way he spoke, so low and velvety smooth, caused her body to heat from the inside out. Abruptly, she was reminded of those minutes in the park when she had become intimately aware of this man's body, and he of hers.

She started when he cupped her cheeks, his thumbs grazing her skin with lazy deliberation. She shuddered at the molten sweetness such a simple gesture inspired.

"Was our kiss really so horrible, Constance?" he murmured.

She didn't have the power to move, let alone speak.

Gideon's lips tilted in a crooked grin.

"I don't think you regret the embrace at all."

Still unable to speak, she could only lick her lips in the hopes that her brain would begin to function again. The action had the opposite effect, when Gideon's eyes flared and his head began to dip.

"I think that you'd like me to kiss you again."

"No," she finally managed to whisper, but he must not have heard the word or read it on her lips, because he didn't stop.

Softly, sweetly, his mouth covered hers. When she sighed against him, he smiled, drawing back enough to whisper, "Relax, Constance. I won't hurt you."

Then his kiss lost all attempt at innocence, and he held her with the passion that she remembered from the previous day. His arms slid down her back, and he pulled her to him, so tightly that she feared she wouldn't be able to breathe.

Moaning against him, she rested her own hands uncertainly at his waist, her fingers digging into the hard flesh.

This time, when his tongue bid entrance to her mouth, she couldn't summon the wherewithal to refuse him. Her senses reeled, and her body seemed primed for some experience that would prove even more startling, even more momentous.

*No!* She couldn't do this. Not with this man, this stranger.

The voice of conscience barely pierced the haze of her emotions, but as Gideon caressed her spine, her shoulders, the warning reverberated, growing stronger until she could not ignore it.

"No!" she gasped when finally she was given the opportunity to breathe.

Wrenching free, she stormed to the opposite end of the room, looking through the barred windows to the bleak alley beyond.

"Mr. Payne. I don't think that I should . . . that you should . . . that we . . ." She took a deep breath and began again. "I must insist that our relationship be nothing more than that of employer and employee."

"Don't worry, Miss Pedigrue, I don't have immediate designs upon your virtue."

So what had that kiss been? An overture of friendship? She wasn't that naive.

"I also don't want you to think that I've made any disparaging assumptions about your character."

"I didn't think you had, Mr. Payne."

Other than that he'd already intimated she was a liar, a sneak, and a wanton.

"You promised to outline my exact duties," she reminded him.

"Of course." Leaning against the desk, he folded his arms over his chest and regarded her intently. "In addition to the tasks I've already mentioned, I need someone to do some simple bookkeeping."

"Fine."

"Cataloging of books and furnishings."

"I can do that."

"I will expect you to handle my correspondence— both personal and business."

"Hmm." She nodded to show she was agreeable.

"You will accompany me during auditions and building site examinations. I have three theaters located within a fifty-mile radius, which will require a small amount of travel but nothing arduous. At times, you may be asked to organize social functions for a few friends or associates."

She was startled by that piece of information, but she said, "I think I'm up to such work."

He didn't immediately reply. Once again, the room filled with a tense expectancy, and Constance found herself wondering if she were being too hasty in her acceptance of the proffered employment.

But what else could she do? She either took the job being offered or made her way onto the streets of New York, penniless and encumbered with an enormous debt.

"Before you accept, Miss Pedigrue, I think you should know that I am a widower."

She had already surmised as much.

"As my assistant, I will call upon *you* to serve as my hostess."

"Really?" She cursed herself for sounding like a besotted fool, but she couldn't help thinking that her inclusion in his personal business affairs gave her job a certain cachet.

"I think that you should also know that I am accustomed to working at odd hours," Gideon continued.

Since he paused, she felt bound to respond. "Yes, sir."

"It will therefore be necessary for you to *share* the same hours."

Constance had thought that point obvious but offered a quiet, "Of course, Mr. Payne."

His eyes were intent as they searched her face, then slowly trailed down to her toes.

"Very well. At least we understand each other." Taking a breath, he bellowed, "Mrs. Potts!"

Footsteps hurried down the outer corridor, and the door whispered open. "Yes, Mr. Payne."

"Take Miss Pedigrue to the town house, and introduce her to Merriweather and Birch."

"Yes, sir."

"Then, as soon as the suite is ready for occupation, put her in the Gold Room."

The woman's eyes grew round and bright. "The . . . G-Gold Room?"

Gideon sighed in impatience. "Obviously, your habit of repeating everything I say is contagious, Miss Pedigrue."

Turning his attention back to the chubby woman, he said, "Yes. Then see to it that the instructions I gave you earlier are taken care of as soon as possible."

Mrs. Potts's eyes threatened to pop from her skull. "Of course. It may take . . . thorough cleaning, shall I . . . have your things put in the Gold Room as well?"

Constance gasped.

Gideon scowled.

"No, Mrs. Potts. This arrangement is for convenience, not for dalliance."

"Very well, sir."

The woman had the grace to look discomfited, but Constance could not ignore the fact that Mrs. Potts had come to a purely logical conclusion. One that many more people would be likely to form.

She gripped her fingers together, wondering if she should say something to Gideon and risk having him retrieve his offer. She was, after all, a woman with a sterling reputation. Her name had never been associated with scandal—or even a hint of excitement, if the truth were known.

The thought speared her to the core. Was that what she wanted from life? To be "constant" to the end? To have lived to a ripe old age without ever having tasted regret, but never having tasted adventure, either?

No.

She would not open her mouth. She wouldn't complain about the arrangements. She wouldn't worry about her reputation.

Looking at Gideon, an effervescent thrill spilled into her bloodstream. She deserved this moment. She deserved the chance to work in a theater—not as a lowly seamstress but as the assistant of the owner. She would not lose the chance to follow such a dream.

Sensing her regard, Gideon glanced her way. His lips quirked ever so slightly—as if he were waiting for some sort of complaint. When she remained silent, his gaze raked over her from head to toe, and he added, "See to it that Merriweather draws her a bath as well. By the looks of her, she came from Boston the hard way."

Constance huffed in annoyance, but Mrs. Potts didn't wait for a rejoinder. The woman bobbed a curtsey and ran back down the corridor—ostensibly to hail a carriage.

Constance knew she was supposed to follow Mrs. Potts, but she'd grown rooted to the floor. There was one thing more she needed to know.

"Mr. Payne?"

Gideon had turned his attention to the papers spread out on his desk, but he stared at her as soon as she'd spoken.

"I thought I made it clear that I wished to have you call me Gideon."

"Yes, but . . ."

"If you are to be my assistant, I insist."

"Very well . . . Gideon."

The unfamiliar arrangement of vowels and consonants felt odd as it formed in her mouth. She was stunned by the intimacy she felt in using his given name. Such a trivial detail shouldn't have mattered, but it did. Somehow, it weakened the emotional barrier she was attempting to construct between them.

"Gideon . . ." Again, she hesitated, then forced herself to continue. "I wondered . . . exactly how much will I be owing you? For the mirror, I mean."

Gideon's gaze dropped to the papers again, and he reached for a stubby pencil at the side of his blotter.

"We can talk about that later."

"I would rather know now. I must insist."

He sighed, his dark eyes so intent that she nearly took a step backward. After several uncomfortable seconds, he relented, opened a drawer, and removed a folder. Flipping through a stack of invoices, he perused the contents and finally pulled one free.

"Here you are," he said, tossing it onto the desk.

Constance had to will herself to approach. Her mind was already whirling with her own estimates. The other theater had offered her a dollar a day—an outlandishly generous amount. Providing that Gideon Payne gave her wages near or equal to that total—and the mirror cost no more than one hundred dollars . . .

The mental gears whirled as Constance hypothesized how much she would need to expend for food and necessities. But the moment her eyes fell to the scrap of paper poised on the edge of Gideon's desk, her mind froze.

Five thousand dollars.

Five *thousand* dollars.

# Six

Gideon watched Constance stumble from the room. Her eyes had been dazed and a trifle disbelieving, but she'd gathered her cat, her bonnet, and her reticule, and followed Mrs. Potts with an obvious show of compliance.

She'd accepted the offer.

Gideon rounded his desk and sank into his chair, his breath escaping in a whoosh. Until that moment, he hadn't realized that he'd been so tense. From the time he'd begun outlining her responsibilities, he'd been sure that Constance would refuse his offer and insist that he allow her to telegraph her solicitors about money for the mirror.

But she hadn't.

She'd taken the position.

Moreover, she'd seemed . . . *pleased*.

So what was he going to do with her? He had never hired an assistant before. He was accustomed to completing his own assignments without an intermediary. Until he could get used to the arrangement, he was going to have to keep the woman busy.

Shaking his head at his own audacity, he fought the

strange swirl of emotions this woman inspired in him each time they sparred. He was still struggling to reconcile himself with her resemblance to Maura. The likeness brought an unbidden wave of remembered anger, betrayal, and lust. But Constance was also able to arouse in him an instant hunger, a patent longing.

Who was she? Who?

And why had fate caused her to stumble into his life? His theater?

Jumping to his feet, Gideon paced the length of his office, then back again.

He couldn't help but remember the day his first burlesque theater house had been completed in Baltimore. His hands tightened. How could he forget the event? It had been the first sign of tension in his new marriage. Maura had inspected her dressing room, then had demanded a complete redecoration of her quarters, since they didn't "befit" a woman of her important social status—as if any of the local blue-bloods would allow Maura to darken their doors.

It hadn't taken long for Gideon to realize that Maura had plans of her own. Since Gideon had a half-dozen legitimate theaters to his name, she'd wanted to cross from the world of burlesque to the more "respectable" roles to be found in the staid dramas and comedies preferred by wealthy patrons.

Gideon had tried his best to convince Maura that even as a dramatic actress, she would never gain the approval of "quality folk." But she hadn't believed him. She'd begun throwing lavish parties, inviting wealthy businessmen and upstart politicians as a means to pave the way for her social "rebirth."

Gideon had been more than willing to humor her. He'd loved her, adored her, showered her with every luxury. Unlike most husbands, he allowed her a free hand with his money, paying the enormous bills from the milliner, couturier, and caterer.

But he'd never thought she would betray him.

Especially with a man he'd considered more a brother than a friend.

Cursing under his breath, Gideon slammed the gate on such memories. It was senseless to think of Maura anyway. She had no place in Gideon's current life. She was a bad episode in his history, and he was well rid of her. Birch had prevented Gideon from eradicating all evidence of her from his house by setting it ablaze, but the somber butler hadn't been able to prevent Gideon from banishing all gentler feelings toward her from his heart.

Gideon was still pacing the room when the door burst open and his stage manager, Lester Grassman, appeared.

"Did you see that woman?" He gasped, obviously out of breath. "She's leaving right now with Potts in tow."

"I know." The words were dark and ominous.

"You saw her?"

"I hired her."

Lester's jaw dropped. "You *hired* her? Are you out of your mind, man?"

Gideon glared at his longtime friend and house manager, but the stout fellow ignored him.

"Didn't you see the resemblance?" Lester demanded. "Clean her up a bit, put her in some decent clothes, and she'll look just like—"

"Maura," Gideon deftly inserted.

That response had the power to seal Lester's lips—if only for a few seconds.

"One of your competitors sent her here to unsettle you and delay the opening of the theater," Lester said after a moment's thought. "That woman's presence here can't be a coincidence."

Gideon shrugged. "Perhaps."

"Perhaps, hell. Just last week, Luther Hayes returned to New York City—everyone knows he was with Maura minutes before she died. Now a woman who is the spitting image of your late wife waltzes into your theater.

You should be scared to death that she's been sent here to wriggle under your skin."

He *should* be afraid of just such a thing, Gideon conceded. But strangely enough, he wasn't. He truly believed Constance's assertions that she had spent most of her life closed up in a house in Boston. The way she'd offered the information, her tone proud but her eyes bleak, had assured him that she was telling the truth.

Besides, this woman was no actress. She was too ingenuous. Everything she thought and felt marched across her face.

"Who is she?" Les demanded.

"Her name is Constance Pedigrue." Gideon collapsed in his chair, tapped his pencil against the blotter, then sighed in resignation as his own suspicious nature prodded him.

Constance might have told him the truth about Boston, but that didn't mean her arrival was completely innocent. Just as Lester had argued, she could have been manipulated into coming here.

By Luther Hayes? The man who had been caught in Maura's bed?

No. Gideon didn't believe it.

"I want you to check into her background. Let me know about her home, family, and education." Gideon took the telegram Constance had dictated for him from his pocket. "Then I want you to contact the solicitors listed here and see if the girl actually had a position with the Theatre Royale as a seamstress. But don't send Miss Pedigrue's telegram itself until you've spoken to me."

Lester took the paper, but it was clear that he still couldn't believe his ears.

"She had a position as a *seamstress?*"

"So she claimed."

Lester stared at the note. "The Royale burned down."

"I informed her of that fact."

Lester's lips thinned. "I bet she had the nerve to act surprised."

Gideon tucked his thumbs into the waist of his trousers. "I'm not sure if *act* is the proper term, Les."

Les shook the paper in his direction. "If she's anything like Maura Kelly, it's the only word to use." He huffed in indignation, then asked, "So what job have you given the woman?"

"For now, she's to become my personal assistant."

Lester's jaw dropped, and Gideon knew why. First, because he'd hired an assistant at all, and second, because the woman he'd hired looked so much like Maura Kelly.

His former wife.

The woman he'd thought would eventually bear his children and supply him with a family.

Gideon leaned back, linking his hands behind his head and staring at the ceiling. He would be the first to admit that his actions were uncharacteristic, but he didn't intend to explain himself. After all, what could he say? That he'd kept the woman nearby because of the proud tilt of her chin and the deep blue of her eyes?

His peers would assume he'd kept her in his employ because she looked so much like Maura. Incredibly alike. *If not for the hint of innocence in her eyes.*

Gideon peered sightlessly into space, seeing Maura as he had the last time. Her golden hair had spilled across the pillow of the bed they shared in the town house. Her body had been twined around that of another man. His former school chum. Her lover.

Luther Hayes.

Echoes of anger rose within him—the same overpowering fury that had caused him to set the curtains ablaze to eradicate all evidence of Maura's duplicity. But as his hands knotted in anger, Gideon dragged his thoughts away from that particular road. He wouldn't think about that right now. Maura had betrayed him, but she was gone.

"Get out of here, Les," Gideon said. There was no sting to his words, merely a weary verbal nudging.

After shooting one last curious glance in Gideon's direction, Les disappeared, closing the door behind him.

For several long, aching seconds, Gideon sat where he was, willing himself not to think, willing himself not to feel.

But when he'd touched Constance, kissed her, he'd been forced to awaken from his long, self-imposed emotional hibernation. And the return to awareness had not been pleasant.

Was he so predictable? Was he doomed to repeat his mistakes with this woman? So much time had passed, he should have been able to look at Constance with complete detachment.

He shouldn't want to hold anything that even remotely resembled his former wife.

He certainly shouldn't want to caress her.

Watch the awareness flicker in her eyes.

Damnation. Why couldn't he force himself to acknowledge that this woman wasn't Maura? She was a stranger. There was no past between them—and there certainly wasn't a future. He should toss her into the street and brush his hands of the whole affair.

He jumped to his feet and strode into the corridor, shouting to anyone who might listen that he needed his horse—a luxury he preferred over a carriage.

By the time he emerged out of the back stage door, the animal was waiting for him, brought by one of the young boys who worked as gophers in the theater.

Swinging onto the animal's back, Gideon spurred it into a gallop—causing pedestrians and workmen alike to take cover. Skillfully, he made his way through the heavy traffic in the main portion of town, needing an outlet for his roiling emotions. But as the congested residential areas led to the squalor of the very poor, he saw that his mind continued to rule his actions.

Both he and his mount were winded as he stopped in front of St. Michael's Orphanage and Foundling Home. His earliest memories were of this place. Although his childhood would take him from one charitable institution to another, it was here that he'd met Luther Hayes. He and the towheaded lad had been inseparable for years. They'd shared secrets, adventures, and the trials of being without parents. Eventually, they had even shared the love of the same woman, a fact that would destroy emotional ties that had already been tempered by the fires of youth.

Sighing, Gideon turned his back on the orphanage, nudged the horse, and headed in the direction of the town house, banishing the taut emotions that roiled within him—remembered rage, wonder, anticipation.

After a few days' work, he would get this woman out of his system, then send Constance Pedigrue away, he decided. With her departure, he would finally rid himself of the burdens of the past.

Just a few days.

Before he found himself wanting far more than kisses from a veritable stranger.

Constance clutched Mr. Bentley firmly in her arms as she stepped from the carriage onto the brick walkway in front of the place that would be her new residence for the next few . . .

Weeks? Months?

Despite the heat of the afternoon, she shivered, looking up, up, up, at the massive neoclassical facade. She would wager that Gideon Payne's town house sat upon a quarter of a city block and was four stories high. Ornate fresco work adorned the fascia, and fretwork edged the windows and roof. Marble columns supported the first floor, the Corinthian carvings layered with gilt.

"Good heavens," she whispered. *"This* is where Mr. Payne lives?"

"It's a bit overwhelming at first sight, isn't it?" Mrs. Potts said as she hastened to disembark from the brougham. The woman had been kind enough to carry the ruined basket, and she paused to study the building as well.

"There was a time when this house was the envy of the neighborhood, I can assure you." Her expression became rapt, her eyes taking on a faraway sheen. "The parties they used to have here were magnificent. Candles burned from every window—and flowers! The whole house smelled continually of roses. There was laughter and music and a constant flow of visitors. Master Payne made every attempt to make the place as warm and welcoming as possible. He proclaimed that this spot would always be an island of safety and contentment in a riotous world."

Mrs. Potts bit her lip and genuflected, then blinked against her sudden tears.

Averting her face, Constance allowed the woman a moment to gather her emotions. Judging by Potts's reaction, this house hadn't always been a happy place.

Remembering that Gideon had spoken of his "late" wife, she realized that the people who lived here had suffered a tragedy in the loss of their mistress—one that Mrs. Potts still felt keenly.

"Ach, now," Potts said, retrieving a handkerchief from her pocket. Wiping her eyes, she regarded the building with her own brand of regrets. "The master had such grand plans for this place. It's a pity his dreams never came to fruition."

"What happened?"

Mrs. Potts made a clucking sound with her tongue. "It was Miss Maura who gave the house its life."

A nervousness gripped Constance's chest.

"Miss Maura?"

Mrs. Potts shot her a measuring glance. "Master Payne brought her here as his bride."

"Maura," Constance echoed, the sound barely managing to escape her lips. So that had been the venerable woman's name.

Mrs. Potts bit her lip as if she feared she'd said too much. Then, leaning close, she gripped Constance's hand.

"Miss Maura was an actress, you know."

Constance hadn't been aware of the fact—hadn't even known of the woman's existence until recently—but she nodded as if she understood.

"She loved to meet interesting people, so she constantly surrounded herself with the cream of society. Even the blue-blooded aristocrats who looked down on her occupation found themselves drawn to her."

"I see."

"It was she who helped to design the house. She patterned it after some of the European homes she visited during one of her tours."

Mrs. Potts pointed to the top floor. "Up there, she made sure there was enough living space for a dozen servants. Below that is a ballroom that encompasses the entire third floor. The second level has the living quarters, and on the ground you will find two libraries, four salons, a study, a solarium, and the kitchens.

Constance's mouth gaped. "It sounds like a palace."

"Very nearly so," Mrs. Potts replied sagely. "I'm sure that's what Miss Maura had in mind."

Constance eyed the woman more carefully when she caught the tightness of Mrs. Potts's tone.

"You didn't approve of her?"

The older woman sniffed. "I neither approved nor disapproved," she stated stiffly. "It wasn't my place to do so."

"But you formed certain opinions," Constance prompted. It wasn't normally in her nature to pry, but she found herself so intrigued by Gideon Payne's late wife that she ignored the fact that she was gossiping in the middle of the brick walkway with a servant.

Mrs. Potts glanced from side to side as if she were afraid of being caught in an indiscretion. Then she leaned close to murmur. "I didn't like the woman in the end," she admitted obliquely. "I could never forgive her for what she did to Mr. Payne."

"What did she do?"

She clucked her tongue. "It was horrible, simply horrible. How the poor man bore it all, I don't know." Her fingers gripped Constance's so tightly that she pinched the skin of her knuckles. "It was only two years ago, mind you, when she—"

"Mrs. Potts, did you say something about picking up a trunk at the railway station?"

Mrs. Potts jumped and glanced guiltily behind her.

The carriage driver glared her way in patent disapproval, and in an instant the moment was lost, and Constance knew she would be receiving no more secrets that day.

Mrs. Potts stiffened. "Do you have your claim ticket, my dear?" Mrs. Potts inquired, but her tone held a formality that had not been present before.

"Yes, of course."

Constance juggled the cat in her arms, wincing as he wriggled and clawed to be free. Reaching into her reticule, she removed the coupons, stating, "Two of my trunks were stolen at the station. There is only one remaining, I'm afraid."

"Poor girl," Mrs. Potts murmured.

Taking the scraps of colored paper, she extended them to the driver. "While you're there, Dawson, will you be so kind as to check on the missing trunks? Perhaps the authorities have been able to track down the miscreants."

"Yes, ma'am."

"As soon as you've returned, have Simpings help you carry it upstairs. Then Birch has been asked to gather the master's things from the theater."

"Very well."

The carriage clattered away.

Constance had hoped that having the man retreat

would encourage Mrs. Potts to return to her confidences, but she was mistaken.

Gesturing for Constance to follow her, Mrs. Potts marched to the shallow steps that led to a pair of oiled mahogany doors. She left Constance with a dozen questions swirling through her brain.

What had happened to Gideon's wife? How had she alienated Mrs. Potts? Why did her memory seem to be shrouded in secrecy?

And what had she done to make Gideon Payne so hardened?

There wasn't a great deal of time for rumination. Moments before they reached the entrance, the panels swung open to reveal the most formidable man Constance had ever seen. He was nigh onto seven feet tall if he was an inch, his body gaunt and squared, his face seeming to have been etched from a block of granite.

Stepping aside, he allowed them to enter a foyer devoid of light and so shadowed in darkness that Constance was barely able to make out the stairs leading to the next level.

"Birch, this is Mr. Payne's new assistant, Miss Pedigrue."

The butler gave no indication whether he welcomed the news or not, but Constance offered him a quick "How do you do?" Squinting into the dimness, she tried her best to see what the man looked like but was unable to make out much more than a craggy, looming shape.

"Don't bother with the niceties, my dear," Mrs. Potts instructed. "He's as deaf as a post."

The information was carelessly tossed in Constance's direction as another servant rushed into the foyer from the rear of the house. Judging by the woman's flour-dusted apron, this was the cook.

"Merriweather, we're going to have a new addition to the household."

Merriweather wiped her hands on her apron, her smile dimming in clear disapproval. "Oh."

Mrs. Potts laughed. "Not *that* sort of addition, Merriweather."

Merriweather's brows lifted.

"Master Payne has hired Miss Pedigrue as his assistant."

"His what?" She squinted in Constance's direction, obviously trying to pierce the gloom of the foyer.

"You heard me. The girl is to be his assistant."

"But he *never* takes an assistant." Merriweather's eyes narrowed even more—as if she feared that Constance had used some means of extortion to arrange the position.

"I'm afraid that an accident at the theater precipitated her position," Mrs. Potts murmured.

When it was clear that Merriweather didn't intend to budge until her suspicions were allayed, Potts sighed and continued, "The men were hoisting the mirror—"

"Which mirror?"

"The big one."

"Not the one from Belgium?" Merriweather gasped.

"The very same, Merriweather—and it didn't come from Belgium, it came from France."

"I thought it was Belgium."

Mrs. Potts scowled. "No. France. In any event, it doesn't matter where it came from, since the mirror has been completely destroyed."

Constance shifted uncomfortably. Even Mr. Bentley had the grace to look somewhat shamefaced.

Merriweather grasped the fabric of her apron to her bosom as if she feared her heart would break.

"No," she whispered in very real despair, although the darkness prevented Constance from reading her expression. "I saw a peek of it just the other day. All that plaster work and filigree and etching."

"Exactly."

"Broken?"

"Into thousands of irretrievable pieces."

Constance fought the urge to wriggle in embarrassment. How many times was she going to be brought to task for that blasted mirror?

"Actually, I suppose I must clarify things and explain that Miss Pedigrue was not personally responsible for the tragedy."

"Oh?"

"Her cat jumped from its basket and tangled with Willoby."

Merriweather swayed as if she'd been informed of a horrible tragedy. "How awful." She turned then to Constance. "How is your cat?"

Constance was so thrown by the change of subject that she stumbled to reply. "Well, h-he's fine." She hitched Mr. Bentley higher in her arms to prove the point.

Merriweather leaned closer to peer at the animal, searching for apparent injuries. "You're quite fortunate, you know. Willoby has been known to eat cats for dinner. Literally. Keep your eyes on the animal."

"Yes, ma'am."

"She's all dusty," Merriweather complained to her companion.

Potts scowled when Merriweather bluntly commented on Constance's state of dress. Too late, Constance remembered she was spattered with mud, wrinkled, disheveled, and decidedly travel-worn.

"She just arrived in New York," Mrs. Potts informed her companion tartly. "She's from Boston. She looks the way she does because she collapsed last night from weariness and was forced to stay at the theater until she recovered. She has been unable to . . . tidy herself since two of her trunks were stolen from the railway office."

"I see."

Constance reeled slightly at the amount of information Mrs. Potts already knew.

Nevertheless, despite the explanation, it was clear that Mrs. Merriweather felt Constance was somehow to blame for the problem. She extended her hand, then, once it had been shaken, dropped it just as quickly.

"Where are we supposed to put her?"

Mrs. Potts bit her lip, then said in a rush, "He wants her placed in the Gold Room as soon as it can be prepared."

Merriweather's brows all but disappeared beneath the ruffled edge of her cap. "You can't be serious," she whispered frantically. "No one has been in the Gold Room since . . . you know."

Instantly, Constance knew there was something about the Gold Room that should cause her to be on her guard. Something ominous, judging by the expressions on the old women's faces.

Mrs. Potts held up her hands in a helpless gesture. "He was quite clear about what room we were to use, Merriweather. The master has spoken, and we mustn't go against his wishes."

The term *master* had been warmly employed, but there was no hiding the fact that these women would do everything in their power to ensure that Gideon Payne's edicts were obeyed.

Merriweather harrumphed and gestured to a long, shadowy marble corridor leading toward the back of the house. "Well, it will take some time to get the Gold Room fixed. Until then, we'll make do with one of the guest chambers."

The sober cook crooked a finger in Constance's direction. "Come along, dearie. You can rest in the kitchen and have a bite to eat. From the looks of you, it's been too long since you had a square meal."

Once again, Constance was reminded that her past life had never been one of abundance. Normally, she wouldn't have given such matters a second thought, but since her clothing was not well tailored or elaborately decorated, she must appear slightly waifish. After seeing the elegant gentlewomen of New York, she knew that her appearance could never be mistaken as that of a fine lady.

A fine lady indeed. She was nothing but the daughter of a former minister.

But she wanted to be more.

She'd *always* wanted to be more.

"Master Payne has said he wishes for her to take a bath as well, Merriweather."

Constance's face flamed at the blunt pronouncement. Somehow, Mrs. Potts made it sound as if Constance hadn't tended to her ablutions in some time.

"Would you like that, dearie? I could put the water on so you could have a long soak."

Constance was pleased by the way she'd finally been given a choice, but before she could speak, Merriweather said, "Well, of course you do. It's obvious that you've only recently arrived here in New York. The maids are busy cleaning, but I suppose you won't mind if Mrs. Potts and I give you a hand."

Again, Constance was left to feel grubby and out of place, but she had no opportunity to speak because she was led into a long, narrow room that was laden in sunlight. After leaving the gloom of the marble-encased hallway with its niches filled with brooding paintings and weathered sculpture, the cheerfulness of this particular place was shocking.

Constance gasped ever so slightly, her steps slowing as she surveyed hardwood tables and cupboards and the finest of modern conveniences. But what caught and held her attention was the wall of windows that overlooked a formal garden abloom with every sort of flower imaginable.

How she loved flowers. Her father had thought them frivolous luxuries, not worth the trouble of tending to them. But Constance had always adored the colors and textures and scents to be found in nature. She had tended to the window box on her bedroom ledge with the same care that a master horticulturist might display for the gardens of Versailles.

"How lovely!"

Mr. Bentley squirmed in her arms, and Constance let him jump to the floor, where he immediately prowled toward a basket of puppies near the fire. Tugging at the ribbon of her bonnet, Constance lifted the hat free and took a step into the buttery sunlight.

"The garden is quite a sight," claimed Merriweather as she moved to the pump situated against one wall. "The master insisted that it be . . ."

When Merriweather's comment died away, Constance tore her attention back to the old woman and was astounded when she found Merriweather staring at her, a hand touching her throat in alarm.

"Sakes alive!" She gasped. "You've come back."

# Seven

Who's come back?" Constance whispered. Then, stamping her foot in irritation, she demanded, "For heaven's sake! What is it about me that continually startles people?"

Since meeting Gideon Payne, she'd become the object of more than a dozen covert gazes and outright stares. The phenomenon was growing positively eerie—as well as completely irritating.

As if to underscore her point, Birch walked into the kitchen, stopped, then stared, all color draining from his skin.

Potts poked Merriweather in the arm, then imperceptibly shook her head at her friend, then the sober butler, before tossing a too-warm smile in Constance's direction.

"Not a thing, Miss," Mrs. Potts said. She threw Merriweather a clear look of warning. "It's just that in the sunlight, your hair is the most incredible shade of gold."

Constance doubted that Merriweather's surprise could be explained so easily—and she was about to remind Potts of her own spilled crockery—but the woman was already bustling toward her.

"Come along, Miss Pedigrue. I'll show you to the bathing room. It shouldn't take but a minute for the water to heat, and while it does, you can hand me your clothes for washing. Once you're settled, I'll tell you where to find one of my wrappers to use—although I daresay it will drown you." She made a clucking sound with her tongue. "Nevertheless, it will keep you free from a chill while you're waiting for your trunk. You can sit by the fire and dry your hair if you'd like."

Although Constance longed to stay until she'd been given a proper explanation of her effect on these strangers, she was propelled forward. Deciding that now was not the proper time to make an investigation, she stepped through a doorway to her left.

To her complete astonishment, she discovered that the house had been equipped with a permanent bathing room. A marble tub lined in tin took up one full wall, the fireplace another, and a huge, free-standing wardrobe a third. There were two straight-backed chairs—one piled high with bath sheets—and a bureau laden with toiletry items.

"How wonderful." Constance sighed, running a hand over the frescoed paintings that covered the entire chamber, giving one the sensation of having just stepped into a garden.

"It is amazing, isn't it?" Potts murmured. Her voice dropped to a conspiratorial whisper. "I don't mind telling you that no expense was spared in decorating this house. None at all."

Constance could very well believe such a statement judging by the furnishings she'd seen so far.

"Mr. Payne must be very rich." As soon as the comment was made, Constance remembered that referring to a person's monetary resources was considered vulgar, but Potts didn't seem to mind.

"As rich as Croesus," the older woman muttered. "I've heard tell he could buy a state of his own, if he wanted."

"He must have come from a very privileged family."

"Ach, not at all. He was a foundling."

"An orphan?"

Mrs. Potts nodded, her eyes growing bright with pride. "He's a self-made man." The woman gestured to the tub. "Have you used one of these before, miss?"

Constance wasn't sure if Potts was referring to the tub itself or the elaborate configuration of spigots, so she shook her head.

"There's a big tank on the other side of this wall next to the stove. As soon as the water on the stove begins to boil, Merriweather will fill the reservoir to the brim. When you want the hot water, you twist this lever here."

Constance nodded, marveling at the luxury of hot running water at the flick of the wrist.

"This lever here controls the cooler water, which is collected in a barrel under the eaves. Rainwater, you know, is the best thing for a head of healthy hair."

"Yes, of course."

Potts lit a pair of faggots and touched them to the kindling that had already been laid in the hearth. When the flames greedily consumed the fuel, she added a larger log.

"I know it's hot as the dickens outside, but this room often feels like an icebox. Its thick walls hold in the chill, and all this marble can get downright icy if a fire isn't laid."

She moved to the huge armoire and flung the doors wide to reveal that the lefthand portion had been reserved for a variety of robes—one of them most likely the one Mrs. Potts had promised Constance could wear. On the righthand side, there were shelves and small brass-trimmed drawers.

"If you look through the compartments here, you'll find towels and soap and all sorts of bath salts, as well as a comb and a brush kept for . . . company."

The way the word was spoken made Constance aware

that Mrs. Potts wasn't quite convinced that Constance wasn't here for some sort of dalliance. She opened her mouth to protest, then realized she had no way to defend herself. She and Gideon *had* kissed, *had* embraced, and to think that such an occurrence would never happen again would border on complete naivety. Constance herself had entertained thoughts that Gideon might pursue brazen intimacies, so she couldn't fault Mrs. Potts for coming to the same conclusion. Especially when her employer was so vibrant and masculine. With his dark hair, flashing eyes, strong arms, rock-hard thighs, he must be considered quite a catch by the ladies of the area.

But she wasn't tempted to chase him herself.

No. Not at all.

Well, not much.

At least, not enough to endanger her future employment in this place.

Even so, it was difficult to banish all thoughts of the man, especially when she had been ensconced so intimately in his home and his life. She would be no casual observer of his daily activities. No, she would be expected to attend to his wishes with all the devotion and loyalty of a—

*A wife.*

No. Not a wife. An assistant. A very capable and professionally minded secretary. She couldn't allow herself to think of her employer striding through the house with his shirt unbuttoned or stripping the clothing from his body to use this very tub.

*Stop!*

Pressing cool fingers to her cheeks, Constance rued her wayward thoughts. Botheration! How many times could a person allow her mind to stray to the borders of impropriety? How many times could a person blush in a single day? Since Constance had played a major part in helping to raise her younger sisters, she'd always considered herself knowledgeable on the ways of the world. Since arriving in New York, this conception had been completely shattered. She had proven to be altogether too unschooled in life to deal with the flood of strange circumstances that currently bedeviled her.

"Are you all right, miss?" Potts asked.

"Yes!" Constance responded much too quickly. More calmly, she stated, "I'm just looking forward to a long soak and a change of clothing."

"If you're sure," Mrs. Potts murmured doubtfully. "You're a bit flushed."

"I'm fine. Just tired, that's all."

"Perhaps you'll have time to take a nap once you've finished."

"That would be nice."

"Very well. Call if you need anything. In the meantime, I'll just leave you to your bath."

She bustled to the door and was about to close it behind her.

"Mrs. Potts!" Constance called. "Why does everyone react so strangely when I am introduced?"

"Strangely?" Mrs. Potts echoed faintly, but it was clear from her troubled gaze that she knew exactly what Constance meant.

"Yes. Mr. Payne's workers stared, you dropped a tray, Merriweather—"

"She didn't act at all untoward."

Constance frowned, offering the woman her sternest glare. "Come now, Mrs. Potts. We both know such an assertion isn't true."

The woman's lower lip wobbled as if she were about to cry. "Please, miss. It wouldn't be right for me to be the one to tell you."

"Tell me *what?*"

When Potts remained stubbornly silent, Constance grasped the woman's arm. "Please! You have to help me understand."

Mrs. Potts shook her head from side to side, but Constance still wouldn't release her. "Try to appreciate my position, Mrs. Potts. I'm a stranger to this city. I know no one here. You must perceive my trepidation— and being a woman, surely you wouldn't be so cruel as to make me suffer with your silence."

Constance was afraid that she'd applied her reasons rather thickly, but Mrs. Potts didn't seem to balk at the melodrama.

Taking Constance's hands, she pursed her lips together as if choosing her words carefully, then blurted, "I hope we haven't offended you—or worried you. Please, don't take our reactions as any sort of slight to you personally. The similarities aren't all that apparent. I'm sure only the staff and those who knew her well have realized how much you look like her."

"Like who, Mrs. Potts?"

"Miss Maura. Maura Kelly Payne, Mr. Payne's wife."

For several minutes, Constance stood rooted in place, numbed to the core.

She looked like Mr. Payne's former wife? The woman who had owned this home and filled it with flowers? The woman who had organized marvelous parties? Who had graced the stage and won hundreds of adoring fans?

Mrs. Potts took that opportunity to slip from the room, closing the door tightly behind her. But Constance hardly noticed the woman's withdrawal. Gazing at the mirror hung over the fireplace, Constance frowned, touching her cheek, her brow.

Was that why Gideon Payne had chased her into the park the day before? Why he'd kissed her? Was that why he'd been so adamant about hiring her? Had the mirror only been a starting point for some other, hidden agenda?

She shook her head. Now it was *she* who was growing melodramatic. Why would Gideon Payne wish to have anything to do with Constance Pedigrue beyond finding a means of reimbursement? The fact that she might bear a slight resemblance to his former wife was coincidental.

*Slight resemblance?* her inner voice mocked. Judging by the reactions she'd seen so far, the two of them must be nearly identical.

Sighing, she reached for the fasteners to her jacket. Her body thrummed with a weariness that was not entirely physical. When she had imagined arriving in New York, she had never dreamed that events could veer so wildly out of control. In her mind's eye, the whole itinerary had seemed so simple.

First, she would gather her things at the station.

But two of her trunks had been stolen.

Second, she would find a place to stay and leave her belongings in her room.

The clerk had been completely forward, and she'd been forced to bring Mr. Bentley with her.

Third, she'd meant to introduce herself to her employer.

The proper establishment had burnt down, leaving her without the means to support herself. To make matters worse, she'd entered the wrong building, allowed Mr. Bentley to escape, and . . .

Mr. Bentley. Tarnation, she'd forgotten about the cat.

Opening the door, Constance was about to rush out to apprehend the rambunctious feline, but she'd no more than poked her head out the door when she heard the whispering from a point somewhere out of her line of sight.

". . . looks *just* like her, she does! It's not merely a casual resemblance. Once she stepped into the light, I saw it plain as day. In different clothes, with her hair combed more elegantly, the two of them could have been twins!" Merriweather exclaimed.

"I know it! The first time I caught sight of her, I thought she'd risen from the dead, I did."

". . . how in creation . . ."

". . . lost his mind for sure . . ."

"Merriweather!"

Constance jumped when the very male voice boomed through the house. Gideon Payne! He'd returned home.

The women were equally startled, because she heard them scurrying toward the front foyer.

Slamming the bathing room door shut, Constance pressed her shoulders against it, breathing heavily.

She could have been Maura Payne's twin? Her stomach roiled, and she had the strangest urge to wipe her mouth with the back of her hand.

She'd been foolish to think that a man like Gideon Payne would be interested in kissing *her* unless he had a shatteringly good reason. He hadn't been attracted to her in the least. No, he'd been drawn to the fact that the embodiment of his dearly departed mate had suddenly appeared at his theater.

Why had she agreed to stay here? Why hadn't she followed her first instincts and run away as soon as she'd had a chance?

Spurred into action, Constance began buttoning her jacket again. She had to get out of this house. She didn't know exactly how or why, but every nerve in her body screamed that she couldn't stay here. Far too many secrets were being kept from her—she felt that fact in her very bones. If she stayed, she would be dragged headlong into the drama surrounding this house and Gideon Payne, and that was something that she could not—*would* not allow.

Pressing her ear against the panels, Constance listened intently for voices, and when she heard nothing on the opposite side, she dared to peek out.

The kitchen was empty.

Tiptoeing as quietly as she could, she made her way to the table. There she retrieved her bonnet and secured it to the top of her head. Grasping the broken wicker basket, she crept to where Mr. Bentley had taken a position on a chair and was staring through the slats, studying the puppies which cuddled in a mass of furry, sleeping balls.

"Come along, Mr. Bentley."

He glanced over his shoulder with utmost disdain, eyed her suspiciously, then glared at the broken wicker container Constance had used to bring him to New York. A low hiss bled from his throat.

Realizing that the cat could be difficult and might decide to bolt, she laid the basket on the table and eased toward the recalcitrant tabby.

"Come here, boy. Come to Mama."

The cat growled, his ears flattening against his head.

"Come on, Mr. Bentley. Come to me. If you do, I'll see to it that you have fish for supper."

The animal cocked his head to one side as if he'd understood and considered the idea, but he did not budge. Instead, his eyes narrowed, and his tail switched in indignation at her interruption of his own pressing activities.

She was almost close enough to grab him, so she continued with her babyish prattle, praying Mr. Bentley would stay in one spot just . . . one . . . second . . . more!

Constance lunged to scoop him in her arms.

The cat yelped and jumped from the chair. Racing past her skirts, he disappeared into the corridor, his claws making a scrabbling sound against the polished hardwood. Even as Constance damned the animal and considered leaving him to his own devices, there was a scream, a clatter, then a smashing, tinkling noise, which could only have been caused by a huge amount of shattering glass.

"No, please, no," she whispered, fearing the worst.

Constance's stomach churned, and she reluctantly moved in the direction of the commotion. Even as she did, she heard a deep masculine roar.

"Miss Ped-i-grue!"

Her feet refused to go any faster than a snail's pace. When she reached the foyer and saw Potts and Merriweather huddled in the corner, Birch tugging at the lax chain that had once supported the chandelier, and the scattered bits and pieces of Austrian crystal littering the floor, she knew immediately what had happened. Birch had probably been lowering the fixture to light the candles when he was startled by Mr. Bentley.

Her eyes closed in dismay. Not again. How could two such calamities occur in two successive days?

"I believe this belongs to you."

She reluctantly opened her lashes and fixed her gaze on the scuffed boots near her skirt hems, then looked up past the masculine legs, narrow hips, and flat stomach to find the wriggling Mr. Bentley held firmly against Gideon Payne's chest.

"Miss Pedigrue," he drawled ominously.

"Yes, sir?" It took all her will to force the words from her mouth.

"I would greatly appreciate it if you would find some way of controlling your cat."

She clasped her hands together to keep them from rising instinctively to protect her face. Had such a thing happened in her father's house, she would have been beaten for sure. Beaten and probably locked in the fruit cellar until she'd atoned for her sins. She couldn't blame this man if he required something similar. She'd done far worse damage to his possessions than she ever would have imagined possible.

Since Gideon was obviously waiting for some sort of response, she whispered, "Yes, sir. I'll do my best."

Patiently, she waited for some means of physical retribution, but Gideon merely extended Mr. Bentley in her direction, holding the cat beneath its arms as if it were something distasteful. After she'd taken the cat from him, he planted his hands on his hips and stared at her in such a way that she felt like wriggling in much the same fashion the cat had done.

His eyes raked her figure from the tip of her head to the dusty toes of her shoes, and he sighed as if severely pained.

"I see you haven't taken your bath yet."

Her throat grew tight with nerves, and she had to clear it before saying, "No, sir. I was just . . . about . . . to . . ."

Too late, she realized that she'd donned her bonnet in preparation for flight. If the old women had told him she'd been taking a bath, he would be bound to reach the conclusion that she'd meant to escape.

"You weren't meaning to leave, were you, Miss Pedigrue?"

Her skin must be blazing again. It felt so hot she was sure that she could have glowed in the dark.

"No, sir." Her response was a mere whisper.

"Because you look as if you were preparing to go somewhere."

"No, sir. I merely meant to . . ." She scrambled for some sort of explanation and found none. "I merely meant to retrieve my cat."

"Ahh. And for that you needed your bonnet?"

An uncomfortable silence shivered in the room around them, and Potts and Merriweather were obviously listening to the entire exchange, but as much as she might want to do so, Constance couldn't move. Gideon Payne clearly didn't believe her explanation.

"No, sir. I . . ."

She what? She wished to wear it into the bathing room? She was afraid that Birch would take it?

"What I meant to say was that . . ."

Vainly, she tried to grasp a logical way to finish her sentence.

"Yes?" he drawled when she didn't speak.

"I wished to . . . keep my belongings together until I was assigned a room."

That piece of information caused his scowl to deepen even more. He turned to Mrs. Potts and Mrs. Merriweather, and the two of them clutched at each other like little children brought before the headmaster.

"I thought I asked you to send for her trunks and install her belongings in one of the guest chambers until the Gold Room could be made available."

It was Merriweather who spoke first. "Yes, sir. But since all of the bedrooms have been closed up for so long . . ."

When her words faded into silence, Mrs. Potts took over.

"We thought it might be best to allow Miss Pedigrue to bathe while Betsy conducted a thorough cleaning."

"Mmm." It was obvious that he was less than mollified. But he dismissed the women with a gesture, then turned to Constance. "Perhaps you should make your way back to the bathing room and wash up for dinner."

"Yes, sir."

"I have some work which will need to be attended to during our meal."

"Yes, sir."

Clutching the cat to her breast, she slowly moved toward the kitchen.

"Oh, and Miss Pedigrue?"

She didn't speak, didn't turn.

"I'll see to it that the price of the chandelier is added to the money you already owe me."

Constance's eyes squeezed closed in dismay.

It would take years to work her way out of this man's debt.

Years.

It wasn't until the hall was completely empty that Gideon willed the muscles in his shoulders and jaw to relax.

What in hell did he think he was doing? He'd all but blackmailed this woman into entering his house and his employ—and why? Because she looked like Maura? Or because she was the first person genuinely to prick his sexual interest in years?

Staring down at the wreckage at his feet, Gideon shook his head. He'd lost his mind, that's what he'd done. In the past, he'd prided himself on being fair with women. He'd never purposely harmed anyone of the gentler sex—and he'd certainly never forced one to live in his house.

But she did owe him for the mirror.

The accident with the mirror had been as much the fault of Gideon's dog as that woman's cat.

What about the chandelier?

Once again, the incident had been unprovoked and unplanned.

So why *had* he arranged for her to serve as his assistant? Did he really think she could rid him of his ghosts?

He frowned. Only moments before entering the town house, he'd been met at the gate by a runner from the theater. Lester had returned with news from the telegraph office confirming that Miss Constance Pedigrue had secured employment with the Theatre Royale. An investigator had already been hired to provide the rest of the information Gideon required.

Not willing to lose sight of the woman until Gideon had all the answers he craved, he'd sent a message instructing Lester to delay Miss Pedigrue's request for funds until he'd had a chance to question his new employee further.

As the boy had run in the direction of the theater district, Gideon had felt a wave of pleasure. So far, Constance's claims had proven true. She had come to New York to work at the Royale as a seamstress.

The thought was enough to send him striding to his

study, his boot heels crunching through the broken crystal. But it wasn't until he caught the stunned expression on Birch's face that Gideon realized he'd been caught smiling.

Evidently, Birch couldn't remember the last time such an expression had crossed his employer's face.

# Eight

*She's come back.*

He leaned against the rough brick in the alley, closing his eyes and breathing deeply to dispel the rush of emotion—elation, fear, relief.

He had waited for this moment for so long, he had difficulty believing that Maura Payne had actually returned. But he'd seen her, in the carriage, the sun flooding her features in a halo of light. She had actually returned to New York.

For him.

*For me.*

Just as she'd promised.

Straightening, he darted a suspicious glance up and down the alley. No one could ever know that she had come back to this place for his sake. He could not acknowledge her presence, he couldn't speak to her, look at her, flash her those silent, passionate messages that she innately understood. No. For all intents and purposes, he had to remain just as he was so no one would suspect their love. Only after she had resumed her position in the theater, in the community, and gained the social stature she craved could he approach her with the final plot in a scheme they had concocted years ago.

To rid Maura of her enemies.

To free her from a husband she didn't love.

To gain control of Gideon Payne's fortune and his theatrical empire.

Only then could they be together. Forever.

Under any other circumstances, Constance was sure that she would have enjoyed the decadent surroundings of the bathing room. After all, she'd never been able to turn a spigot to adjust the temperature of her water before. Nor had she ever had a tub that would allow her to wallow in water up to her ears.

But she was so conscious of the man who lurked somewhere on the other side of her door, in some other portion of the house, that she couldn't relax. Her ablutions were finished in record time, all amid the yowls of protest from a cat who was distraught about being forced to wait in a room dominated with water.

Taking a robe from the armoire, she wrapped it around her naked body, praying that her own trunks had arrived so that she could dress as soon as possible. She didn't feel safe wandering around this house without proper clothing.

Perhaps *safe* was too strong a word, she admitted to herself as she peeked around the edge of the door and found Merriweather slicing vegetables on the heavy block table.

"Mrs. Merriweather?"

The woman looked up, automatically wiping her hands on a towel. Her expression remained guarded, and Constance rued the absence of the obvious warmth that had shone from the cook's eyes before the older lady had discovered Constance's resemblance to Maura Payne.

"Are we really so much alike?" she asked tentatively, causing Mrs. Merriweather to start.

"I beg your pardon, miss?"

"Mrs. Payne and I? Are we so much alike?"

Merriweather's eyes darted around the room as if she were searching for some avenue of escape. Finding none, she was forced to meet Constance's eyes again.

"There is an uncanny resemblance," she mumbled, chopping the vegetables with far more vigor than was necessary.

"But it is only a slight likeness," Constance insisted.

The woman opened her mouth as if she were ready to agree, then shook her head. Her expression revealed a very true regret. "It is a very pronounced likeness, miss."

Constance's throat grew tight with nerves. "I understand she . . . died," she said carefully, knowing that a true gentlewoman would not tread into such dangerous conversational waters but needing to know more about this woman whose memory was still so strong.

Again, Merriweather looked around her as if she feared that someone had entered the room without her knowledge.

"Yes, miss."

"When?"

"Two years ago May Day."

*Two years.* And the angst of her death had not abated?

"How did she die?"

Merriweather shuddered as if she'd been caught in a brisk draft. "It was horrible, Miss Pedigrue."

"Why?"

Merriweather glanced down at the vegetables, which were swiftly turning to mush. The knife clattered from her hands, and she rubbed her palms down her apron. "She took her own life."

Of all the things Constance had expected to hear, this was not one of them. "She committed suicide?"

"Yes, miss."

"But why?"

Merriweather turned sharply away and began clanging the lids of the pots on the stove. "I really would rather not talk about this, if you don't mind."

Constance was disappointed by Mrs. Merriweather's decision, but she couldn't fault the woman for wishing to change the subject. Her former mistress had succumbed to a horrible tragedy—one that must have affected the entire household. Constance had no right to pry.

"Would you like some tea, Miss Pedigrue?"

"That would be lovely. Thank you."

The woman used the corner of her apron to lift the kettle. Constance could not have missed her obvious relief at the change of subject.

"Which would you prefer? Chamomile or one of Mr. Payne's Chinese acquisitions?"

"Chamomile would be fine."

Mr. Bentley sauntered into the room, made his way to the puppies' basket, then hissed. Seeing him, Mrs. Merriweather offered, "Mr. Payne chained Willoby to the tree outside."

"Willoby?"

"The dog."

"Won't the puppies need to be nursed?"

Mrs. Merriweather chortled, lightening the atmosphere of the room. "Willoby's a *male* dog, Miss Pedigrue. Unless he's changed his sex in the last hour, he'll be of no help."

Constance padded toward the basket. Mr. Bentley was avidly sniffing the puppies now.

"Where is their mother?"

"She died after the birthings, poor thing. We've been feeding the puppies by hand, we have."

"That must be quite a job." Constance counted six healthy pups, and she imagined the constant nursing they'd demanded the first few weeks must have tried everyone's patience.

"I'm sure it did, but for the first month, Master Payne took charge of the entire operation. He only sent the puppies here a few days ago. They're at an age where they need space to run about, and the theater isn't a place for gamboling pups. They've missed the master's doting, of that I can assure you."

Gideon Payne? Doting?

Constance had a difficult time resolving the hard, stoic man she'd encountered with the patience and coddling these puppies must have demanded. Somehow, the same hands that had gripped the rope at the theater had cradled a wriggling newborn dog, had loved it, soothed it.

The image caused an inexplicable tingling deep in the pit of her stomach, and Constance pushed it aside. Knotting her wrapper more firmly around her waist, she asked, "I wondered if my trunks had arrived yet so I could—"

"They aren't here yet."

Constance froze, one hand flying to grip the neckline of her robe as she whirled and discovered that Gideon Payne had opened the door from the garden and entered the room without having made the slightest noise.

Automatically, her gaze bounced guiltily against Mrs. Merriweather's. Thank heaven the man hadn't returned a few minutes earlier. If he'd caught them gossiping together, there was no telling how he might have reacted.

His eyes immediately raked over her—from the damp hair that tumbled over her shoulders and down her back to the heavy cotton robe that skimmed her figure.

Constance wished she could sink unnoticed into the floorboards. Not a week earlier, she'd lectured her sisters upon the hazards to be found in the real world. She reminded them about the importance of wearing their woolen underwear and carrying a hat pin for protection. Yet here she stood in a stranger's kitchen, dressed in little more than a borrowed robe.

His mouth slid into a crooked grin.

Embarrassed at his intense scrutiny, she stood with one foot on top of the other, damning the fact that the wrapper she'd selected barely covered her calves.

"You look very fetching, Miss Pedigrue."

There was no missing the bite of amusement to his tone.

"Somehow, that wrap never looked that good on me."

"I beg your pardon?" she asked in a horrified whisper. But she knew. This robe belonged to Gideon Payne.

"That is my garment, Miss Pedigrue."

Her nose twitched as she realized that when she moved she caught a faint trace of sandalwood.

"I haven't worn it in ages, so you needn't worry that you've inconvenienced me by borrowing it."

And what was that statement supposed to mean? That he had another robe somewhere else? Or that he had grown used to traipsing about without any sort of covering whatsoever?

Her embarrassment grew tenfold. Why hadn't she been more careful? Mrs. Potts had offered her own wrapper, but since she had never brought a robe to Constance, Constance had assumed that one of the cotton cover-ups in the armoire belonged to the woman. She should have known better. After all, the bathing room was probably reserved for members of the household, not its staff.

Not sure how best to handle the situation, Constance cleared her throat and tried to appear unconcerned—a very difficult task indeed since she was naked as a jaybird beneath the robe in question.

"Please allow me to apologize, Mr. Payne. I didn't know that—"

He waved away her explanation in mid-sentence. "I don't care about the robe, Miss Pedigrue. Right now, I'm concerned with more pressing matters."

*Such as a broken mirror. A ruined chandelier.*

Constance shivered as he approached, his body bringing with it a potent male energy that she was finding difficult to ignore. Goosebumps popped up over her still-damp flesh as he circled her as if she were some sort of mare on the block.

An invisible hand constricted her chest, squeezing the

air from her lungs. What did he see when he looked at her? The image of his wife? Or a simple spinster from Boston?

"Sir?" she whispered when she feared she would not be able to endure his scrutiny a moment longer.

"You're not exactly what I expected, even after a bath."

Constance wasn't sure why, but she was immediately insulted.

"Mr. Payne," she began firmly.

But he didn't let her finish.

"You're far too thin, you know."

She gasped at the effrontery of his remark. "I don't think that's any of your concern!"

"But it is. I can't have the competition thinking I don't pay my employees."

"What the . . . *competition* thinks is neither here nor there."

He'd made a full circle, but his scrutiny hadn't eased. "On the contrary, Miss Pedigrue. Appearances are always important, I assure you."

He grasped her chin, holding her face up to the light. "Especially yours."

The room became so still and brittle that Constance shivered. A hardness had entered her employer's green eyes, and there was no sound at all from Merriweather. It was as if the room had shrunk to hold only the two of them.

"Where did you come from, Miss Pedigrue?" Gideon murmured.

Constance opened her mouth to respond, then grew silent when she realized he was speaking rhetorically. The way he was watching her, the glimmer of recognition, surprise, and wariness was back in his eyes, making her wonder what he thought when he stared at her for so long. What sorts of images raced through his head?

She opened her mouth to ask him, but he released her so abruptly that she nearly fell.

"Do you have anything in your still-to-be-delivered trunks more suitable than what I saw this morning?"

"Sir?"

Mrs. Potts chose that moment to bustle into the room. Humming, she darted into the bathing cubicle and emerged again, carrying Constance's dusty traveling clothes.

Gideon snagged the bonnet from the top of the pile. "Do you have anything more feminine than the things I've already seen?"

"I don't understand."

He sighed shortly, as if his patience were sorely tested. "I detest black on women."

"But I'm in mourning." She would have thought such a state obvious, until she remembered that black was not an unusual color for traveling and Mr. Payne had only seen one of her suits to date.

Merriweather and Potts exchanged glances, but it was obvious that Gideon was unimpressed.

"Are you?" The query vibrated with doubt. "For whom?"

"My father."

"How long has he been gone?"

"Less than a month."

"Do you miss him?"

She opened her mouth, then was struck by the odd nature of his question. Did she miss her father? Not in the least. But that didn't mean that she should flaunt her secret disrespect.

Avoiding a direct answer, she said instead, "I don't see why I should be forced to respond to such a personal question."

"And I would hope that you would answer my query without hesitation, Miss Pedigrue. After all, you are the stranger in this household, and you already owe me a great deal of money. I should think you would wish to present yourself in the best light possible."

Constance pressed her lips together at the unsettling reminder, but she could not escape the truth. Until her debts were paid, she was at this man's mercy.

"Did you love your father, Miss Pedigrue?"

She should have known this man would have caught the nuances of her tone when she'd spoken of her father. He knew she hadn't loved Alexander Pedigrue. He *knew*. Even so, she couldn't admit such a thing out loud.

"How can you even ask such a thing?" she asked tightly, knowing she should be forthright in her answer but fearing his reaction if she were.

"Because you don't look all that grieved to me. Except for the fact that you're nothing but skin and bones, you appear too healthy to be in mourning. Your cheeks have a good deal of color, and your eyes are clear and bright."

She huffed in indignation at such a remark, but he ignored her, tossing the bonnet back onto the pile.

"I have changed my mind, Miss Pedigrue. We will dispense with conducting business tonight. Since your trunks have not arrived—and I refuse to have you dress again in these unsightly rags—I will meet you at nine o'clock sharp in the vestibule tomorrow morning. I hope you have something in the trunks arriving from the station that will do until these can be properly cleaned."

With that comment, he strode from the room, slamming the kitchen door behind him.

Constance jumped as wood met wood, then gazed at Mrs. Potts and Mrs. Merriweather in confusion.

They both shrugged, obviously not in the least surprised by their employer's display of temper.

"He really does prefer to see women dressed in colors," Mrs. Merriweather murmured. "He says any attempt to dim a woman's natural beauty is an affront to the gentler sex."

Mrs. Potts scowled in her direction, obviously displeased that Merriweather felt the master's moods needed any explanation at all.

"But why? There is absolutely nothing wrong with wearing black—nor with my wardrobe. That bonnet was purchased only a few weeks ago, and my gown the month before last." She huffed in indignation. "In my opinion, his attitude is completely baffling. I would think he'd want an assistant to be dressed as plainly as possible."

Merriweather shrugged. "There's a logical enough reason for his views, I can assure you. Ever since the missus said she was with child and he—"

"Merriweather!"

Mrs. Potts dumped the clothing on the table and whirled to face her companion. It was clear from her expression that Merriweather had said more than she should.

But what exactly had she said that could be considered indiscreet? She'd merely stated that since Mrs. Payne had been with . . .

*No.*

*Not that, too.*

Constance's heart ached as she looked from woman to woman, knowing that what she had surmised was true. Gideon Payne had lost not only a wife but a baby.

Her eyes flew to the closed door, and she was immediately contrite about what she'd said to him. Why had she failed to remember that Gideon was a widower—moreover, that his wife hadn't died of natural causes? She'd taken her own life. Any of these facts would explain why he hated black, why he despised those who merely appeared to grieve, and why everyone kept staring at her as if she were some sort of interloper. His staff probably thought that she'd come to the house as some sort of replacement for the late Mrs. Payne.

*No.*

*Dear heaven, no.*

"I'll be taking you up to your room now," Mrs. Potts said, sweeping a hand in front of her to show that Constance should precede her.

"Fine," Constance replied absently.

"I'm afraid it will be some time before the Gold Room is fit for habitation."

The statement jolted Constance from her reverie.

"But the Peach Room should suffice until we can get you properly settled."

"That will be fine," Constance murmured, as if she knew why Mrs. Potts was so concerned about the change in arrangements.

As she climbed the rear servants' staircase, the scent of sandalwood hovered around her like an invisible cloud. With each step she took, Constance tried to block out all she'd seen, all she'd heard.

But just as the scent wriggled into her consciousness, her own thoughts could not be completely banished.

*Had* Gideon Payne brought her here for some reason other than to become his assistant?

If he had, what was she prepared to do to thwart him?

For the next few hours, Gideon tried everything in his power to drive Constance Pedigrue out of his thoughts. He'd completed reams of paperwork, fed the puppies, even roughhoused with Willoby. But none of those activities had managed to dissuade him from thinking about the woman ensconced in his own home. If anything, the time apart had merely underscored how little he knew about her.

And how much more he longed to know.

Huffing in impatience at his own avid curiosity, Gideon abruptly rose from the tin-lined tub, causing the water to rush around his body and slop onto the floor of the bathing room.

Ignoring the puddle he'd made, he stepped onto the hooked cotton rug and poured himself a glass of whiskey from the bottle he'd left on the mantel. Staring down into the flames in the fireplace, he cursed the restlessness that thrummed through his body, filling him with a vague sense of dissatisfaction.

Dammit, what was the matter with him? He was generally an even-tempered man whose days were consumed by business and his nights by . . . well, a variety of entertainments.

So why did he feel so dissatisfied?

So frustrated.

So empty.

He drained the whiskey in one gulp and reached into the armoire for his robe, only to remember that it had been borrowed by Miss Pedigrue.

Miss Constance Pedigrue. He grunted, knowing instinctively that a portion of his emotions stemmed from his encounters with the woman—even though he wasn't quite ready to admit such a thing to himself.

The fact that she looked so much like his former wife would have unsettled any man in the same predicament, yes. So why did he find himself thinking less and less about the resemblance and more about Constance herself? She was everything that he had once thought Maura to be and more. Her gentleness was genuine, her fears real, her manner unrehearsed.

So why had the fates sent her his way?

The question reverberated in his head, and he grimaced ruefully, wrapping a bath sheet around his hips. Grasping the bottle of whiskey, he made his way through the house, dousing the lamps which had been left aglow for his benefit.

"Good night, Birch," he said to the man who waited at the foot of the stairs, holding a lamp for his master. Gideon knew the butler hadn't heard him, but the man nodded all the same, then backed into the shadows. Gideon had forgotten how attentive Birch had been to him and Maura years ago.

Feeling a weariness that tugged at his spirit, Gideon made his way to the upper hall, taking a deep swallow from the bottle as he went.

Unable to still the impulse, Gideon turned, making his

way to the east side of the house. Taking a deep breath, he opened the door to the Gold Room.

He'd forgotten what it looked like. His first glimpse in two years caused the whiskey to lurch in his stomach.

Some effort had been begun to make the room habitable, but the chamber remained in an obvious state of disrepair—a fact that would not change as quickly as he had at first supposed. Dust and mildew permeated the air, a condition caused by the window that had shattered when Luther Hayes had attempted to escape. The gaping aperture had been boarded up but never properly repaired. Mice had chewed at the bedcovers, which were still ripped and strewn over the floor. Broken glass was scattered on the dressing table, and Maura's clothing littered the floor. But what drew his attention over all of these details was the scorched painting hanging on the opposite wall.

This portrait was quite different from the one stored in the theater. It had been Maura's wedding present to him. She lay on a velvet tufted couch, clutching a sheer scarf to an otherwise naked body.

This was how he remembered her. Completely sensual, driven by her passions for success, money, and fame. As a lover, she had been incredible. As a wife . . .

Something had been lacking in her nature—that effortless devotion he had seen in other married couples. In all truth, he supposed that Maura had been wed to her career and Gideon had been a means to further her notoriety. Even so, he should not have trusted her so completely.

He should have seen her faithlessness.

He should have suspected she'd been having an affair.

Maybe then he wouldn't have been so stunned by her betrayal with Hayes.

Sighing, Gideon padded forward, surveying the still rumpled bed. In his mind's eye, he could see Maura and the tall, lanky frame of his childhood friend as plainly as if the event had occurred only yesterday. He could see her straddling the man's hips, bringing him to an ecstatic release. Then she'd looked at Gideon and smiled as if she'd expected him to enjoy what he saw, to be aroused by it. When he didn't respond, she called out his name, softly, questioningly. At that instant, Luther had scrambled free, scooped up his clothing, and crashed through the window that led to the balcony.

Maura had rushed after him, but when her lover disappeared down the trellis and ran into the trees, she screamed for him to come back, to take her with him. Then, with one last look of defiance in Gideon's direction, she'd climbed atop the railing and leaped to her death.

Driven by pain and anger and guilt, Gideon had erupted into rage. Grasping a nearby lantern, he'd crashed the chimney against the wall, then had touched the flame to the draperies in an effort to burn the evidence of betrayal and suicide from his memory and from this room. If not for Birch, he probably would have succeeded, too. But the butler had discovered Gideon's intent, and he'd doused the velvet draperies with water from the wash set before any real damage could be done. Then, turning in Gideon's direction, he'd bodily carried his employer from the room and locked them both in Gideon's study until Gideon regained his senses.

In the years that had passed since that night, Gideon had wondered how much Birch knew about what had occurred to make Gideon lose control. Had he suspected that Gideon had found his wife in the arms of Luther Hayes? Had he guessed that Maura had deliberately jumped to her death? That she hadn't fallen, as Gideon had later claimed to the police?

Worse yet, had Birch been more than aware that Maura would rather kill herself than forsake her lover and remain faithful to her husband? Could he possibly understand the anger and betrayal that Gideon still felt toward Maura and Luther Hayes?

Shaking free of the morbid memories that twined around his chest and threatened to squeeze the breath from his body, Gideon backed away from the ruined bedroom.

Potts and Merriweather would have it put back to rights eventually. Indeed, they would have fixed the room already if Gideon hadn't forbidden them to touch the place so that he would be forever reminded of what had happened on that night so long ago.

Gideon's eyes fell on the entrance to the Peach Room and the sliver of light that crept beneath the door. A curious warmth slid into his chest, lightening his gloom.

It was time that the whole house was aired of the bitterness that had festered here for some time. Placing Miss Pedigrue in the Gold Room would be the first step toward putting the past in its place.

Yet even as his mind insisted that his reasons were purely practical, his conscience whispered that Miss Pedigrue would probably not have found a place in his employ, let alone his home, if her response to his kiss hadn't caused his body to burn with a very sensual need.

# Nine

Louise Chevalier rose from the dressing table in her changing room at the Bristol National Theatre. A brief, familiar knock had signaled that her carriage had arrived to take her home.

Her carriage and Etienne.

The mere fact that he waited in the corridor near the wings of the stage filled her with anticipation. Etienne was so strong, so masculine, so irretrievably in love with her that the mere thought of his presence was enough to spark her into motion. Throwing her cape around her shoulders, she grabbed her reticule, then threw open the door.

"Good evening, Etienne."

"Madame."

Their greetings were formal, as was their manner whenever they were at the theater.

"This way."

Etienne ushered her outside, one hand on his revolver at all times. Such measures had proven necessary over the past few years, as Louise's fame had grown and she'd begun to receive disturbing letters from avid fans who wished to make private acquaintances as well.

Her bodyguard kept a watchful eye on the alley as she climbed into the carriage and settled against the squabs. As Etienne swung onto the running board, he shouted to the driver, then climbed in beside her, pulling the curtain over the window.

"Well?" she asked, impatient for the good news about her daughter, which would allow her to freely marry this man.

"There has been . . . a problem."

Her stomach knotted at the words. "No," she breathed in disbelief. "How is it possible that my plans for my daughters should be disrupted on three separate occasions?"

Etienne did his best to look stern, but the chuckle that rumbled in his chest ruined the effect.

"I really don't think she's in any danger, Louise. In fact, she's muddled her way into a similar situation."

Louise scowled. "What do you mean?"

"You wished for your daughter to spend time working as a seamstress at the Theatre Royale."

"Yes?"

"It burned down before her arrival."

"Burned down!"

"As near as I've been able to determine, your daughter reported for work as scheduled but misread the information she'd been given by her solicitors and wound up at Gideon Payne's new establishment on Kensington. Evidently, there was some sort of accident, and Constance was responsible for part of the damage, so Gideon put her to work."

"Gideon Payne has given my daughter a job?" she repeated in disbelief. "You mean she's been employed as a burlesque performer?"

Her voice rose with each word, and, laughing openly, Etienne framed her face in his hands. "Relax, *ma petite.*"

"Relax! My daughter has been hired as some sort of circus act—or, worse yet, as a stripper—and all you can say is relax?"

"She has not been hired as a stripper. Gideon has given her the position of his personal assistant."

"Personal assistant?" Louise whispered in horror.

"My dear, you seem to be repeating everything I say."

"That's because I don't believe it. I can't believe it."

"I thought the man was married. You can't possibly believe that Gideon Payne would have nefarious designs on your daughter. Granted, he's a scoundrel, but he's got his scruples."

She shook her head. "But he's *not* married. That's the problem. His wife died from a horrible fall years ago, one that was so shrouded in secrecy I suspect she may have . . . done herself in, so to speak—although, if you ask my opinion, the man is better off without her. I had the misfortune of meeting Maura Kelly Payne during a reception. Personally, I found her to be very grasping and manipulative. I didn't see what Gideon found attractive about her at all, other than the obvious. She had the face and figure of a goddess."

"Is that why you broke off your association with the man and refused to consider performing in one of his legitimate theaters?"

"Of course. That and the fact that I was doing my best to keep my name free of scandal, while Gideon . . ." She smiled indulgently. "That man attracts scandal like a magnet, damn his hide." Her features immediately grew serious. "Which is why I balk at having Gideon Payne serve as any sort of a benefactor to my daughter."

Etienne grimaced. "I suppose that means I'll be arranging for a train to take us to New York. Good thing I checked with the railway station before heading to the theater and your car will be ready to leave in an hour."

She threw her arms around his neck in gratitude. "Thank you, Etienne. You always know exactly what I need."

"And what about my needs, Louise?"

It was the first time that she'd ever heard a note of

impatience from Etienne, and she peered up at him. "I'm sorry. It isn't fair to keep you waiting."

"So marry me. Marry me tonight."

She was tempted, severely tempted, but at long last she shook her head. "I can't. I've managed to win Felicity's and Patience's goodwill—and if there is a hope of garnering Constance's as well, I want them to be there when we wed. Please understand."

He sighed, kissing the tips of her fingers. "I do," he murmured regretfully, then speared her with a direct gaze. "As long as you remember that there will come a time when I will expect you to damn the world and damn your family in order to put me first."

She cupped his cheek. "You are always first in my heart, Etienne."

"Really?"

"Really."

Mary MacClannahan bowed her head against the driving sleet and curled her hands more snugly beneath the flapping edges of her cape. Hurrying down the length of Beakman Avenue, she ignored the queue of restaurants, specialty shops, and hotels that huddled in the early morning shadows, and strode toward the towering structure of the Wellington House of Burlesque on the corner of the next block.

Despite the early hour, Mary felt the press of time like a heavy breath against her neck. After last night's debacle in fitting Madame Bernoulli's costumes for her "Dance of the Seven Veils," Mary had little more than three hours to see the muslin shells picked apart, new alterations made, and pieces sewn back together. All of the tasks would have to be finished before the burlesque house's premier performer arrived for a special call prior to her morning rehearsal.

At that thought, Mary's pace increased until she nearly ran the length of the last block. She paused only once, at the edge of the curb. For a moment, she thought she'd heard something—the soft stamp of a footstep, the snuffle of a horse. But there were no sounds now. At least none but her own breathing.

Shrugging, Mary hurried across the road and ducked into the side alley. Without pause, she climbed a rickety set of steps to the second-story entrance of the theater. Sniffing, she patted the ledge over the door, searching for the key. Encountering its cold iron shape, she blessed the costume master who'd remembered to hide it there despite his drunken stupor the night before. Mary hadn't looked forward to rousing him at his boardinghouse had he forgotten.

Unlocking the heavy door, Mary gathered her skirts and slipped over the threshold into the musty backstage area, where props and scenery pieces were stored between shows. Without bothering to light a lamp, Mary threaded her way with practiced ease through the clutter of gaudy flats and began to climb the staircase that led to the costume workshop. If she hurried, she could brew a cup of tea while she waited for the irons to—

"... *Maaary* ..."

Her name melted out of the darkness, and Mary hesitated, gripping the rickety banister more securely. Cautiously, she peered into the shadows around her. Not so much as a wisp of movement relayed whether the eerie sound had been real or imagined.

"Who's there?" she called, waiting, listening.

No one answered. Nothing stirred.

The theater shivered in expectation.

Harrumphing to herself, Mary decided she'd imagined the whisper, shrugged, and climbed another step.

*"Maaary* ..."

Once more, she thought she heard a voice. Softer this time. Ethereal.

Bewildered, intrigued, Mary paused again. She glanced over the edge of the staircase to scan the storage room, then climbed the steps to the landing above. "Who's—"

A velvet cord whipped around her neck, dragging her into the blackness.

Mary's scream tore through the arching confines of the stage, then shuddered into a choked moan. Her hands groped; her mind fought. Slowly, ever so slowly, muscles trembled and grew weak, thought clouded, and her body crumpled to the floor.

Thick silence shrouded the theater. A step creaked in the darkness. Two. A piece of heavy parchment fluttered to the floor, settling beside Mary's outstretched fingers. In an ornate scrolling hand, three words had been inscribed upon the heavy paper.

"For you, Maura."

# Ten

She didn't have a blasted thing to wear. Not a thing.

Constance surveyed the trunk that Birch had delivered to her room late the previous evening. Grimacing in dismay, she surveyed the gowns, underwear, and shoes she'd strewn around the Peach Room. There really wasn't all that much to choose from. Other than yesterday's traveling costume, she had two more skirts, both black, four shirtwaists, a capelet, and a pair of sweaters.

Unlike her sisters, who had used the money they'd been given for the journey to augment their wardrobes, Constance hadn't seen a need to do much more than replace a few of her more threadbare garments. After all, she was going to be employed as a seamstress, not a performer, so she'd given no thought to buying anything pretty.

Now she regretted the impulse. She was about to begin an entirely different type of employment, as an assistant to a widower who had a reasonable aversion to black. At the very least, she should have something in her possession that wouldn't remind him of his grief.

But she didn't.

Almost everything she owned was black.

Not for the first time, she cursed the part of her that seemed so concerned with public opinion. It was hypocritical of her to wear mourning for a man she was secretly glad had passed on, but she would rather die herself than admit such a thing. Such an absence of love for her father revealed a horrible flaw in her nature. She wasn't sure how, exactly, but there must be something wrong with her if she wasn't capable of loving a man who'd been her own flesh and blood.

Sinking onto the bed, she sighed, closing her eyes. As was her habit when she despaired of her relationship with her father, she found herself thinking back, back, to happier times. She remembered the log house in the midst of a huge rolling plain, her mother's dark, smiling eyes, Mama's kindness, her infinite love.

Constance's hands clenched into the clothing she'd crushed beneath her, and she rued the sense of loss that flooded through her body.

Things would have been so different if Mama had lived.

*No!* She couldn't think about that now. She couldn't believe that Alexander Pedigrue had . . .

Killed his wife.

*No.*

But her denial was weaker this time. She couldn't help but remember how her father had precipitously moved them to Boston and in doing so had become completely cold and rigid. He'd seemed intent on driving some unseen sense of evil from his daughters' natures, thereby alienating himself from their affections entirely.

"Miss Pedigrue!"

She jumped when the deep voice bellowed at her from the floor below.

"It is now eight fifty-five. I hope you're damned well ready!"

Constance scrambled into action, knowing that it wouldn't do her any good to sit and mourn what she didn't have. She would have to make do with the clothing she owned.

Generally, it took her the better part of an hour to dress, but since she knew Gideon would come looking for her if she were very late, she dragged three petticoats over her head, rather than the usual five, and tugged on her corset cover, her shirtwaist, and a black taffeta skirt. Then, after twining the single plait she'd formed from her hair into a knot, she pinned it in place, grabbed her bonnet, and threw open the door.

Gideon stood poised on the other side, his hand reaching for the knob that was no longer there. Constance blushed when she realized he would have thrown open the door without knocking if she'd been any tardier.

"I thought I told you to meet me at nine."

"Yes, sir. I know, sir. But I had trouble with my . . ." She searched for something that would not sound too personal, failed in the attempt, and blurted, "With my buttons, sir."

Too late, she realized she should have thought of something, *anything,* else. His gaze dropped to her chest, and he studied the small pearl disks.

"They are still fastened wrong, Miss Pedigrue."

Horrified, she looked down to see that the placket of her shirtwaist was crooked. Whirling, she quickly set them to rights but became completely flustered when she realized that she'd performed the entire action in complete view of the mirror over her dresser.

Her cheeks grew red as the man behind her chuckled.

"You needn't appear so horrified, Miss Pedigrue. I've seen it all before."

She searched for some suitable reply but found none. Therefore, she decided she would remain silent. In doing so, however, she allowed him the opportunity to absorb the state of her room.

"Are you always this . . . enthusiastic with your personal preparations, Miss Pedigrue?"

"I . . ."

He brushed past her, regarding the clothing she'd strewn over every available piece of furniture.

She burned with embarrassment. Never in her life had any man been allowed the slightest intimacies. She'd had no suitors to hold her hand or whisper sweet nothings in her ear. To have Gideon Payne enter her bedchamber and inspect her clothing was completely mortifying.

"Your only hat?" he asked, lifting her bonnet.

"Yes." She did her best to resist the impulse to snatch it from his hand.

"And these are your skirts?"

"Yes."

"Mmm."

When he reached for a petticoat, she could no longer bear standing idle.

Stepping in front of him, she said tartly, "These are the only clothes that remain in my possession, Mr. Payne. Other than this trunk, which your butler delivered at an unconscionable hour"—she paused to make it clear that the man had roused her out of bed—"I have no other baggage. Two of my trunks were stolen en route to New York, and what you see here is all that remains."

"Ahh."

Too late, Constance noted that in trying to stop him from going through her things, she'd put herself nearer to him than was comfortable. Indeed, the heat of his body was seeping through her clothes, and the familiar scent of sandalwood tickled at her nose.

"You have very . . . practical tastes," he said after some time.

Constance shifted uncomfortably, sensing the none-too-subtle chiding.

"I am a practical woman."

"Hmm."

Without warning, he bent and took one of her stockings, rubbing the black cotton fabric between his finger and thumb.

Constance felt a bolt of sensation race through her body, and she snatched it free, completely horrified. No man had ever dared to touch her intimate apparel. In fact, no man had ever dared to touch anything at all that belonged to her. Why Gideon found it necessary to do so was completely beyond her ken.

"Mr. Payne!" she huffed in indignation.

"Yes, Miss Pedigrue?"

His response was far too smooth, far too knowing.

"I have taken your offer of employment on good faith, believing that there would be no . . . shenanigans involved."

"Shenanigans, Miss Pedigrue?"

His grin was completely innocent, but the light in his eyes contained a devilish merriment.

"You know precisely what I mean."

"No. I don't. Perhaps you should be more clear."

She held her breath, counting to ten to control her temper.

"I am an honest, God-fearing, Christian woman."

"I don't know what that means, either."

"It means that I do not indulge in improprieties."

He made a *tsk*-ing sound with his tongue. "You keep employing euphemisms that are completely vague."

She pressed her lips together to keep a hasty response from springing free. Gathering the last shreds of her composure, she stated, "I think that you are being purposely obtuse, Mr. Payne." Dropping the stocking onto the bed, she brushed past him. "I believe it was time we were leaving. Isn't that why you came up here in the first place?"

She thought she heard him chuckle, but she wasn't sure. "I suppose you're right, Miss Pedigrue."

But when she took another step, he grabbed her elbow and forced her to turn and face him.

"However," he continued, "before we get started with today's activities, I have a few questions that need answering."

"What sorts of questions?"

"The same inquiries any employer would demand that you answer."

Her heart made an odd leap in her breast. "Have you received a reply from my solicitors?"

"Yes. They confirmed your position with the Theatre Royale."

"And the money I requested?"

"As yet . . ." He paused an inordinate amount of time. "No funds have been sent."

Constance bit her lip. She should have expected as much. Five thousand dollars was beyond the yearly stipend her father had promised his daughters.

"May I continue with my interview, Miss Pedigrue?"

Her lips pressed together in evident irritation, but with an abrupt nod she signified that she would do her best to satisfy his curiosity.

"How old are you?"

She gasped at his audacity. "Don't you know it's impolite to ask a woman her age?" she blurted, then wished she'd remained silent.

"I've never been a keen advocate of society's little rules," he remarked. "How old are you?"

Seeing no way to avoid the issue, she muttered, "I have passed my twenty-first birthday, so I am a legal adult."

He frowned at her evasiveness but didn't press the issue further.

"You're from Boston?"

"You already know that answer."

"Were you born there?"

"No. My family once homesteaded a portion of land in Illinois."

"You mentioned you had siblings."

"Two sisters."

His eyes narrowed as if the information interested him immensely. "What about your mother?"

She stiffened, wondering how this aspect of her background had anything to do with her employment. Choos-

ing the safer road, she offered the same explanation
Alexander Pedigrue had used for Louise's absence. "My
mother abandoned the family when I was small."

The man's eyes narrowed even more.

"So you were in charge of raising your sisters?"

She shrugged. "In a manner of speaking. When we
were children, we had a succession of governesses,
housekeepers, tutors. But as the years passed, my father
became something of a recluse."

"Until the household dwindled to just the four of
you."

Her chin tilted to a proud angle. "Mr. Payne, I fail to
see how any of this information is applicable to my
position as your assistant."

His thumb moved against the hollow inside her elbow,
and she pressed her lips together to squelch the automat-
ic sigh that would have melted from her lips otherwise.

"I like to know everything I can about my employees."

Obviously, he thought the statement was enough of an
explanation, but Constance demanded, "Why?"

He thought carefully before saying, "I don't like surprises."

"What sorts of surprises?"

"The kinds one encounters when employees are running from something in their past."

She huffed. "I can assure you that I have no *past.*"

He shifted, and his hand cupped her jaw, forcing her
to tilt her head up to his inspection. His scrutiny was
intense, his features sober.

"No, I don't suppose you do," he murmured.

For some reason, Constance felt vaguely insulted.

"Your father probably never allowed you to flirt with
scandal."

"You sound as if you disapprove of such a fact."

"In some ways, I do. Everyone should be allowed to
sow the wild oats of youth." He was inching closer and
closer, his hand spreading across her nape. "You should
have been allowed to do a good many things."

Then there was no time for a rebuttal, because his lips were brushing against her own, softly, gently, filling her with a roiling mix of emotions—yearning, regret, and foreboding.

When finally he drew back, she felt dazed and uncertain of what she should do, where she should look.

"Has no one ever kissed you like that, Constance?"

She was growing tired of his continual reminders of her sheltered life.

"You assume too much, Mr. Payne. I have been kissed by dozens of men. Dozens and dozens."

"Who?"

"I don't think that's any of your business."

"I suppose not, but I enjoy watching you blush."

Damning the telltale heat of her cheeks, she harrumphed in disapproval. "If this interview is finished, I think it's time we both went to work, Mr. Payne. Don't you?"

Then, ignoring his all-knowing smirk, she twisted free of his grasp and made her escape.

Gideon watched in amusement as his new assistant sashayed past him with all the dignity and grace of a queen. Chuckling softly to himself, he followed her, intrigued by the angry swish of her skirts as she descended the front staircase.

He wondered what she would think if she knew that he'd spent a sleepless night on her behalf. After visiting the Gold Room, he'd found himself haunted by memories—not of Maura. No, he'd found himself remembering instead what it had been like to share his life with someone else. To share his bed.

Long ago, Gideon had decided that he wanted to marry and raise a family. He couldn't remember the number of times he'd been passed from orphanage to orphanage all over New York State—with no companions other than Luther Hayes, who was considered as "unadoptable" as Gideon.

*Luther Hayes.*

Pushing the name from his head, Gideon remembered instead how his luck had changed. Already on the brink of manhood, he'd been unofficially adopted by a boisterous farm couple with thirteen children. With them, he had learned what it could be like to grow up surrounded by siblings, and he'd vowed to have such a situation for himself and his own heirs one day.

In the interim, he'd been determined to earn his fortune by owning a dozen theaters. He'd managed to build several legitimate performing halls by the time he reached his mid-twenties. In marrying Maura, he'd been so sure that the rest of his dream would come true. In no time at all, he would have a wife and children of his own.

But Maura had been hesitant about having a baby so soon. She'd wanted to pursue her life on the stage as long as she could.

Only later did he realize that her explanations had been strictly calculated. She hadn't wanted a husband at all, let alone children. She'd merely wanted to further her career—and she'd thought that marrying Gideon would be the best means to obtain such an end.

Still, he couldn't fault the woman entirely. She'd taught him to be less trusting, to refrain from wearing his heart on his sleeve. In a business dedicated to survival of the fittest, Maura had helped him to see that everyone had a hidden agenda, personal goals, bent values, and that he would be better off discovering such flaws before committing himself to any relationship. Professional or personal.

Striding into the sunshine, he shook himself free of his morbid thoughts. After braving the stern looks of warning he'd received from Potts and Merriweather, he knew that they were still suspicious of his motives for bringing this woman into his house and making her his assistant. He was well aware that they were puzzled by his behavior. But he wasn't about to attempt explaining something that was confusing to himself.

His eyes narrowed, fixing on Constance's profile for the hundredth time that morning. Upon climbing into the carriage, she'd done her best to focus her attention on the houses lining either side of the road, but he wasn't fooled by her attempts at nonchalance. She was well aware of his scrutiny, and it bothered her.

"Who sent you here?" The question was meant to be rhetorical, but Constance answered him immediately.

"I told you. My father's solicitors arranged for a position at the Theatre Royale."

"They must have known the place burned down."

"The arrangements were made several weeks ago."

"Upon your father's death."

"Exactly."

He climbed into the carriage, causing Birch, who was at the open door, to watch him with narrowed eyes, since Gideon had always been very vocal about his preference for taking his own mount.

As the driver eased the conveyance into the morning traffic, Gideon watched Constance with great care. If she wore some decent clothes and did something softer with her hair, he was sure that more of her natural beauty would shine through.

"Why do you keep staring at me, Mr. Payne?"

The woman's question split the silence, and she immediately flushed. She hadn't meant to say such a thing aloud. Her consternation was obvious.

Gideon decided to be honest. "You are a very beautiful woman, despite your plain clothes and schoolmarmish bonnet."

Her lips pursed in that prim line he was growing accustomed to seeing.

"I wish you wouldn't speak that way," she protested.

"What way?"

"I wish to keep our relationship on a purely professional footing, Mr. Payne."

"As do I."

"Then you must understand that any comments of a . . . personal nature, are completely unacceptable."

"Why?" He couldn't resist goading her. She looked like a preacher's wife with her hands folded demurely in her lap and her hair scraped away from her face like a schoolgirl.

In that respect, this woman was Maura's opposite. Maura had been born a sensual creature, and she had wielded her talents as a temptress from the moment Gideon had set eyes on her.

"Mr. Payne, as I have told you several times, I come from a very strict and simple family."

"Meaning?"

"Meaning that I am accustomed to a certain amount of respect, especially from my elders."

He winced at that remark. Her elders? How old did she think he was?

"Have I given you any indication to suppose that I *don't* respect you, Miss Pedigrue?"

"No. But I would prefer having you desist from making such intimate comments."

"Why?"

Again, she looked on the verge of losing her temper, and he had to tamp down a chuckle of delight. He enjoyed pushing this woman to the limits of her endurance. He'd known her for less than a day, yet he already knew just what to say to bring a flood of color to her cheeks.

"Why would you like me to dispense with personal comments, Miss Pedigrue?" he asked when she didn't respond.

"Because I am bothered by such familiarities."

"Are you?" he offered. "Why?"

The carriage rolled to a stop, and he realized he would not have his answer. But when he would have jumped down in order to help her alight, he was surprised by the way she willingly detained him with a touch on his arm.

"Mr. Payne, I really must have your word that you will be a proper gentleman in my presence. Otherwise, I feel strongly that our arrangement should be terminated. I will find some other means of employment to reimburse you for the mirror."

"And the chandelier."

Two spots of color blazed on her cheeks. Lovely cheeks. Velvety cheeks.

"And the chandelier," she agreed.

Knowing that if he pushed her much further she would leave without ever satisfying his curiosity about her odd arrival in his life, he nodded. "Very well, Miss Pedigrue. I will be a perfect gentleman. I promise."

Nevertheless, he couldn't deny that when she had touched him of her own volition, so softly, so hesitantly, his thoughts were not those of a gentleman.

From the opposite block, Luther Hayes paused, his hand clenched around the gold handle of his walking stick. There in the distance was Gideon Payne. The man who had dogged Luther's every thought for years.

He rubbed at his brow, remembering the last time he'd seen his old friend. Gideon had approached him at Maura's funeral—and a brawl would have ensued if Birch, Gideon's butler, hadn't pulled his employer out of the funeral parlor. The entire incident had caused a good deal of speculation. No one had ever believed that Maura's death had been an accident, and Gideon's behavior had provided more grist for the gossip mills.

To this day, guilt seared Luther's heart. When Gideon had won Maura's affections, Luther had been miffed but resigned. Nevertheless, he'd never intended to indulge in an affair with his best friend's wife. Then Maura had come to him for "solace." She'd been so beautiful, so bewitching . . .

He sucked a deep breath into his aching lungs, but even the cooler air couldn't ease the tightness of his shame. Luther had cuckolded his best friend. There was no getting away from the fact.

But there were things Gideon should know, secrets Luther had kept for years.

Even so, the truth couldn't completely exonerate Luther's actions, so why try to explain things now?

Frowning, he watched as Gideon spoke to a woman whose face Luther could not see. Then they both disappeared into the theater.

*Confront him,* his conscience urged. *Tell him what possessed you to succumb to Maura's spell.*

But, curiously, as much as he had dreamed of just such a meeting, Luther stood rooted to the pavement.

He'd waited two years to approach Gideon Payne.

He could wait a little while longer.

# Eleven

Constance was not completely swayed by her employer's earnest avowals of discretion, but she didn't comment on her own misgivings. Not when she'd managed to sway him to her wishes in this respect at least. If he would only try to be more circumspect in her presence, she was quite sure that she could bear whatever surprises the rest of the day might bring her way.

As soon as they arrived at the theater, there was no more time to brood. The craftsmen had arrived before them and were already hard at work on their various tasks. Among the carpenters, the set decorators, and the masons, a constant din made anything but the most necessary dialogue impossible. As Gideon strode through the bevy of workers, she rushed to keep up with him in order to receive her instructions.

"Miss Pedigrue, on my desk you will find a pad of paper and a pencil. Retrieve them, please."

"Yes, sir."

As best she could, she made her way in the direction she thought held his office. Yesterday, she'd been so rattled by the time she'd left the place, she hadn't paid much attention to her surroundings. But today, she found herself wide-eyed as she walked over ornate embroidered carpets that resembled blooming gardens of roses and tulips and wisteria. Around her, the walls had been covered with a rich garnet-colored silk edged with gilt and brass, while overhead, the ceilings had been painted with elaborate murals of . . .

She stopped, her jaw dropping. Her eyes squinted in an attempt to clarify the drawings. But no matter how she looked at them, there was no mistaking that the pictures were of women. Dozens of women. Naked women.

She unconsciously touched the buttons at her throat as if to ensure that they were still fastened.

A loud clatter from the lobby caused her to jump, and she hurried further down the corridor.

What on earth had possessed someone to paint the ceiling of a theater with nudes? She was the first to admit that an artist should be allowed some freedoms, but, in her opinion, this particular painter had gone too far. How was a woman supposed to enter this theater on the arm of her companion without being mortified to the core the moment he looked overhead?

She would have to mention the fact to Gideon. Perhaps, being a man, he hadn't considered the indelicate situation he perpetrated.

Filled with resolve, she searched more doggedly for Gideon's study. Twice she had to retrace her steps until she finally found the paneled room. Grasping the notepad and pencil, she hurried back to the lobby.

Except for a brief frown of impatience at the amount of time she'd spent gathering the items, Gideon paid her little mind. In fact, she began to feel like some sort of expendable plebe as she trailed after him, making notes of the tasks that needed the laborers' attention. There were sconces to install, railings to attach, draperies to hang, and a huge mirror to be reordered for the lobby.

She grimaced at the last instruction, but Gideon

hadn't referred directly to her in the better part of an hour, and she saw no need to attract his interest.

When Gideon began climbing one of the two staircases that spiraled from the lobby to the balcony level above, she trailed after him, ignoring the curious gazes she received from his employees.

Upon reaching the landing, Gideon wrenched open one of the heavy doors. Constance dodged in behind him, moving so quickly that she nearly ran headlong into his back when he came to an abrupt stop. Regaining her balance, she peered around his shoulders, then gasped at the view that opened in front of her.

A huge chandelier hung high over their heads, its crystals shooting myriad rainbows onto the walls. The fixture hung suspended from the middle of a ceiling that had been painted to resemble a moonlit sky complete with wisps of clouds and bright sparkling stars. Below that, tier upon tier of gilded box seats surrounded the main level of cushioned benches and a gleaming hardwood stage. Garnet velvet curtains trimmed with heavy gold fringe had been looped around the proscenium arch with all the care of a master decorator, while in the wings a bevy of carpenters worked on an elaborate gazebolike set.

"Archie!" Gideon called, startling Constance, who had been awed by the near-reverent silence that shrouded the inner theater.

A portly, balding man squinted up in the direction of the balcony.

Since the only light came from the lanterns that had been lit around the outer walls and those at the base of the stage, Constance doubted that the man could see Gideon too easily—and she prayed he couldn't see her. She was growing tired of the way Gideon's workers kept staring at her.

"How long before the set is finished?"

"It should be done by tomorrow at the latest."

"The performers are arriving on the late afternoon train."

"It'll be done."

Not bothering to offer his farewells, Gideon marched onto the landing again.

"Come along, Miss Pedigrue."

She jumped a little when he called her by name, but her reaction was not noticed since another of Gideon's employees was racing up the stairs to meet them.

"Gideon! Have you heard the news?" He gasped as he stumbled to a stop in front of them. Constance immediately recognized the gentleman, Lester Grassman. Gideon had introduced him earlier that morning as the theater's house manager.

Gideon's brow creased. "What news?"

"From Wellington—our competition."

Gideon shook his head.

Les gulped air into his lungs to calm himself, then said, "There's been a murder."

"Murder!" Constance gasped without thinking.

Les didn't seem to mind her interruption. He nodded and said, "They found one of the seamstresses early this morning. She'd come to work early. It appears she was attacked on the stairs—strangled."

Constance's hand reflexively flew to her throat.

Les's gaze bounced from her to Gideon, and it was obvious he debated whether or not to continue.

"Well, man. Speak up," Gideon urged.

"There was a note left at the scene by the murderer."

Gideon scowled, and Les hurried to elaborate.

"It read: 'For you, Maura.'"

A chilling silence settled upon the landing. Constance tried to avoid looking at Gideon—she studied Les's features, the floor, the staircase. But soon she found herself watching Gideon, seeing the tightening of his lips, his jaw.

"Do they know who committed the crime?" he asked in a tight, low voice.

Les shook his head. "Other than the note, no real clues were left at the scene. A pair of policemen are waiting to speak to you in your office."

Without another word, Gideon brushed past Les and hurried down the staircase.

Constance stood uncertainly on the landing, sensing she wasn't meant to follow him but not really knowing what she should do until he emerged again. Needing something to dispel the awful quiet, she asked, "Who was the girl?"

Les clucked in regret. "Poor Mary MacClannahan. She used to work for Maura as a personal maid of sorts during the early years of her career."

A tightness was gripping Constance's throat, and she fought to swallow past the barrier.

"Why would anyone want to kill her?"

"I don't know," Les murmured sadly. "She was a sweet thing. If it weren't for the way Maura took a dislike to her, I'm sure Gideon would have employed her here in some capacity."

"What happened to change Maura's attitude toward her?" Constance asked, caught by that one kernel of information.

Les shrugged. "Maura accused her of stealing a diamond brooch. The jewelry was never found—and I would bet money that Mary didn't have a hand in its disappearance. But Maura wouldn't be satisfied until the girl had been punished in some way, so Gideon was forced to let her go. Even so, he made sure she had work with another company."

With that, Les turned and disappeared through the doors leading to the balcony.

Constance stood for some time, absorbing what she'd learned, her heart still beating a trifle fast.

Murder.

That poor girl had been murdered.

For Maura? That's what the note had said.

*But Maura is dead.*

Shaking her head to rid herself of such morbid brood-ings, Constance sighed and made her way down the staircase.

Not quite sure what she should do while she waited, she meandered in the general direction of Gideon's office, becoming further shocked by the statuary being moved into several recessed alcoves. Good heavens! Was everything in this building based on a motif of nude women?

Averting her eyes, she saw that the office door had been firmly closed—meaning she had the choice of standing in the hall like some sort of displaced minion or making herself useful.

Eyeing another door across the hall, she noted that it had been left open a crack. Seeking somewhere to wait out of sight, she pushed at the panels, then gasped in delight at what she saw. Props and costumes had been stacked willy-nilly against the walls and piled on the floor, leaving little more than a narrow path for walking.

She stepped further inside, and her smile widened as she saw that one entire wall had been devoted to a series of built-in shelves, drawers, and pegs to house the collection of clothes.

Without thinking, Constance set her pad and pencil aside and began to explore the plethora of theatrical supplies that had been left here—all under the guise of organizing the items and placing them in the storage wardrobe.

Time slipped through her fingers as she found hats and scarves and diaphanous gowns. There were drums and gaily colored hoops, hair extensions, brocade boots, and glittering faux jewels.

Constance had cleared nearly half the room when she became aware of a presence. Immediately, she knew who had stepped into the doorway, and she turned, clutching a sparkling tambourine to her chest as if it could shield her against Gideon's intensity.

His arms were braced on either side of the doorjamb, making her completely aware of the leanness of his body, the width of his shoulders.

"You've been hard at work, I see."

His voice offered no hints about whether he was annoyed at her presumption in cleaning the room.

"I thought it would be best to keep busy."

"Mmm."

Still unsure of his reaction, she waited for him to say something more. Finally, he offered, "You are a very resourceful woman, Miss Pedigrue."

How was she supposed to respond to such a comment?

"You also have a great knack for organizing chaos."

"Yes, sir," she whispered.

"Tell me," he urged, his voice silky smooth. "Is it only outer chaos that you have the ability to cure?"

She frowned. "I don't understand what you mean, Mr. Payne."

He stared at her for several long, hard moments—so much so that she felt her pulse begin to pick up speed.

"Perhaps I will explain about the nature of my own inner chaos someday," he murmured, so softly that she nearly didn't catch the words. Then he straightened, his mood changing so swiftly that Constance could scarcely credit the businesslike air that settled over his shoulders.

"Come along, Miss Pedigrue. I've finished speaking with the police—who thought I might have had some hand in Mary's murder."

Constance's fingers clenched. The note Lester had referred to must have led the police to Maura's next of kin.

"Thanks to you, Potts, and Merriweather, I have a solid alibi, and I've been scratched from the suspect list. For that, I thank you."

"Thank me?" she parroted in confusion.

"If you hadn't stumbled into my theater, Miss Pedigrue, I might still be sleeping in the upper storeroom."

Straightening, he said, "You have worked hard enough for your first day. Since we've caught up on our work, I think it's time we ran some errands on your behalf."

She stumbled slightly. *"My* behalf?"

He glanced at her, briefly, but it was long enough for a strange weakness to invade her knees.

"I think it's time we saw to your wardrobe."

"But—"

Again, he looked at her, and this time his expression brooked no argument. "I've seen the extent of your wardrobe, and, frankly, you've nothing at all in your possession that befits the position you hold in my theater."

She stiffened. "I cannot allow you to buy clothing for me. It wouldn't be seemly."

He sighed. "I had already intended to offer you a clothing allowance as part of your salary, Miss Pedigrue. As my assistant, your appearance is extremely important, and it will be necessary for you to have several different costumes—some for work, for travel, for dinner, parties, balls, as well as several evening gowns for the theater performances we will attend."

"Oh." Constance couldn't prevent the way the single word emerged so small and meek.

He prowled toward her like some jungle cat, and she jumped when he tipped her face up to meet his gaze. Long, silent moments passed between them, growing so fraught with tension that she froze, wondering if he meant to kiss her. Here. Where anyone could stumble across them.

Instead, he released her.

"You needn't look so stunned, my dear. I have no designs upon your virtue. As for your shopping, you needn't worry that I will become involved in such a delicate matter as choosing whether you'll have cotton or silk for your chemise."

A burning indignation flooded her body at such an

intimate subject, but before she could remind him of his promise to remain a gentleman, he continued.

"I believe we'll call on a friend in town. She'll see to it that you purchase all the necessities." His gaze remained stern. "But remember. Nothing in black. If you wish to mourn, do so in gray, brown, or blue. But not black. If I see one stitch of black, I'll add the amount to the money you already owe me."

# Twelve

Gideon's parting comment set Constance's teeth on edge. *What a horrible man,* Constance decided as the carriage drew to a stop in front of a delicate white house. *What a thoroughly disagreeable man.* Never in her life had she met anyone who disturbed her so completely. Nor had she met anyone who seemed bent on provoking her each time they exchanged words.

If it weren't for the fact that she owed him so much money, she would trot out of his life and . . .

*And what?*

True, Gideon Payne was completely without decorum, but there was also a tiny part of her—a *very* tiny part— that admitted there was something about him that thrilled her. She wasn't sure why. It might be the spirited bantering. Or the intensity of his emotions.

*Or his kisses . . .*

Constance had never been allowed any time in the company of men. When she was younger, such a fact had been a case for heartache. She'd longed to attend balls and entertain beaux, but her father had strictly forbidden any such exercises.

Yet here she was, in an unfamiliar city, her surroundings mimicking so many of her dreams—complete with an exotic, mysterious man who was slightly improper and oh, so attractive.

*Constance!*

Her thoughts came to a screaming halt as she tamped down the corner of her heart that had dared to think such a thing. This man was her employer, nothing more. She couldn't possibly allow herself to believe that he might . . . that they could . . .

Kiss again—even more passionately?

*No!*

Savagely, she focused on her surroundings, on the gaily decorated town houses and the arbor-lined boulevards. Ignoring the man who sat on the opposite seat, ignoring the strong hands resting easily on muscled thighs, she forced herself to speak.

"Mr. Payne, did I hear you correctly when you stated the theater will open in two weeks?"

"We've set our last dress rehearsal for two weeks from today. The theater itself will open the night after that."

She couldn't be sure, but she thought his eyes sparkled with sudden devilment.

"I estimated it would take at least that much time to make some temporary arrangements to cover the spot where the mirror was supposed to be."

Her lips thinned. Would he never cease to remind her of her debt to him?

"I would be more than happy to help you hang an extra set of draperies, should it prove necessary."

"Is that what you would suggest?"

She shrugged.

"I was thinking more along the lines of a painting. I've already hired an excellent artist, and he's all but finished with the ceiling murals."

The image of naked flesh and round, pink women draped in little more than feathers and silk slid into her mind.

"I would not recommend his work for the main lobby."

"Oh?"

She tried her best to appear knowledgeable, but to her disappointment, she knew she sounded far too prim.

"I saw the paintings he did on the ceiling."

"They're magnificent, aren't they?"

He was watching her so intently, she sensed he was trying to trap her verbally, but she wasn't sure how.

"I suppose that someone such as you might think so."

"Someone such as I?"

"Yes. You are . . ." She hesitated, wondering how far she dared to go with her employer.

"I am what, Miss Pedigrue?" He leaned forward, his hands loosely clasped between his knees in such a manner that she couldn't help but study them, note the strong, slender fingers. He had such sensitive hands. The hands of an artist. Hands that could touch a woman and make her feel cherished and . . .

*Stop it, Constance!*

"You are a man, Mr. Payne."

"I am well aware of the fact, Miss Pedigrue. But I do not see how that changes my appreciation of art from your own."

"Men are prone to certain . . . vulgarities."

One of his brows lifted. "Such as?"

"Such as dwelling on carnal matters."

"Ahh." He leaned back again. "So you view the paintings as being carnal."

"I don't think even you could deny such a fact."

"But I think the female form is beautiful."

"Then you should keep your thoughts to a more appropriate setting than a theater lobby."

"What would you consider a more appropriate setting?"

"I suppose a gentlemen's club or . . ." She snapped her lips closed, knowing she was pushing the conversation into places she would rather not go.

"Or what, Miss Pedigrue?"

His tone brooked no refusal, so she tipped her chin at a proud angle and said, "Or a bordello, Mr. Payne."

"What would you know of such places?"

"I know enough, Mr. Payne, to make an educated deduction."

His grin was far too potent, far too smug. "We shall have to see about that, won't we?"

She was about to ask him how he intended to make such a decision when the carriage rolled to a stop. Turning, she gasped slightly when she saw their destination.

The town house in front of them had been painted entirely in shades of purple, from the deepest violet to the lightest mauve.

"Good heavens," she muttered.

"It is a bit of a shock to the system, isn't it? But I assure you that Penny's taste in clothing is impeccable. She'll have you out of those crowlike outfits and into something attractive within the hour."

Gideon stepped onto the carriage block and held out his hand.

Huffing in indignation, she refused his offer and jumped from the carriage without his assistance, marching to the door of the house without so much as a glance in her employer's direction.

To speak of her lack of clothing was one thing. To warn her about his distaste for black was quite another. But to intimate that her own judgment could not be trusted, and that he intended to enlist the help of a "friend" to augment her wardrobe, was completely insulting. Especially if Constance's suspicions proved correct and his "friend" was someone with whom he'd once engaged in a liaison.

Damn the man. She didn't care that she owed him money. He was asking too much of her this time. He really was.

Gideon rang the doorbell, and she knew he was eyeing

her questioningly, but she refused to acknowledge him. If he insisted on this shopping expedition, she would comply—if only for appearance's sake. But she would not buy a thing this woman suggested. Not a single item.

The door opened to reveal a tall, regal woman with dusky skin and Indian features which were nearly obscured by the silk headdress and veils she wore.

Constance gaped at her. *This* was the person who would dress her? *This?* Well, Mr. Payne had another think coming. She wasn't about to swath herself in gossamer fabrics, let alone leave her arms and midriff bare.

"Good day, Rasha. Is your mistress at home?"

"Yes, *sahib*. This way."

Constance realized to her own chagrin that she had mistaken the housekeeper or a personal maid for the mistress of the house. Nevertheless, she found herself tugging at Gideon's sleeve.

"I don't think this is a good idea," she whispered.

"Nonsense. This is a wonderful idea."

Gideon's eyes sparkled with amusement, and she glared at him. She was growing infinitely tired of having him regard her as some sort of huge joke. Not for the first time, she rued the fact that she had been put in such a situation by a cat. A mangy, battle-scarred, lop-eared tabby cat.

They were led down a richly paneled corridor lined with objets d'art. Constance's eyes widened as she noted the amazing number of nude sculptures placed in every possible niche. Either the woman was an avid collector of Greek art, or she, like Gideon, didn't see the wisdom of saving such intimate subjects for more private places.

"Here you are," the servant murmured, pausing in front of a set of double doors. "If you will wait here for one moment, please."

Rasha disappeared inside the shadowy interior, then swung the doors wide, ushering them into a bedroom—a *bedroom,* for heaven's sake.

Constance stiffened in disapproval. She might not be an expert on worldly affairs, but she did know that no one respectable entertained guests in the boudoir.

"Gideon, darling!"

Constance knew that her mouth had dropped wide, but she couldn't seem to help herself. A woman more beautiful than any other Constance had ever known rushed toward them. She was enveloped in a gown trimmed with feathers and silken petals, and in her left hand she held a thin cigar.

"It's been ages, darling. Simply ages!"

She enveloped Gideon in a scented embrace, then held him at arm's length to study him.

"When did you get back from your business trip?"

"A few weeks ago."

She pouted. "And you didn't bother to visit me until now?"

"I've been rather busy."

She glanced at Constance and smiled. "I can see that." Leaning close to his ear, she whispered, "She isn't really the sort you usually—"

"She isn't a performer or a personal acquaintance, Penny."

"Oh?"

She stared at Constance with much more avid interest than the situation warranted.

"She's lovely, Gideon. But surely you've noticed how much she looks like—"

Again, he interrupted her, taking her arm in a grip that deftly demonstrated he was the person in charge of this discussion. "That isn't the point, either."

He nodded to Constance, who was growing increasingly tired of having them refer to her as if she were some inanimate object. "Miss Pedigrue is my new assistant."

"Assistant?"

"Yes."

"But you've never—"

"Regardless of my past habits, Miss Pedigrue will be working closely with me over the next few weeks . . ."

Penny giggled.

". . . and she will need some help to reconstruct her wardrobe."

"I should say."

Constance flushed.

"I'd like to see her in colors."

Penny's eyes narrowed, and she studied Constance as if she were an unfinished canvas. Then she made a complete circle around Constance, murmuring, "Yes, yes, I see what you mean. Black tends to make her skin very drab and sallow. Blues, I think. Pinks. Yellow—but only a touch."

"She may insist on wearing mourning."

Penny peered at Constance yet again. "Pity. Mourning doesn't suit her. Not with that coloring."

Gideon leaned back against the hearth, looking far too pleased with himself. "You'll help us, then?"

"I'd be honored. I have a dressmaker who's a dream and a milliner who can work miracles."

Constance stiffened. She'd never considered herself a person in need of "miracles."

"I suppose this little escapade has a budget?" Penny inquired.

Gideon shrugged. "Have them send the bills to me." He was partway out the door and stopped to poke a finger into the air. "And make sure she's got something to wear right away."

Then the door slammed with enough force to make Constance jump.

Penny giggled and took a long drag of her cigar. "He can be a beast, can't he?"

"Yes. He can."

Constance's reply was so adamant that Penny's brows rose. Very slender brows. Obviously plucked, then darkened with kohl.

Shocking. Absolutely shocking.

Penny approached, clamping the cigar in her mouth and holding out her hand. "The name's Penny. Penny Whistle."

*Penny Whistle?* The woman couldn't be serious.

But when she continued to hold out her hand, Constance realized that the statement hadn't been meant as a joke.

"Constance Pedigrue," she replied, taking the woman's proffered hand.

"And you're from . . ."

"Boston."

Penny's eyes twinkled in delight. "Boston, hmm." The way she repeated the information held so much secret amusement that Constance shifted uncomfortably. "I should have known that Gideon would have been brought down by someone from Boston."

"I assure you, I haven't—"

"But you *have!* The whole situation is positively marvelous, don't you see? Gideon Payne never associates with anyone from work. Never. Since his wife's death, I think I can lay claim to being the only actress he's struck up an acquaintance with—and even then, he wouldn't give me the time of day until I retired."

Actress? Retired?

"He's always been a closed sort of person, you know what I mean?"

Constance shook her head, thoroughly confused. "No, I'm afraid I don't."

Penny's eyes widened in delight. "Then I shall have to fill you in on all the details, won't I?"

She linked her arm through Constance's, pulling her resolutely toward the hall. "But first, I think we should be getting under way, don't you? We've so much shopping to do, and so little time."

Constance had no real opportunity to object. Before she knew what had occurred, she had been installed in Penny Whistle's opulent carriage. An *open* carriage. One that left her vulnerable to the gawking passersby.

And there were plenty of those sorts lining the streets, craning their necks when the white and gilt conveyance rolled past them. Constance was vividly aware of the way chins dropped and mothers drew their charges more closely against their skirts.

The whole situation was completely vexing. Constance had spent the better part of her existence seeing to it that she remained as invisible as possible. She'd learned early on in her father's house that to attract attention would incite Alexander Pedigrue's wrath. For some unknown reason, he'd considered his daughters to be prone to sin, and any hint of transgression was rewarded with serious and immediate punishment.

She did her best to sink more completely into her seat, all to no avail. People couldn't help but notice her, she realized as she studied Penny, who waved to the strangers as if she were Queen Victoria with a smoking habit. The woman had donned an elegant coat littered with beading and tassels. Her bonnet held a huge spray of egret plumes that ruffled merrily in the wind, giving her the appearance of an exotic fowl.

Constance brushed at her own skirts. If Penny was an elegant bird of paradise, then what was she? A wren?

She frowned, scolding herself for such a comparison. After all, she was in the right here. She was dressed appropriately for an afternoon of shopping. She was modest and feminine and wholesome.

But judging by the amount of male attention Penny was attracting, such qualities weren't in high demand here in New York.

Constance wriggled in shame. She shouldn't allow such thoughts to enter her head. She shouldn't care whether or not she attracted a man's attention. A sigh lodged in her throat. At twenty-five, she was a confirmed spinster—there was no way to escape the fact. She would be much better off accepting her fate and dealing with her lonely future with as much decorum as possible. She wouldn't be one of those simpering females who, having found herself past her prime, began wearing extravagant clothing and putting on airs in an attempt to catch a husband.

"It's invigorating, isn't it?"

Penny spoke so suddenly that Constance was caught off guard.

"Beg pardon?"

"I do so love a good morning ride." Penny's grin was entirely saucy. "Especially when there are men about to make a woman feel appreciated."

The woman's comment was so close to her own thoughts that Constance didn't know how to respond. She didn't suppose there was a right way. Not without betraying herself far too much.

"It's so gratifying to know that my work is still remembered."

"Your work?"

"On the stage."

"Oh, yes. Of course."

Penny took a deep drag of her cigar, then leisurely blew the smoke above her. "I did so love performing. I miss it horribly sometimes."

"Why did you retire?"

*"Amour."*

"Beg pardon?"

"I fell in love." She sighed, the sound mixed with pleasure and regret. "Alas, my dearly beloved wished for all of my future performances to be private ones."

Constance couldn't help herself. She blushed.

Penny's laugh was as delicate as a silver chime. "My dear! I don't think I've seen a woman blush in ages! How delightful."

Feeling the need to explain herself, Constance admitted, "I am not accustomed to such frank speech."

"Of course not. You're from Boston." Penny chortled again and reached to pat Constance on the knee. "But don't you worry, my dear. Men are absolutely enchanted by such naivety, I can assure you." She rapped her hand against the side of the carriage. "This is the place, Peter!"

The conveyance pulled to a stop in front of an elaborate storefront, and somehow the driver managed to secure a spot for them to alight right next to the walkway, despite the teeming traffic.

"Wait here, my man," Penny said as a liveried footman helped her down. Constance couldn't help thinking that the uniforms Penny's servants wore made them look out of place and entirely conspicuous.

"We shouldn't be too long, I don't think. An hour or two at most," Penny breezily informed the man.

*An hour or two?* Constance thought helplessly as she followed Penny.

"Miss Whistle, I don't think—"

"Call me Penny, my dear girl. There's no need for ceremony between us."

"But I don't think that I—"

"Don't think, Constance. It's time to shop. And since Gideon is footing the bill, you should take advantage of his offer."

*Gideon is footing the bill. Take advantage of his offer.*

The little voice in her head used a tone that was positively wicked, tempting her to spend a great deal of money and show him that he might think he was in control, but only so far as she allowed him to be.

But even as the idea appeared, she rejected it. After all, if he were displeased with her, he would add the total to the amount she owed him. Of that she was sure. No. She would be sensible in her choices. He would find no fault with her selection.

As soon as she entered the shop, however, Constance wished she didn't have to be so responsible. For a reason known only to Penny, the woman had decided to begin their expedition at the milliner's.

Constance had walked little more than a yard into the store when her heart began to pound and her mouth grew dry. All her life, she had been restricted to simple black bonnets that could serve for church and everyday use as well. Her father had insisted that his daughters' headdresses be made from a practical color completely free from all forms of frippery.

Yet in this single establishment, there were hats topped with velvet flowers, miniature birds, tassels, lace, and netting.

"Oh, Penny," she breathed.

"I knew you'd like this boutique. I just knew it!" Penny took her hand, squeezing it. "We're kindred spirits, you and I. I sensed it from the moment Gideon brought you to me." She swept her arm wide. "Now, choose what you like. Then we'll see what we can do to find gowns and shoes and gloves to match."

# *Thirteen*

He waited for Maura to reemerge, even though he knew it had been foolish to follow her here. But when he'd seen her climb into Gideon Payne's carriage, he'd felt a need to follow her, to reassure himself that she was really in New York, ensconced in her husband's house.

Settling onto a park bench where he could see through the shop windows and catch a glimpse of her now and again, he had to smile. What a masquerade she'd concocted. It had taken some careful maneuverings for him to discover the details of the charade she played, but he had finally determined that she was pretending to be a spinster from Boston. A look-alike.

And Gideon Payne had been too stupid to realize that there could never be another beauty like Maura. Never in a hundred years.

He itched to talk to her, touch her, if only to take her hand in some darkened corridor, but he knew such a feat would be impossible. First, he needed to prove to her that his devotion had not wavered during her absence.

Soon, he was sure she would hear about the terrible fire that occurred at Theatre Royale. During the early years of her career, the owner of that establishment had

refused to pay Maura for a month's worth of performances—citing poor ticket sales as the reason for his
woes. Maura had sworn she would get even with the man
one day.

Then there had been Mary MacClannahan. She'd
known too many secrets about Maura Payne. When
Maura had tried to arrange her dismissal, Gideon had
interfered, finding her another means of employment
within the city.

His smile deepened in satisfaction. The girl would not
be telling any tales now.

So what next? What more should he do to prove his
adoration?

His eyes fell on a wooden newsstand plastered with
posters and advertisements. One day soon, Maura's face
would outshine all of the other upstart actresses who
dared to compete with her.

*Who dared to compete . . .*

His jaw hardened, and he stared into the window of
the milliner's shop again, hoping to catch a glimpse of
his soulmate.

*I will help you any way I can,* he vowed silently. *Soon.
Soon . . .*


Louise Chevalier stepped from her private railway car,
taking the hand of her bodyguard.

"I want to see her immediately," she said under her
breath.

Etienne squeezed her hand in warning. "You can't do
that."

"Why not? I'm her mother."

"But she hasn't seen you since she was a little girl. You
can't simply burst into her life and demand that she
listen to your misgivings."

She frowned, then quickly rearranged her features into
a welcoming smile as she saw the reporters and fans who
waited in a cordoned area next to the station.

"How did they discover I was coming to New York?"

she hissed in irritation even as she waved and smiled even more warmly.

"How do they ever find out?" Etienne asked matter-of-factly. "Frankly, I think this crowd is an even stronger reason for planting yourself in a hotel and plotting your movements quite carefully. Otherwise, your efforts will appear as the top headline on the gossip column of every newspaper in the city."

Sighing, she realized Etienne was right. As much as she might wish to rush to Constance's side, she couldn't. Not yet. Not until she had more facts about the situation surrounding her daughter.

"Very well," she murmured, barely moving her lips. "But as soon as we arrive at the hotel, I want you to locate Constance *and* Gideon Payne. Then I want you to ensure our man continues to follow them until I can intervene."

Etienne's lips twitched. "Your wish is my command," he said under his breath, his tone rife with teasing. "Now, put on your happy-actress expression and greet your public."

By the time Constance returned to Gideon's town house, she was exhausted. Evening shadows were gathering in the alleyways, and a distinct air of abandonment was beginning to infect the city—as if all that had been stately and circumspect had dissolved along with the night.

As she bid Penny good night, Constance discovered that she barely had the energy necessary to climb the front steps. Fortunately, the door was opened by the butler, and a fussy Mrs. Potts rushed to greet her.

"You poor, poor dear. You look worn to a frazzle."

"Yes, I—"

The woman didn't allow one word. Taking the hatbox from Constance's hand, she ushered her inside.

"We kept water for your bath on the back burner for the better part of the evening, so you go right into the bathing room and have yourself a nice, long soak. I'll bring a plate of sandwiches and a pot of tea. I'll bet you haven't had a bite to eat all day!"

"No, I—"

Her explanation was given no heed, so she didn't bother to finish her sentence. She allowed herself to be ushered into the bathing room, where Mrs. Potts helped to divest her of everything but her chemise. Then, leaving a tray of food on a low stool, Mrs. Potts left the room altogether, allowing a potent stillness to settle over Constance's shoulders.

Constance hadn't known until that instant how her day had been filled completely with chatter—either from Penny or from one of the many store owners. Now that she had the evening to herself and the silence of this garden-painted chamber, she felt the kinks that had settled into her shoulders loosen and her spirit relax.

Slipping into the tub, she immersed herself in the hot water, congratulating herself on her restraint. Despite Penny's urging, she had purchased a nightshift, a chemise, and three pairs of stockings to replace those that had been in the stolen trunks. Then she'd bought two white shirtwaists, a navy skirt for work, a simple green woolen gown for traveling, and a violet merino for special occasions. Other than matching ribbons, which she could form into clever hair ornaments, she had purchased only a single bonnet. A wide-brimmed straw edged in lace.

Considering the plethora of choices extended to her, even Gideon couldn't fault her disciplined choices. He wouldn't dare.

From somewhere inside the house, a commotion ensued—the tramp of footsteps up the stairs, the banging of doors, murmured calls. But she ignored them all, taking her time, enjoying the endless supply of hot water available to her from the brass spigot.

By the time she had washed and soaked and scrubbed her hair, she was as wrinkled as a raisin, but she didn't mind. She could very well become accustomed to such luxuries.

Mrs. Potts had left Constance's sensible cotton wrapper draped over a chair. Since Constance's packages had surely been delivered to the house, she slid into the robe without donning her chemise. As soon as she reached her own quarters, she would don her new underthings and the light cotton nightshift.

Gathering the clothing she'd littered on the floor in her haste to bathe, she wadded the items against her chest and tiptoed forward. The door squeaked slightly as she emerged. Constance winced when she noted the empty kitchen and the velvet darkness. A glance at the clock informed her that she'd closeted herself in the bathing room for the better part of two hours.

She was thankful there was no one near to witness how long she'd lingered. Otherwise, she was sure she would be scolded for such hedonistic indulgences. Her father would have been livid if more than a quarter hour was spent on a person's ablutions. Of course, Constance had never been tempted to spend longer than that in the cold tin washbasin the family used as a tub.

"There you are."

The low voice snaked out of the quiet so suddenly that Constance gasped and whirled, nearly upsetting herself in the process.

"Mr. Payne!" She gasped, clutching her black gown and limp petticoats to her chest as a makeshift shield. To her horror, the action caused one stocking to wriggle loose and fall to the floor, then her bonnet, and finally her corset.

A heat flooded her cheeks. She could have borne having the man witness her guilty retreat, but to leave a trail of apparel was completely mortifying.

"Did you enjoy your day?"

The question hung in the air like a ribbon of silk, the tone of his words somehow gossamer, ethereal, but hinting of a hidden strength.

"Yes, I suppose."

"You suppose."

Instantly, she regretted her lukewarm response, but she didn't feel it would be prudent to appear too enthusiastic, since her employer, like her father, might regret parting with his money.

"I had a very enjoyable time."

"In what way?"

"Penny is very engaging."

"How?"

Constance was at a loss regarding how he expected her to respond. "She is very . . . vivacious."

"You don't approve?"

"On the contrary. I found her company to be delightful."

His eyes narrowed as if he doubted her statement. "There are some women who would refuse to spend time in her presence."

It was her turn to be surprised. "I don't see how that could possibly be true."

"Penny once graced the stage."

"She told me as much. Even so, I don't see how her former profession could be held against her."

"You don't, hmmm." He began to close the space between them. "Then you don't disapprove of her avid love for the theater?"

"I don't believe in such old-fashioned nonsense as actresses being considered women of easy virtue."

"You don't?"

"Not at all. Just because she chose to make a living by immersing herself in make-believe is no reason to judge her character so harshly. In my opinion, such a reaction is as unreasonable as the first novelists being branded liars and heretics because their prose was not based on their own life experiences."

"You seem to have given the matter a great deal of thought."

Constance was poised to respond, then hesitated.

After all, would it be wise to admit to this man that she herself had longed to "tramp the boards"? That she had even considered running away from home on several occasions? That if it had not been for her younger sisters, she would not have waited so long to follow her own dreams for the future?

Since Gideon Payne was regarding her with narrowed eyes, she prevaricated by saying, "There are many vagaries of society that have garnered my attention, Mr. Payne."

"You love a good debate, eh?"

Again, she hesitated in revealing too much, in informing him of how her father had considered her far too headstrong and impulsive and her views far too frank.

"I think it is much too late in the evening to indulge in any such forms of dialogue, Mr. Payne."

"No doubt your shopping wore you completely out?"

"Yes, sir. In a manner of speaking. Your friend was very exuberant and insisted that I follow her to most of the ladies-wear establishments in New York."

"That must be the reason you were willing to drop your customary reserve and spend my money so freely."

Constance's body was suffused in heat, then an icy foreboding. She shouldn't have chosen two shirtwaists. One would have sufficed—and the bonnet she'd brought from Boston was more than enough for her needs.

"I'm sorry, sir," she whispered.

Throughout their exchange, Gideon had moved closer and closer until barely a foot stretched between them. When he bent, scooping up her corset, she could have withered on the spot.

"There's no need to apologize. I look forward to seeing what you've chosen. Besides which, I'm sure that the work you provide me with in the future will be well worth the sums incurred today."

"Yes, sir," she whispered miserably.

He placed her stays on the top of the pile of clothing, then reached to stroke her cheek.

"Don't fret, Miss Pedigrue. I have more money than God, so I don't mind surrendering a portion on your appearance."

How was she supposed to react to that comment?

"That's why I sent Penny Whistle with you in the first place. I knew she would encourage you to spend freely."

Thank heaven Constance had refused Penny's urgings to use even more of Gideon Payne's money. If she had, she could imagine the scolding she would have received from this man. Then she found it difficult to think of anything at all as her employer rubbed the pad of his thumb over her cheekbone.

"How old are you, Miss Pedigrue?"

She wished he hadn't asked that. She was far too old to be trembling at his touch.

"I believe we've had this conversation before."

"Yes. But you refused to give me a clear-cut answer."

"As I stated before, a true gentleman would never demand such information."

"I don't give a damn. I want to know."

Since she saw no way of avoiding the issue, she reluctantly supplied, "I am twenty-five, sir."

"A bit on the shelf, wouldn't you agree?"

She gritted her teeth to hold back her anger. "I wouldn't know, sir."

"Something tells me that you aren't accustomed to pretty things, that no one ever indulged you."

"My father wasn't prone to . . . *indulgences* of any kind."

"What a pity. A woman such as you should definitely be spoiled with all sorts of trinkets. You really are quite beautiful."

The words flowed through her veins like a potent wine, and she struggled to keep her wits about her. "I really don't think that you should—"

He laid a finger over her lips. "Don't think. Neither of us should think."

The words were spoken more to himself than to her.

Bending, he caught her at the nape, pulling her inexorably closer. His mouth ravaged hers, demanding an immediate response—one she was helpless to prevent. Her body leaned into his, and she rose on tiptoe, reveling in the heat and lightning that swept through her body.

When Gideon's tongue slid across her lips, it was she who deepened the caress, she who explored the sweet depths of his mouth. She was astounded by her own audacity, but she was also honest enough with herself to admit that she had been longing for this to happen since she had encountered Gideon early that morning. She wanted to feel his body pressed against hers. She wanted his hands to roam along her back and hips through the thin cotton of her wrapper. She wanted him to make her feel pretty and alive and cherished.

Gideon lifted his head and stared deeply into her eyes. In the darkness of the room, she was unable to read his expression, but the ragged nature of his breath and the pressure of his fingers digging into her skin filled her with a certain triumph.

"This is a dangerous situation, Constance."

Her heart flip-flopped at the gentle way he used her name.

"Why?"

"I'm not the sort of man you should allow to kiss you. As you stated before, I am not a gentleman. I have never taken much stock in the niceties imposed by society. I tend to take what I want and damn the consequences. You shouldn't become embroiled in such a situation."

"I think that we have already established the fact that I am an adult. As such, I am more than capable of making my own decisions."

He frowned, his entire body becoming fierce and intense. "Dammit, Constance," he rasped. "You don't know anything about me. You don't know anything about this house and the things that have occurred here. If you did, you'd run into the night."

"I know I look like your dead wife," she said boldly.

He grew perfectly still. "How did you—"

"Surely you didn't expect the fact to remain a secret. I've had people staring at me from the moment I entered the city. Sooner or later, I was bound to pull the pieces together."

His hands dropped to her arms, and he shook her slightly. "So, you think I've decided that you're some kind of substitute for Maura?"

A sliver of hurt shot through her heart when he echoed her most secret fears. "Am I, Gideon?"

His fingers dug into her flesh, but he didn't speak.

"When you look at me, touch me, argue with me, do you see Maura?"

Her stomach knotted as she waited for his response, waited for him to reassure her that she was her own person. Any similarities to his late wife were fleeting and barely worth noticing.

But when he stepped away, dropping his arms, she knew instinctively that she would receive no such solace.

"Yes. I see Maura in you. I hear her in your voice. I taste her on your lips. All that has prevented me from taking you to my bed was the fact that you didn't know about my wife's existence."

Constance was not prepared for the all-consuming defeat she felt at his words. The inexplicable hurt. The palpable pang of rejection.

She was nothing to this man. Nothing but an employee and a substitute woman. She would never be anything more.

She began to shake—with rage and disappointment and loss. Just when she feared the trembling she experienced would sap the strength from her bones, he retreated another step. Two.

"Forget I said that. Forget I said anything at all," he ground out between clenched teeth. He offered her a curt bow. "Once again, I have strayed over the border of good manners. Good evening, Miss Pedigrue." Then he melted into the darkness as quickly as he had appeared.

For several minutes, Constance waited, sure that he would come back. He couldn't leave her this way. He couldn't blurt such confessions then abandon her before she had made some attempt to heal her pride. She should have been offered the opportunity to call him a cad, to rail at him for his injustice, to demand an apology.

But he hadn't lingered, and he didn't return to the kitchen.

Blinking away the tears that sprang to the surface, Constance gathered her scattered belongings and raced up the staircase. After throwing open the door to the Peach Room, she dumped the pile on a chair, then used the weak glow emitted by the hall sconces to light her own lantern.

Only then did she shut the portal and lean back against the heavy wood, squeezing her eyes shut.

Not for the first time, she wished she'd never met Gideon Payne, wished she'd never become indebted to him. How could she possibly work for the man now? Each time they met, her emotions disintegrated into chaos. She'd thought such a reaction would ease in time, but tonight, when he'd touched her, kissed her, she'd lost all sense of reason.

She shuddered at the memory.

Until she'd come to New York, no man but her father had ever held her hand or tipped her cheek. Then, during her journey to New York, she'd been kissed, jostled, and propositioned. Yet none of those brushes with intimacy had aroused in her anything more than irritation.

Until Gideon had caressed her cheek as if she were a woman worthy of love.

Then her pulse had pounded, her breathing had grown labored. If he'd pressed her to continue, she would have been severely tempted to succumb to his advances completely.

*Even though he was thinking of Maura, using me in her stead.*

Constance swiped at the tears that rolled down her

cheeks. No. She couldn't think about that now. Nor could she allow herself to dissolve into such schoolgirl nonsense as believing that—in time—she could heal this man and make him forget Maura.

No. She could not become entangled in Gideon's affairs. She must remain clear-headed and unconcerned, as professional and single-minded as she could manage. Otherwise, her servitude would become unbearable over the next few months.

Constance inhaled sharply, bidding the thumping of her heart to return to its customary pace.

She would not allow Gideon Payne to hurt her, she told herself again, erasing the last of her tears with her palm.

She would be strong.

She would be immovable.

She would be constant.

Her head bobbed in agreement, and her eyes opened. Blinked. Stared.

The room was completely filled with parcels and hatboxes, baskets, valises, trunks, and assorted feminine paraphernalia.

"There must be some mistake," Constance whispered to herself, opening the first package. When she encountered a dozen pairs of clocked hose in shades of pale pink, yellow, blue, and peach, she frowned. Constance had never ordered such impractical colors, even though Penny had insisted that she . . .

*Penny.*

Penny was responsible for all this. Constance rushed from box to box, exposing frothy petticoats, boots, slippers, and mules, gowns of every description, hats aplenty.

When Constance had refused to buy everything she'd been offered, Penny had insisted that there was no need for such restraint—indeed, she'd seemed nearly put out by Constance's frugal ways. But then, by the second shop, her mood had miraculously improved. Constance had assumed the woman had finally conceded to Constance's wishes. Now it appeared that the former actress had been ordering merchandise without Constance's consent.

Her hands flew to her hot cheeks. No wonder Gideon had asked if she was worth the expenses she'd incurred. He must have thought her incredibly irresponsible. Then, when he'd kissed her and she'd responded so avidly to his embrace, he must have assumed that she meant to . . . "thank" him. With her body.

No. No, no, no! She couldn't allow him to entertain such a misconception. Especially now that she had forced him to admit that he would willingly put her in Maura's place as his lover.

She reached for the doorknob, ready to race through the house, find him, and explain that she had never ordered these clothes. But when she encountered the cool brass, she grew still.

No. Not tonight. Too many things had already been said, too many secrets shared, too many emotions expended.

She would explain everything to him in the morning and point out that his misconception of her gratitude had caused them both to react hastily.

Yes. That was what she would do. Tomorrow. When the cool shadows weren't so disturbing.

So tempting.

And she could remember why it was so important to remain completely aloof from Gideon Payne.

# Fourteen

Gideon spent an hour on the back verandah, sitting in one of the old wooden rockers that had been his inheritance from the closest thing he'd ever had to a mother. Closing his eyes, he could see Elizabeth Kincaid on the chilly January morning when she had informed Gideon that he would be living with her and her husband and children instead of in a foundling home in Buffalo.

Naturally, Gideon had been suspicious of the idea. After all, what sort of family would unofficially adopt a boy well into his teens? But Elizabeth had drawn him into the family as naturally as if he were a long-lost son. He probably would have stayed on the Kincaid farm in Indiana for the rest of his life if she hadn't died soon after his eighteenth birthday, leaving him this rocker in her will—as well as a host of happy memories.

Sighing, Gideon supposed that Elizabeth would have been shocked and appalled at his most recent misbehavior. Although she had grown to expect some outlandish shenanigans from Gideon as well as her own eight boys, she had strictly informed them that they should treat a lady with respect.

Any lady.

Even if she happened to look like Maura and drive him to his wits' end.

Pushing at the floor with his toe, Gideon rocked back, staring into the darkness and wondering what had come over him since Constance had stormed into his life. He was normally a calm man—a sane man. But she had the ability to drive true reason from his brain. When he was near her, he forgot all codes of ethics and morality and thought of only one thing.

*Possessing her.*

As soon as the words shot through his brain, he grimaced, realizing he'd danced around the issue long enough. He'd tried to convince himself that Constance was nothing more than a curiosity, a riddle to be solved. But his interest in her ran much deeper than her surface resemblance to Maura—no matter what he'd told Constance earlier.

Dropping his head against the back of the chair, Gideon listened to the familiar creaks and groans of the chair. He was amazed at how quickly his household had changed in only two days. Women's frippery was scattered in the bathing room, and the air held the faint scent of perfume. There had been shopping parcels and hatboxes being delivered, as well as sashes and aprons being ironed. Even Mrs. Potts and Mrs. Merriweather seemed to feel a more genuine sense of purpose as they bustled through the house, making it "fit for a lady."

Gideon found the whole situation remarkable. For two years, he'd been unable to step into this house or live any sort of a "settled" lifestyle as befitting a man in his mid-thirties. He had shunned female companionship, devoted himself to his work, and steered clear of gaming halls, shooting clubs, and the like. All in an effort to drive Maura and her treachery from his mind. Yet here he sat, on his own back porch, content to rock and ponder his situation as if he were a married man again.

Idly, he supposed that having a woman around the place was the main reason for his change in attitudes.

There was a sense of completion that came into a man's home when a woman shared the same domicile. The whirlwind pace of business eased, and Gideon found himself wondering if he could find some way to make the arrangement . . .

*Permanent?*

There was no hope of that. Not since he'd spouted all that nonsense in the kitchen about regarding Constance as his wife's double. Constance would probably never speak to him again, let alone allow him to kiss her.

Grimacing, he mourned such a loss. He hadn't meant to speak to her in such a manner—he knew he'd bruised her tender emotions. But he'd felt driven to warn her away from him, to make her completely aware of the current status of his life—even if he'd been unable to push her completely away. He was not some innocent schoolboy who would trail along behind her. Nor was he the honorable sort of gentleman who would patiently wait years for the consummation of his passions. He couldn't court the woman, and he certainly couldn't marry her.

Not at all. He might enjoy having a woman back in his house, but he wasn't about to marry again. Not in this lifetime.

Nevertheless, he wouldn't mind a mistress. He would even be willing to set Constance up in her own house, should she agree to such a proposal.

*She won't do it. Not after the things I said in the kitchen.*

No. Constance was a sensible woman. She'd willingly agreed to become his assistant to fulfill her debts. If he agreed to release her from such a burden, perhaps she could look upon him as a man instead of a mere employer.

*Doubtful. She would probably spit in my eye at the mere suggestion.*

But she had responded to his kisses. He knew she was attracted to him, that he could rouse her to passion.

*Could such a flurry of desire persuade her to abandon her views on the roles of a proper gentlewoman?*

Possibly. If he could hold her again, kiss her, she might lower her defenses enough to reason with her. He could show her the deliciousness to be found in such an intimate relationship. He could offer her the world she longed to experience. They could travel to exotic locales, live the life of wealthy aristocrats. He might even persuade her to go on the stage.

His lips curved in a slow smile. Yes. That's exactly what he would do.

His decision made, Gideon stood, stretched, and yawned. Tomorrow he would set his plans in motion. He would do everything in his power to weaken Constance's puritanistic ideals.

Even so, he wasn't so naive as to think that Miss Pedigrue would readily agree to his plans. Not at all. She was from Boston. She had been raised with all the strict morals and values that Gideon had abandoned as soon as he'd left the orphanage. But there was a fire to her spirit that he was sure he could trap. She wasn't as well suited to her structured lifestyle as she might suppose.

He merely had to find a way to convince her of that fact.

When she awoke, Constance focused on the mounds of dresses and scarves and shoes. Groaning, she knew she was not going to be given an opportunity to ignore her original problem: how to make Gideon believe that she wasn't a greedy woman bent on relieving him of his fortune.

Pressing her palms against her eyes, she did her best to form some course of action.

She could wear her own clothes to breakfast.

But he grew so moody when she wore black.

There was no way around the issue. She was going to have to don one of the purchased gowns. But, she thought as she swept back the covers, at least she could keep her costume as simple as possible. She would choose one of the shirtwaists that she had originally ordered and a simple taffeta skirt. Even Mr. Gideon Payne couldn't fault her for such an ensemble.

Unfortunately, after nearly a half hour of searching, she was forced to admit that the plain blouses and skirts were nowhere to be found. Evidently, Penny Whistle had been quite free in taking charge and had canceled Constance's original order.

Botheration. What was Constance supposed to do now?

Grimly, she searched through the items again, settling on a white piqué suit, a frilly black and white striped blouse, and black boots. Savagely taming her hair in a pair of braids, she wound them at the nape of her neck, then secured a small black bonnet to her coiffure with an ebony hat pin.

Knowing that if she dallied any longer she would be tempted to closet herself in this room for good, she threw open the door.

"Good morning, Miss Pedigrue."

Her heart jumped when she found Gideon waiting for her on the opposite side of the threshold. He leaned indolently against the far wall, one leg crossed over the other as if he'd been waiting a good long time and had prepared himself to wait even longer.

"I'm so pleased that you decided to join me."

She sensed a thread of censure in his tone and immediately stiffened.

"I'm sorry, sir, if I detained you. But you did not specify a time for us to meet."

"No. I didn't." He crooked his finger, signaling for her to come forward. Once she'd reached the center of the hall, he motioned for her to stop. Then he circled her, studying every aspect of her attire.

Constance felt a raging heat rise into her cheeks. She might be beholden to him, but that didn't mean that he had the right to circle her as if she were a piece of bric-a-brac to be purchased.

"Very nice, Miss Pedigrue—although I see that you've managed to include some black in your ensemble."

"The color is considered fashionable this season."

"Only because Queen Victoria, who dictates what women of breeding should wear, is also in mourning."

Constance wouldn't have thought that Gideon could have been so astute. Nevertheless, she was pleased that he approved of her appearance for the day.

"You've chosen wisely, Miss Pedigrue. You look quite smart—just the sort of image I want in an assistant."

The compliment seeped through her veins with a potent sweetness, managing to unnerve her even more. The sting of indignation and hurt, which had lingered in her heart since retiring to her room, eased.

"You have better taste than I would have expected."

The smile that had been hovering at the edges of her lips faded completely.

"What *did* you expect, Mr. Payne?"

He shrugged. "Something matronly."

She pursed her mouth to prevent a scathing reply. When she felt calm enough to speak, she inquired, "And what might a 'matronly' woman wear?"

He was still studying her, paying far more heed to her tightly corseted waist and the tailored lines of her bodice than she would have liked.

"You know. Boring skirts and white shirts. One bonnet for all occasions."

She started, glaring at him, sure that he knew of her original purchases and was making fun of them. But he appeared completely sincere. Too sincere. As if he'd summed up her character, classified it as being uninspired, and now sought evidence to support his assumption.

"I wouldn't have thought you so daring as to clear the district of ready-made samples."

Again, he was hinting at her supposed extravagances.

"I believe that there has been a mistake."

"Oh, really? Are there more items to be delivered later?"

She nearly huffed aloud in indignation. "Indeed not. As a matter of fact, these things"—she waved an arm in the general direction of her bedroom—"are not mine."

His eyes narrowed. Again, his attention seemed to focus on the general vicinity of her bosom. "They seem to fit."

"That isn't what I meant."

"Then please explain."

"Yesterday, Penny and I made the rounds of her dressmakers and milliners."

"Obviously."

She shot him a withering glance for interrupting. "I explained to Mrs. Whistle time and time again that I would be working as your assistant, and as such, I would need a very limited wardrobe."

"How prudent of you."

Again, she sensed his sarcasm. "I can assure you, Mr. Payne, I *was* very prudent. I purchased less than a handful of items. Yet this"—she waved her hand again—"is the result."

"Your logic still escapes me."

She could have stamped her foot in frustration. Was he being purposely dense? "Mr. Payne. I never would have presumed upon your . . . kindnesses to order such a plethora of supplies. I fear that Penny took it upon herself to circumvent my wishes and order all of these gowns."

The hall pulsed in silence for several long minutes, and Constance was sure that she would be chastised for her carelessness. But the man's only response was, "Thank heavens someone took you in hand, Miss Pedigrue. Come along. There's work to do."

"Your tea, Miss Caruso."

The exotic actress looked up from the makeup she had

been carefully applying to her cheeks and eyes in order to hide the encroachment of age.

"Put it on the table, Nannette."

Her maid curtsied, set the silver service on the table, then left the room as quietly as she'd come.

Carlotta frowned, studying her reflection in the mirror.

There had been a time when an hour had been more than enough time to finish her performance preparations. She'd been so young and lithe and beautiful then. Her only real rival in the business had been that upstart Kelly woman who had married Gideon Payne and forced him to send Carlotta to a less prestigious theater to work. Even so, Carlotta had brought most of her male fans with her, and in time even Maura had been obliged to admit that Carlotta's talent and winsome ways were a force to be acknowledged.

Rising, Carlotta poured herself a cup of tea, added a dollop of cream, and mourned the time when her tea had been thick with the stuff and she hadn't worried about gaining an ounce from the indulgence.

Idly stirring the brew, she preened before the mirror, noting that her arms were still firm, her legs long and lean. What did it matter that her breasts were no longer high and proud? Or that her costumer had been instructed by the management to devise clever ways to bone Carlotta's garments to disguise a thickening waist? The men still adored her burlesque routines.

She smiled, taking a sip of her tea. Less than a month remained before Gideon Payne would be opening his new burlesque house. As soon as he began selling tickets, she planned to approach him about working with his establishment. She no longer wished to work at Bartholomew's Burlesque. Carlotta was tired of the owner's roaming hands and his stingy salaries. Gideon Payne had always treated her like a queen—and she was sure he would do so again.

Humming softly, she took another sip of her tea,

frowning when she detected a slightly bitter aftertaste. She would have to talk to Nannette again. The girl often used a too liberal hand with the tea leaves.

Coughing, Carlotta set her cup down, then tried clearing her throat again when a strange burning sensation threatened to shut off her breathing.

"Nannette?" she called, her voice emerging as little more than a croak. "Nanne—"

She rushed to the chamber pot in the corner, suddenly overcome with a wave of nausea. Bracing her hands against the floor, she whimpered when a series of sharp pains began stabbing into her muscles.

*Dear heaven, what is happening to me?* she thought desperately, as her body began to twitch uncontrollably and she fell onto the rough floor. The room swam around her, and she fought to pull at the decorative shawl draped over her bureau. If she could tug the perfume bottles and water bottle off the edge, she was sure that the noise would attract someone . . . to help her . . . help . . .

Squeezing her eyes closed, she tried to focus. But she couldn't seem to see anything at all. Her hands were so numb she couldn't feel the cool silk . . . soft fringe . . .

*Please . . . help me,* she whimpered silently.

Then she was consumed by an implosive sensation in the region of her chest, and all conscious thought shattered into the encroaching gloom.

The door squeaked slightly as he let himself into Carlotta's dressing room, locked the door, and stood hidden in the shadows. He waited patiently for Carlotta's body to grow still and her eyes to dim to a waxen sheen. Then, kneeling beside her, he brushed a lock of hair aside so that he could study her more carefully.

"You were never a threat to her, you know," he murmured. "You were more of a nuisance. I would have left you to make a mess of your own career if I hadn't decided to show Maura the extent of my loyalty."

The woman did not respond—and he hadn't expected her to do so. It had been so simple to slip into the theater and dose her special stash of tea with poison. He was merely disappointed that he hadn't thought of such a course of action earlier. He should have killed Carlotta years ago—from the moment he'd unearthed the depth of Maura's hatred for her rival. But Maura had claimed all of his attention back then, and he hadn't found the time to deal with Carlotta.

Now that Maura had returned, what better way to show his devotion than to make an example of her rival? Maura would laugh in delight at such a solution to her problems.

Just as she would love him, body and soul, when she appeared again and he could inform her of the extent of his preparations for her return to the stage.

# Fifteen

For the next week, Constance followed Gideon like a lapdog, assisting him in his various offices and helping him with dozens of errands around town. There were workmen to pay, shipping clerks to inform, and train schedules to check—and other than a point when Gideon asked her about the quality of a fabric intended for cushions to be made for the dressing room of one of his divas, she could have been a spot on the wall for all the notice she was given.

Nevertheless, Constance was thankful for Gideon's busy schedule. She was kept so occupied with business that she didn't have to think about Gideon's reaction to each new gown she wore or the way her body tensed with anticipation whenever he was near. And if at times she thought she'd detected a hint of possessiveness in his gaze, she ignored the sensation. Such an idea was preposterous. If she'd seen anything hot and deliberate in his eyes, the reaction wasn't to the alteration in her wardrobe but to her striking resemblance to Maura. That reminder was enough to make her immediately wary and cool so that she easily maintained her standoffish attitude.

So far, Constance had seen three of Gideon's New York theaters. Ruby Hall—the name of the theater where she'd first encountered Gideon Payne—was by far the most elegant, in her opinion. The Crystal Palace, where an opera was currently being rehearsed, was filled with gilt and greenery but was much too fussy for her taste. The Diamond Pavilion, where an English comedy would soon be offered, had been decorated in cool marbles, wrought iron, and antique baroque furnishings.

Much to Constance's dismay, the visits to the theaters had generally occurred early in the day—which had allowed her little contact with the performers and only glimpses of the elaborate sets, costumes, and properties being prepared for the shows. In fact, she was lucky to have the opportunity to leave Gideon's offices in the various buildings.

He had obviously been without an assistant for some time, Constance had decided after only a few days in his employ. Each of his offices was small, cramped, and cluttered with his own brand of haphazard organization techniques. Her days had been filled with filing, tidying, and cataloging. Nevertheless, she kept thinking that once she'd neatened his work areas, Gideon would be sure to assign her to tasks in other parts of the theater. Then, at long last, she could drink in the heady atmosphere of fantasy, glamour, and drama that clung to the stage area like a potent perfume.

"Is something wrong, Constance?"

Constance blinked, becoming aware of the way the carriage was making its way through the crowded streets next to the docks. Rousing to a semblance of attention, she belatedly realized that Gideon had called her "Constance," not "Miss Pedigrue"—something he had not done since their altercation in the kitchen.

"No, Mr. Payne," she said coolly. "Nothing is wrong."

"You're sure?"

"Quite sure."

"You seem rather . . . subdued," he commented as the carriage drew to a stop in front of another of Gideon's many suppliers. "You haven't spoken once without my asking a question."

"I see no need to bother you with endless chatter."

He eyed her consideringly, then said, "I have never once heard you 'chatter,' as you put it. In fact, you are a remarkably calm woman. That is a quality I haven't experienced a great deal with the fairer sex."

"And I'm sure you've had a good many encounters with the opposite sex to use as a comparison."

The moment the words passed her lips, she wished she could retrieve them. What in the world had possessed her to comment on this man's personal conquests?

Rather than appearing offended by the remark, Gideon chuckled. "There is something to be said in favor of a man having some experience with women, don't you think?"

"I wouldn't know."

"But I think you do, Constance." He leaned close under the guise of standing to whisper. "Otherwise, you might not melt so completely in my arms each time I kiss you."

Constance's huff of outrage was drowned by his laughter.

Climbing from the carriage, he opened the tiny door and unfolded the steps. "I trust that you have a good supply of evening gowns in the cache of clothing you and Penny selected," Gideon said, startling her with the quick change of subjects.

Constance pulled her attention away from the flash of women in jewel-toned afternoon dresses who hurried down the walkways intent on their shopping. In the dappled, latent sunshine, his features were softened, relaxed, drawing attention to the strength of his jaw and the wind-tousled waves of his hair.

"I have one or two things that would suffice, yes."

"Good. Tonight we have a date at the opera."

Her heart skipped a beat. The opera. He could have promised her the moon and she would not have been so instantly alive.

"Really?"

His eyes crinkled at the sides in amusement, but he didn't tease her about her immediate excitement. "Mozart. *The Marriage of Figaro.* Surely you were aware that the opera was about to open?"

"Yes, but I didn't know that I . . . that you and I . . ."

His smile was rich and tender. "I attend every opening of every performance as long as business permits." His voice lowered to a tempting murmur as he added, "I believe you will be seeing a great many operas and plays in the next few weeks."

She didn't dare breathe for fear she would discover that she was dreaming.

"Come along, Miss Pedigrue. There's work to be done."

Without further preamble, Gideon left her sitting in the carriage and strode toward the office, leaving her to scramble from the conveyance on her own. As she glared at Gideon for forgetting the most basic gentlemanly courtesies, she wished there was some way she could put this man in his place. He really was too high-handed where she was concerned. Somehow, some way, she would have to find the means to set him down a peg or two. And by thunder, she would, too. If she could only find the means to humble him.

Louise Chevalier watched Gideon stride into the warehouse without so much as offering his hand to help Constance alight. Impatiently, she shifted in the squabs of her own covered carriage, trying to catch her first glimpse of Constance's face. But the woman's posture and the brim of her hat made such an act impossible.

"The bastard," she hissed. "The least he could have

done was wait to ensure she safely reached the walk-way."

Etienne hid a grin behind his hand. "Mayhap Constance does not want his help or his attention."

Louise glared at him. "What on earth do you mean?"

This time, he could not prevent his laughter. "My dear, surely you could feel the sensual tension between those two even from this distance."

She gasped. "You can't possibly mean that Constance and . . . that *man* have . . . *feelings* for each other?"

"I think they do."

She sniffed in disdain. "You've lost your wits, Etienne."

"Not at all. I am merely stating the obvious."

Louise bit her lip. "We must take her out of this situation—this very afternoon."

"Why?" he calmly inquired.

She swung her hand wide. "B-because that man isn't right for her."

"He might be."

"Nonsense. He owns a *burlesque* theater."

"He also owns a dozen legitimate stages and three opera houses."

"But he's far too . . . worldly for her."

"After her rigid childhood, she might need a taste of the world."

Louise's lip quivered. "He will hurt her, Etienne," she said with infinite despair.

Etienne leaned forward, grasping her hands. "You cannot save your daughter from life's trials, Louise. I know that you've missed a good portion of her life. I know that you want to make up for Alexander's harsh upbringing. But if you shield Constance from all the evils in the world, you will prevent her from finding the joys as well."

"But Gideon is so . . ."

"You know as well as I do that he is a good man at

heart. You've performed on several of his stages, and you've always remarked on how kind he has been to you."

She sniffed and hunted through her reticule for a handkerchief. "I know that. It's just that after his wife died, he became so . . . hard. Almost cruel."

"He was in mourning, Louise. You can't judge a man on emotions he experienced two years ago."

"I suppose." She dabbed at her eyes. "Nevertheless, I want both of them followed around the clock. If Gideon Payne does one thing to hurt her—"

Etienne placed his fingers over her lips before she could utter the words. "If he hurts her, I will handle him myself, Louise. I promise you, he will not escape retribution."

She blinked at Etienne, then threw herself into his arms despite the fact that the shade had not been drawn over the window. "I love you," she whispered into his neck. "I love you so much."

"I know," he murmured against her neck. "And very soon you will be my bride."

When Gideon's carriage pulled to a stop at the front mounting block of the town house, Constance breathed a silent sigh of relief. They had been working since seven that morning—and, judging by the church clock in the block beyond, she would have very little time to ready herself for the theater that night.

"You look tired," Gideon said as the wheels squeaked to a halt.

"Not at all, sir," she murmured, fearing that he would rescind his offer to take her to the opera. "However, if you don't need me for the next few hours, I believe I'll have Merriweather fix a tray for my room instead of joining you at dinner. That way I will be ready to accompany you this evening." The last was said with a note of defiance, daring him to ruin her day by refusing to take her to *The Marriage of Figaro*.

"I believe this is the servants' day off."

"Oh."

The prospect of searching the larder for something to eat, preparing it, and lugging it to her room seemed suddenly overwhelming considering the need to look her best that night.

"If you would allow me, I'd be delighted to take you out to dinner, Miss Pedigrue."

*Out* to dinner? At a restaurant?

Constance had never eaten at such an establishment. Except for train stops on her journey, she'd never been to a place where the tables were draped with snowy linens and the food was presented on delicate china plates.

"Well? Are you game?"

She bit her lip in hesitation, knowing she should allow herself as much time as possible to dress. But the growling of her stomach and her innate curiosity proved to be her Waterloo.

"Thank you, Mr. Payne. I would like to accompany you to dinner."

"Then I will meet you in the front foyer in an hour."

*An hour?* She gulped at the impossible task that lay before her, but managed a calm "Very well."

As soon as she'd been ushered into the house, she nearly ran up the staircase and closeted herself in her room.

Praying that her inexperience at such elaborate measures would not betray her, she hung her curling irons in the chimneys of the lamp on her dresser, stripped off her working ensemble, washed, then began to study the garments hanging in her wardrobe.

For once, she thanked Penny under her breath as she surveyed the dozens of gowns the exotic woman had chosen.

What did women wear to the opera? Something dramatic and daring, no doubt. But even though Constance's new wardrobe was more exotic than anything she'd ever had before, she doubted she could compete with women draped in jewels and couturier gowns.

Deciding to constrast with such women rather than compete, Constance decided to search for something simple and elegant.

As she heard the carriage roll to a stop in the street outside and the driver urge his apprentice to knock on the door, Constance took one last look in the mirror.

Although her father would have been appalled at her vanity, she could not help but be pleased by what she saw.

Knowing that she hadn't the talent for the masses of ringlets popular with fashionable women, she had drawn most of her hair into a thick braid and wound it over her head like a crown. Then, taking the lock of hair she'd left loose behind one ear, she had formed one thick sausage roll that fell over her shoulder. A bare shoulder.

Constance shivered slightly at the unaccustomed reflection of her own skin in the lamplight. The gown she'd chosen was of a rich, dusky lavender satin trimmed with bands of black velvet at the hem, cap sleeves, and bertha collar that skimmed the contours of her breasts and hugged her shoulders. As accents, she'd donned black gloves, a black ribbon at her throat, and a frilly black hairpiece.

Since she was not certain she had the courage to spend the entire evening in such daring décolletage, she quickly slid her arms into the matching satin jacket. The compromise proved to be warm in the summer stillness, and she prayed for a breeze outside to keep her cool until the sun dropped from the sky.

The distant *bong* of the clock in the foyer pronounced the hour, and she gathered her reticule, hurrying to meet her employer.

To her surprise, however, the area at the bottom of the staircase was empty and shrouded in its customary shadows.

At the sound of a footfall she turned, a welcoming smile spreading over her features. It wasn't Gideon who greeted her but the solemn countenance of the butler.

"Good evening, Birch," she said without thinking. Then, remembering his deafness, she wondered if she shouldn't have spoken at all.

Rather than appearing put out, the man dipped his head in acknowledgment. The effect may have been caused by the lantern he held beneath his chin, but she thought his features lightened and his mouth parted slightly.

But if the unaccustomed movement of his lips was a smile or a grimace, she would never know. In that instant, Gideon clattered down the steps, still fastening one of the buttons to his formal black jacket.

When he reached the bottom, he glanced up, then drew to such a sudden halt that Constance couldn't help but warm with pleasure. His eyes widened in pleasure as he looked her up and down, instilling her body with a heady warmth.

"You look lovely, Miss Pedigrue," he said, the comment holding a tinge of surprise that nearly—*nearly*—spoiled her mood.

Before she could speak, however, he held up a finger. "One moment, please."

He disappeared down the corridor, and Constance waited in the uncomfortable silence that spilled into the foyer when once again she found herself abandoned to the company of a deaf man. He, too, seemed to be eyeing her closely—so much so that she began to wonder if perhaps she had been *too* daring in her choices for the evening. As Gideon's assistant, was she supposed to cling to restraint and prim decorum in her dress for the theater performances as well?

Gideon returned before she could give the matter much thought. As his fingers curled around her elbow, squeezing slightly, she forgot her doubts and threw caution to the wind. Tonight she was attending her first opera. Nothing could spoil the evening. Nothing at all.

Gideon murmured a few instructions to the driver, and they were soon clattering through the streets, competing with the buggies and hacks that were filled with people intent on their own diversions.

Just as Constance feared the rumblings of her stomach might grow insistent enough to be heard by Gideon, the driver stopped the team in front of an imposing brown brick building. Except for a well-polished door and a shiny brass plaque that proclaimed the place to be "The Oasis," there was no evidence of a proper restaurant.

This time, Gideon helped Constance to step from the carriage. Keeping a gentle hand on her elbow, he led her to the door and knocked twice with his knuckles.

"I apologize for the informality, but since we've a limited amount of time before the opera begins, I chose our surroundings for their excellent service. The proprietors are more than aware of my schedule on an evening such as this."

Not sure how to reply, Constance remained silent as a tiny window slid open to reveal a pair of suspicious eyes. Then the panel slammed shut again, and the door swung wide.

"Mr. Payne!" proclaimed a stout gentleman dressed in a black frock coat and a snowy-white shirt. "Welcome. Welcome!"

They were ushered into a narrow foyer and from there to an archway that led to the main dining hall. The lighting was dim, intimate, the slight draft caused by their arrival making the flames flicker and dance.

Constance peered warily at the occupants of the room, noting in an instant that most of the customers were men. A few had female companions at their tables, but most sat alone or in groups of two or three.

Constance tugged at Gideon's sleeve.

"What sort of place is this?" she whispered, the atmosphere of the room inspiring an almost sepulcher-like reverence.

Gideon leaned close to whisper, "It's a private club. A men's club."

"But they permit women to enter?"

"Occasionally . . . a certain kind of woman."

There was no time to question him further since the maitre d' had approached.

"This way, Mr. Payne."

They were led to a table situated in an alcove, its opening swagged with gossamer draperies.

"Would you like the curtain open or closed, Mr. Payne?"

"Closed, please."

Since Gideon was holding her chair, Constance didn't have time to protest the fact that their private hidey-hole was about to grow even more intimate.

"Is something wrong?" Gideon asked as he took his seat.

"Wrong?" she echoed weakly, her gaze flitting from the closed curtain to the man who'd brought her here. "What could be wrong?"

"You seem nervous."

"No. I don't think so."

But his expression of amusement told her eloquently enough that he didn't believe her protestations.

"I promise, I won't do anything you won't agree to, Constance."

Her breath caught in her throat. What exactly did he mean? That he intended to make advances but that he was sure that she would agree to them?

Suddenly, she knew exactly what "sort of women" were allowed to frequent this establishment.

"Those ladies out there are courtesans, aren't they?"

Gideon's eyes shimmered with mirth. "What a lovely—if antiquated—way of putting it."

Constance jumped to her feet in alarm, a heat rushing to her cheeks as she wondered who had witnessed their arrival. "What possessed you to bring *me* here?"

"The food is excellent."

"Forget the food. What about my reputation?"

"I assure you that the staff and its guests are completely discreet."

"I don't care if they're all deaf, dumb, and blind. I wish to be taken to the theater."

"Not until we've eaten. I, for one, am starving."

"Please, Mr. Payne. I would be more than happy to cook something for you at the town house later."

He shook his head, openly grinning. "Relax, Miss Pedigrue. The curtains have been drawn to maintain your privacy, and anyone who saw you enter will be eager to keep their own guests anonymous, so I'm sure they gave you barely a second glance—although you may have attracted a bit of attention in that costume."

She gasped, automatically smoothing the fabric of her jacket. "I thought you approved of my attire."

"I do." The words were husky, low, and filled with overtures of the most sensual variety. "However, I must confess that I have grown so accustomed to your . . . conservatism that you have completely bowled me over tonight. You will have to pardon me if such a reaction is not one I wish to share with the other patrons of this establishment."

The compliment was so unexpected and so revealing that she was stunned into silence.

"If you'd like, you may remove the jacket. It's very warm in here tonight."

She automatically shielded her throat with her hand—as if he could see the brevity of her neckline beneath the fabric.

"I'm rather chilly myself," she said, clutching her buttons, fearing he might take it into his head to force the issue, but he merely shrugged.

"Fine. Do whatever pleases you."

His tone was so affable, she was sure he was mocking her refusal somehow. "Mr. Payne, I think that—"

She was interrupted by a waiter who slipped through the curtains and presented them with a pair of huge menus. Distracted, she forgot her pique and ran a finger over the gilded bird that graced the cover.

"How lovely," she breathed.

"The Oasis is known for its elegant details."

Opening the heavy binder, Constance bit her lip to keep from exclaiming in delight over the hand-printed lettering interspersed between delicate watercolor birds.

"As I said before, the food is very good here, so feel free to order whatever you'd like," Gideon said.

"Oh, my," she whispered in astonishment as she drew her gaze away from the artistry of the pages themselves and surveyed the lists of appetizers, entrées, and desserts. Each dish had been inscribed in French, then translated in elaborate script below its title.

Her mood lightened considerably, buoyed by the promise of food. Gideon was right. A curtain shut them both in a cocoon of anonymity. What would it hurt to eat here? Just this once?

Sensing Gideon's gaze, she peered at him over the edge of the leather-bound sheaves. He hadn't picked up his menu at all. Instead, he watched her with an air of bemusement.

"Is something wrong, Mr. Payne?" she asked imperiously.

"Not at all. I am merely enjoying your enthusiasm."

She grimaced. Evidently, her efforts to hide her reactions had not been completely successful. "You must think me something of a simpleton."

"On the contrary. By watching you, I am reminded of my own reactions to such ordinary pleasures."

"Not so ordinary," she murmured under her breath.

"Perhaps so, but I have grown accustomed to many of life's luxuries over the years."

"Then you weren't born to such wealth?" she asked,

not about to reveal to him that Mrs. Potts had already disclosed that Gideon was orphaned as a child.

"Hardly."

The single-word response was more intriguing than she would have thought possible, but since the waiter had arrived for their order, she allowed herself to be distracted from the tidbit of information about Gideon's past.

Searching the items printed on the speckled vellum, she inwardly debated what to order. There were no prices included—a shocking oversight, in her opinion—and she knew she should keep her expenditures to a minimum. But without the proper information, how was she supposed to make any sort of decision?

"Well, Constance? What will you be having?"

Her stomach grumbled at the catalog of exotic dishes, and she longed to try them all, but she finally stated, "I'll have the soup of the day," then closed the booklet with utmost decisiveness.

"That's all?" Gideon inquired.

"I'm not very hungry."

"Liar."

The waiter's lips twitched infinitesimally at the soft rejoinder, but he didn't speak.

"Paul, bring us a small portion of everything on the menu, please."

"Yes, sir."

The black-clad waiter disappeared, and Constance eyed Gideon in distress.

"You really shouldn't have done that."

"You'd be hungry again in an hour if all you ate was a bowl of soup."

"I assure you, I am accustomed to a light repast."

"So your father starved you as well as beat you?"

She scowled at him. "I wish you would refrain from criticizing a man you never knew."

"I'm beginning to believe that it's a good thing your papa and I never had an opportunity to meet."

"Why?" She was astonished at the fierce expression that flooded his features.

"Because I despise meanness, especially in men who think that it is their role in life to dominate women."

"Your views are very . . . liberated."

"Not at all. I have merely learned to appreciate women."

She swallowed against the inexplicable tightness gripping her throat. "I'm sure you have," she retorted with great meaning. Gideon had already informed her that— before Maura—there had been dozens of lithesome ladies in his life. Why did he feel it necessary to underscore such a point time and time again?

Gideon's chuckle was low and dark and husky. "What's the matter, Constance? Are you afraid that you've aligned yourself with a masher?"

"I'm no longer sure."

"At least you're honest," he muttered ruefully. He leaned forward, taking her hand before she had a chance to snatch it out of his reach. Resolutely, he turned her palm up. "I think it's time that I was honest with you as well, Constance."

She could not have moved if her chair were on fire.

"I *do* have ulterior motives for employing you."

"Oh?" she whispered.

He nodded. "I think you are a beautiful woman."

She frowned. "No, you think I look like Maura."

She couldn't ignore his quick inhalation.

"You don't pull any punches, do you?"

She was immediately contrite. Had her manners abandoned her entirely? She should know better than to speak so frankly with a widower about his dead wife.

"I'm sorry," she whispered, but when she would have drawn away, he linked their fingers together more securely.

"Don't be. You've been the first person in years who hasn't pussyfooted around the truth or avoided speaking your mind. I appreciate that quality."

Constance couldn't account for the way his compliment caused her to warm. It shouldn't matter to her what Gideon Payne thought. It shouldn't matter at all.

But it did.

"You've also been the first person since Maura's death to capture my . . . interest."

A frisson of sensation raced down her spine at the pronouncement, but she forced herself to say, "I do not intend to become a substitute for your wife."

"I didn't ask you to be."

One of his fingers moved to the single button that held her mitt closed.

"No, but you have already stated—quite clearly—that you regard me as nothing more than a reminder of your spouse."

"I lied."

The words were offered so matter-of-factly that she blinked in surprise.

"I told you such a thing because we were alone in a dark room and the taste of your lips was still heady on my own. I knew that if I didn't push you away, I would have been carrying you upstairs to my room."

When she didn't offer a stinging rejoinder, he added softly, "And I think you would have come quite willingly."

She dipped her head, taking an inordinate amount of interest in rearranging her napkin even as she shamefully admitted that Gideon was probably right. "So why are you telling me these things now?"

"Because I regret hurting you." He tipped her chin up, forcing her to acknowledge the sincerity in his eyes. "I have missed you, Constance."

"I haven't gone anywhere, Mr. Payne."

"No, but you've been quite distant these past few days, and I regret that it was my own hasty words that caused such a rift between us."

"So what are you suggesting? That I return to being

the naive, trusting young woman who first entered your house?"

He shook his head in honest regret. "I know such a thing would be impossible. Too many things have passed between us for either of us to return to such . . . innocence."

His thumb traced the line of her jaw and caressed the fullness of her lower lip. Constance found it difficult to concentrate on anything at all but that tiny point of contact. A hunger flared in her breast, and she wondered if surrendering to this man could be so wrong.

"No, Constance," he continued, his voice low and entrancing. "I'd rather take things as they come . . . see what progresses if we allow nature to take its course."

The boning of her corset seemed to constrict her lungs. "Mr. Payne—"

"Yes, Miss Pedigrue?" he interrupted with a lazy smile.

"Could you clarify your statement?"

"In what way?"

She tried her best to offer him a carefree shrug, but the task was difficult since he'd begun to tug at the tips of her glove. "Such a pronouncement sounds very much like a . . . proposal of marriage."

# Sixteen

Gideon's lips quirked again, and Constance found herself floundering in the dark depths of his eyes.

"Not at all, Miss Pedigrue."

She relaxed ever so slightly, even though she could not account for a wayward twinge of disappointment.

"No, Miss Pedigrue, my statement was meant as a warning."

As quickly as she'd succumbed to her relief, she grew tense again, her body shifting from hot to cold, her limbs trembling with a nameless emotion she'd never experienced before.

He slid her glove free and dropped it to the table, exposing the sensitive skin of her palm.

"I've given a good deal of thought to the situation, Miss Pedigrue. I can no longer deny that I am attracted to you, and have been since the moment we met."

"You were very irritated with me, as I recall," she reminded him primly.

"Yes, but that does not preclude an attraction."

"You can't possibly think of me in any way other than a ghost of your wife."

"Actually, the two of you are quite different. Maura was much more . . . voluptuous."

She grimaced at her apparent shortcoming.

"She was also very worldly."

"What do you mean?"

"She was a woman who was well acquainted with the pleasures of the flesh, where you . . ." He lifted her hand and placed a kiss in the center of her palm, and Constance couldn't prevent the gasp that escaped her lips. "You are still quite untainted."

"But you have designs on that very purity you claim to admire."

"I suppose I do."

"Surely you can't mean to destroy that quality?"

"Not destroy. Enhance. Educate."

She snapped her hand free from his disturbing caress. "I see. You intend to make me into one of those women out there." She waved at the room beyond them with a vague hand. "You intend to steal my chastity—"

"I won't steal it."

"—my good name—"

"Not at all."

"—and what shreds of a reputation I have left after serving as your employee."

"I assure you that if you agree to my proposition, you will be well compensated. I would even be honor bound to erase all your debts."

She stared at him in horror, realizing that he meant to *pay* her, to *employ* her as his mistress. Somehow, he actually believed that her emotions would be involved no more than they already were as his assistant.

Her fingers curled into tight fists in an effort to restrain her temper when all she wanted was to leap across the table and pummel the self-satisfied expression from Gideon's face.

"You seem to have all the details worked out."

"I've been giving the matter a great deal of thought."

"I see. And I suppose that you've taken every contingency into account."

"I think I've planned ahead for most."

"How very thoughtful of you." She made her voice sorghum sweet, but she sensed that Gideon had caught her tinge of sarcasm. "And how very level-headed."

"There's no reason to become emotional over such things."

*One, two, three,* she counted in an effort to control her temper, but the old habit wasn't having much effect.

"I assure you the arrangement would be beneficial to us both, Constance."

"In what way?"

"I would have . . . companionship again, and you would have—"

"Money?"

"Security," he amended.

"Ahh. And *then* what will happen to me?"

His eyes narrowed. "What do you mean?"

"Once you've tired of me, once my . . . *newness* has worn off, I will be tossed into the streets like a discarded toy."

He frowned. "I would never—"

"Wouldn't you, Mr. Payne? Then how else would you handle me? Especially if I should grow attached to my position in your house. What if I should decide to make life difficult for you and your next paramour?"

"I never referred to your position as being my para—"

"You might use nicer words and employ all the euphemisms at your disposal, Mr. Payne, but there is no whitewashing the truth behind the utterances. You mean to seduce me, isn't that correct? You've taken the notion into your head—and even if I refuse the offer of a position in your household, you intend to use all of your resources to change my mind. In effect, you mean to beguile me."

He leaned back in his seat, regarding her with something akin to astonishment. "I suppose that's true."

"Then you have a very high opinion of your own charms, Mr. Payne. In order for a seduction to succeed, you must persuade me to participate—that is, unless you intend to *coerce* me into such an arrangement."

His features darkened even more. "I have already told you that I won't *coerce* you to do anything."

"How can you say that when, somehow, your will must overpower mine? In order to feel so confident, you must think yourself quite a lover."

She was being far too brazen, she knew, but at the moment she felt helpless to stop. Her heart thundered in her chest, but she steeled her spine and adopted her sternest "schoolmarm" mien. His pronouncement that he found her worthy of a sensual campaign had shocked her to the core, but she knew instinctively that it would be a mistake to make him privy to such a reaction.

"You must also think," she said stiffly, "that the fact that I've been locked away from masculine society makes me easy prey."

"If I had, I'm sure I would be revising my opinion now," he said tightly.

"And so you should, Mr. Payne. I might have spent the better part of my life in a seclusion of sorts, but that does not mean I've just fallen off the turnip wagon." Her voice rose as her self-righteousness grew. "I am a woman of impeccable manners and morals, Mr. Payne. I can also prove to be quite intractable when my mind is set. My sisters have often commented that rather than 'Constance,' my name should have been 'Pig-headed.' I can assure you, Mr. Payne, that if I put my mind to remaining cold and distant, your plans of seduction will never come to fruition."

"Is that a dare, Miss Pedigrue?"

She opened her mouth to retort, then shut it again with a snap. How could she have been so stupid? She'd set a trap to catch a wolf, then had turned it against herself.

"Well, Miss Pedigrue? Are you extending a challenge in my direction?"

Constance prayed for some sort of guidance. Then, when the heavens refused to help her, she said, "You may do whatever you wish, Mr. Payne. I'm sure that you will anyway."

The light in his eyes became positively devilish. "Yes, I suppose so."

She was spared any sort of response when the waiter appeared with a tray laden with food.

Gideon didn't know what had prompted him to be so forthcoming with Constance Pedigrue. He hadn't meant to blurt out his plans for seduction—and in fact, he hadn't really decided whether or not to embark on such a venture.

But in that moment she'd defied him, he discovered that his motives had shifted. No woman had ever challenged him—least of all to a sensual campaign of wits. The entire idea was completely unorthodox. So much so that he found his body thrumming in anticipation— another sensation that he hadn't experienced in far too long.

As he watched Constance eat—with reluctance at first, then with complete enjoyment—Gideon studied her with something akin to awe. Since Maura's death, he'd purposely devoted all his energies to his work. He'd amassed a fortune double that which he'd acquired during his brief marriage with Maura, but his financial success hadn't made him happy. There had been something missing from his life, a reason for existing other than habit.

Looking at Constance in her elegant evening gown, her hair coiled about her head, black lace brushing her chin, he knew he shouldn't allow himself to entertain anything but the most respectable thoughts. But as he watched his unlikely companion sip her soup and close her eyes in abject enjoyment, he admitted that a part of him had died long before that night Maura had leaped from her bedroom balcony. Years of foundling homes and orphanages had caused him to steel himself against truly surrendering his emotions, and now that same corner of his soul was returning to sentience. With such a change came the same pleasure-pain a numbed limb might feel as the nerves quickened and jerked to life.

*I will have her.*

The thought sprang into his head so suddenly and so resolutely that he knew he could not deny its power. Something beyond his own reckoning had brought the pair of them together.

And now he was destined to see this drama through to the end.

By the time they'd finished with their meal, many of the diners had already left for other evening activities. What few murmurs of conversation could be heard were too distant to understand, and only a hazy glow from the candles on the tables revealed that they weren't alone.

"Are you ready for the opera, Constance?"

"Mmm."

Her expression was filled with a potent combination of eagerness and a sleepy contentment from the rich food they'd both consumed.

"Then I suppose we'd better go," he murmured, helping her to rise and barely resisting the urge to cup her shoulders with his hands.

Not yet. If he touched her now, he would not be able to stop—and Constance would not see her opera.

Putting a step between them, Gideon made his way to the slit in the draperies. He was about to pull the fabric aside when Constance stopped him with a hand on his elbow.

"Must we parade in front of the other guests as if I'm some sort of trophy on your arm?"

He turned slightly to face her, and she hadn't realized how close he stood until his knuckles grazed her cheek.

"I really have been abominable to you, haven't I, Constance?"

She eyed him in confusion, wondering if he were sincere or if this were some new gambit to undermine her defenses.

"I should have remembered that we are from very different upbringings."

"Not so very different, I shouldn't think." She could not prevent the way the words emerged in a confidential murmur.

"You have no idea."

"Then why don't you explain things to me?"

"What is there to explain?"

"I know you were an orphan, but other than that I know very little about you."

He considered the idea for some time, then nodded. "Very well. For the next few days, Constance, my life will be an open book. Ask whatever you will, and I will do my best to satisfy your curiosity."

The offer was more than she ever would have expected, and oddly it filled her with a sense of power. If she could only uncover what past events had formed such a man, she would surely understand him.

"Very well, Mr. Payne. I will compile a list of questions."

He chuckled. "I'm sure you will."

Taking her arm, he led her through a slit in the rear of the curtains.

"Come with me. We'll escape through the back door."

He waited for an hour. Two. Three. As the minutes ticked past with aching slowness, he wondered what was happening behind those curtains. Was Maura flirting with Gideon? Was she toying with him like a cat batting a mouse?

Or was he drawing her into his web? Just as he had so many years ago?

His hand bunched into a tight fist, and he ordered another whiskey—this time tossing it back and swallowing the fiery liquid in one gulp.

Dammit! Why was she tormenting him this way? Why hadn't she offered him some small smile, some hint that she knew he was watching, waiting.

A cold hand clutched his heart. Surely she didn't doubt his adoration. He'd done his best to prepare the way for her triumphant return to the stage.

But maybe he hadn't done enough.

Abruptly rising, he threw several coins onto the table, then marched toward the alcove. But when he swept the curtain aside, he found nothing but a startled waiter cleaning up the debris of the evening meal.

Without explanation, he ignored the waiter, turned on his heel, and left the Oasis behind.

He had plans to make. Evidently, Maura hadn't noticed his efforts to this point. He needed to work harder. Something elaborate.

Something she could never ignore.

Gideon had long ago grown immune to the allure of the theater. If he concentrated hard enough, he could easily remember the thrill he'd felt the first time he and Luther Hayes had sneaked into a playhouse to watch their first performance.

Nevertheless, he hadn't anticipated the rapture that spread over Constance's features the moment the Crystal Palace came into view.

"Are you familiar with Mozart?"

"Oh, yes." Her response was eager, but he could tell by the way she craned her neck to obtain the best view out her window that she was distracted by the delights to be found outside. "Mozart was often played in our church."

Gideon grimaced, realizing that Constance probably had but a passing acquaintance with the man's music.

"You will probably be pleasantly surprised with the opera, then," he informed her. "I can assure you that you will find this evening much more enjoyable than church."

With that, he rapped on the side of the carriage, instructing the driver to take them through one of the alleys so that they could miss the crush of patrons.

In the cool shadows next to the performers' entrance, he helped Constance to step down, delighting in the delicate fragility of her hand in his own. She was so delightfully eager, so charmingly vulnerable, that he couldn't help tucking her arm in the crook of his elbow and drawing her close to his side.

"Perhaps I should have taken you through the front door," he murmured. "That way, your first glimpse of the stage and the costumes would be as the curtain rises. Since I value your honest opinion of the production, I've been very careful to keep you away from the stage as much as possible to date."

"I don't mind," she breathed, and he knew in that instant that a glimpse of backstage chaos was an event she had longed to experience for years.

Pausing at the shallow steps that would lead them inside, he turned to face Constance. Something akin to reverence stole through his body as he looked down at her. She was so beautiful, so . . . real.

How had he ever fooled himself into believing that Maura had the qualities he longed to find in a woman? Until meeting Constance, he had never realized that Maura had been lacking everything Constance possessed—empathy, enthusiasm, a passion for life.

And dare he hope . . . a passion for him?

Tipping her chin up with his thumb, he bent to brush a soft kiss over her lips. His body responded instantaneously, a molten heat tumbling through his veins at the simple caress.

"Tonight will be special for both of us," he whispered when he forced himself to step back.

She nodded, her eyes wide and filled with her own secret wonder.

Touching the tip of his finger to her lips, he said, "Come along, Constance. Fairyland awaits."

# Seventeen

Constance woke to sunshine streaming through her window. Hugging a pillow to her chest, she smiled into the sweet-smelling linens, wondering if she had ever been so happy in her entire life. She was quite sure she hadn't, just as she was completely certain of the reason for her joy.

Gideon Payne.

The previous evening he had promised her fairyland, and he hadn't disappointed her. From the moment they'd stepped into his opera house, she had been treated to sights, sounds, and rich perfumes that she had never encountered.

His hand had been warm against her back as he'd led her through a forest of men and women dressed in bedazzling costumes that would have shamed the royal heads of Europe. She'd been introduced to the reigning diva, a corpulent tenor, and a bass with the profile of a god.

From there she had been taken through the back corridors to mingle with the waiting patrons. Gideon had even brought her a glass of champagne, and, abandoning her code against spirits, she'd sipped the intoxicating liquor while her body had warmed even more beneath the pride that Gideon displayed toward her as she was introduced to his business associates and friends. Not as his assistant but as his "companion for the evening."

Constance shivered in delight. At that point, she'd been so sure that nothing could top the experience. But when Gideon had led her to his own private box—one draped with heavy velvets and furnished with wide settees and a side table of refreshments—her heart had felt ready to burst. She hadn't even demurred when—as the overture swelled—Gideon insisted on helping her to remove her jacket. To her dying day, she would remember his whispered "Constance."

The tones had been so filled with desire and wonder that she almost missed the way he slid the ribbon around her neck free and replaced it with a glittering jet necklace. Not until he leaned closer to whisper, "I knew you'd wear something that would look lovely with a sparkle of jewelry, but I had no idea . . ."

From there the evening had continued its magical course. Taking her hand, Gideon had sat beside her on the settee—much more closely than necessary but still too far away to ease the pounding of her pulse. Throughout the evening, he'd translated the words of the arias, toyed with the ringlet at her nape, and brought her to a fever pitch of excitement.

Yet, despite his avowals of seduction, when he'd brought her home and accompanied her to her bedroom door, he'd offered her one rich, searching kiss.

Nothing more.

Nothing less.

Sighing, she wondered if a person could dissolve in the midst of such rapture. She could only wonder what the next few hours would hold. Before leaving her, Gideon had reminded her that she had promised to spend some . . . personal time with him so that he could satisfy any questions she had compiled about his past.

Dipping her head, she wondered what to ask first.

*Do you love me?*

No. Neither of them was in love, she chided herself. They were simply . . .

What?

Attracted? Quite definitely. Impassioned? Oh, yes. But such emotions did not constitute love.

Without warning, her bedroom door whipped open, slamming against the opposite wall. Constance gasped, scraping the covers to her chin.

Gideon grinned at her from the threshold. "Good. You're up."

"You could have knocked!"

"Why? This is my house."

"But this room has been assigned to me," she pointed out needlessly.

"Only because the Gold Room wasn't ready at your arrival—a fact that is subject to constant delay since the delivery of the new bedclothes, wall coverings, and draperies has been changed yet again. In the meantime . . ." His lips tilted in a lopsided grin, and he mockingly rapped the open panel. "Miss Constance Pedigrue, I beg the honor of your presence."

She frowned at him. "You needn't be so flippant, Mr. Payne."

"It's the only way I know how to be." Offering her a mocking bow, he said, "Get dressed—and wear one of those awful black skirts you brought."

"But you hate seeing me in black."

"I know, but today the color will prove practical."

"Where are we going?"

"I plan to take you to a few of my old haunts. Since many of them are located in out-of-the-way places, it will prove necessary for us to ride on horseback."

Constance felt her body grow weak. "Horseback?" she echoed.

"You can ride, can't you?"

She shook her head from side to side.

He sighed as if extremely put out. "Then I suppose we'll have to teach you." He eyed her consideringly. "Perhaps I should offer you a pair of trousers. Maybe Penny has some you can wear."

Her cheeks flamed at the very idea. "I will *not* be wearing trousers—yours or anyone else's." The idea of parading in front of this man in such a costume made her positively . . .

*Weak.*

He shrugged. "You might reconsider once you've tried a side-saddle."

"I doubt very much that my opinion will be altered when the alternative is riding astride."

His eyes glinted with humor. "I suppose it would be too much to ask a woman such as yourself."

"What do you mean?"

His eyes twinkled with a hidden mirth. "A maiden lady couldn't possibly risk riding astride. Not when she might spoil the fun her husband would have on their wedding night."

Constance squealed in outrage, reaching for the vase of flowers Birch continually replenished and left on her bedside table. But when she launched it in his direction, he'd already closed the door, and she could hear his throaty chuckles as he made his way down the hall.

"Blasted man," she muttered under her breath, ruing the day that she'd ever had the misfortune to enter his theater.

But then, as her giddiness from the prior evening returned, she admitted to herself that she wasn't nearly as upset as she pretended to be.

Gideon knew the precise moment Constance entered the dining hall. It wasn't the rustle of her clothing that had alerted him or the sweet scent of her perfume. No, it was the way his body grew taut and instantly alert.

Glancing over his shoulder, he noted that she had followed his instructions. She was wearing the detestable black skirt, but, to his relief, she wore a frilly shirtwaist above and had cinched her waist with a bright red sash. Another scarlet ribbon had been wound through the plaits of her hair, and she held a straw bonnet with a red and black band to complete the ensemble.

"You look very fetching, Miss Pedigrue."

The look she threw his way conveyed clearly enough that she didn't care what he thought about her appearance, but he was also aware the emotions were a sham.

"Good morning, Miss Constance," Mrs. Potts sang out as she bustled into the room, and Gideon chuckled when Constance offered her a pointed look of welcome.

"Good morning, Mrs. Potts. How is Mr. Bentley this morning?"

Mrs. Potts giggled. "That wretched beast has taken to mothering those puppies."

"You can't be serious."

"I am, miss. He's giving them all a bath even as we speak. Last night, I believe he was trying to teach them to catch mice."

Chortling to herself, Mrs. Potts laid a silver platter filled with fried eggs, bacon, sausage, and potatoes in the center of the table.

"There's coffee in the pot there, fruit and bread under the covered dishes. Let me know if you need anything more."

"Thank you, Mrs. Potts," Gideon said, feeling the odd need to reassert his own position as man in charge.

The woman rushed from the room with her usual efficiency, then closed the door discreetly behind her.

Gideon watched Constance as she chose a sliver of melon, a small slice of sweet bread, and a cup of coffee.

"Surely you plan to eat more than that."

She offered him a crooked grin. "I have to maintain my girlish figure."

"Girlish, hell," he muttered, his eyes roaming over the swells of her bosom and the narrow span of her waist.

There was nothing at all girlish about Constance. She was a woman through and through.

Leaning back in his chair, Gideon pushed his plate away and studied her even more thoroughly. The morning light streamed through the window, caressing her delicate features and highlighting the hints of red buried deep in her hair. Her skin was fine and clear, her eyes bright—and her obvious joy with life filled him with a longing to be a part of her wonder.

Scowling, he realized that he had probably already ruined such hope. Since he'd proclaimed that he intended to make her his mistress, she would be on her guard night and day. Worse yet, with the situation turning into something of a dare, her pride wouldn't allow her to give in to him.

"I have changed my mind, Miss Pedigrue."

She looked up from the bite of bread she'd just taken, and he watched in amusement as she hurriedly chewed, swallowed, then asked, "We aren't going riding?"

"Yes. We'll leave as soon as you finish."

"Then what did you mean about changing your mind?"

He took a deep breath, wondering for a moment if he'd lost his mind. If he followed his gut instincts, there would be no seduction, but there might—just might—be a chance to make this situation real, to have Constance at his table every morning.

The germ of an idea began to blossom in his head, filling his mind with the images of a doting, headstrong wife and a house filled with laughter. Perhaps even children.

He automatically balked at the idea, but the yearnings of his heart soon drowned out all caution.

Why hadn't he accepted the possibilities before? Why hadn't he allowed himself to consider making his arrangement with Constance permanent—*ensuring* it was permanent?

"I have decided that I will not seduce you," he said quietly, gauging her reaction. To his infinite delight, he thought he saw a gleam of disappointment deep in her blue eyes.

"I see." She carefully dabbed at her lips with her napkin, but he knew the gesture was merely a ploy to hide her expressive features. "When did you come to such a realization?"

"Just now."

"May I ask why?"

So she *was* disappointed.

"You are the kind of woman Elizabeth Kincaid warned me about."

Her lips pressed together, then she blurted, "Another of your conquests?"

His bark of laughter was genuine. "No. Elizabeth raised me."

"I thought you were an orphan."

"Yes. But at the ripe age of thirteen, I befriended another young fellow who had come to New York to visit his aunt. Harry Kincaid told his family about me and my situation at the foundling home. His mother, Elizabeth, decided that with thirteen children there was room for one more."

"Thirteen!" Constance echoed in disbelief.

"They were a very close-knit family, full of fun. They worked hard to make a success of their farm, but they always had time for one another."

"Such a change must have been wonderful for you."

"It was. I learned a good deal about what I wanted out of life."

"Such as?"

"Ties. People who love you." Deciding he was growing maudlin, Gideon abruptly stood. "Are you ready?"

She set her napkin beside her plate but did not rise. "I don't think I'll ever be ready to ride a horse."

He chuckled, moving toward her to help with her

chair. As he did so, he leaned close to utter, "Relax. After witnessing your obvious trepidation, I ordered a buggy to be brought around."

She was so visibly relieved that he couldn't help bending to brush a kiss over the top of her head. "Put your hat on, and we'll begin our adventure."

Constance was not sure what to expect from the day ahead of her as she climbed into the narrow buggy and moved her skirts so that Gideon could take his place beside her.

Soon they were barreling through the streets of New York, and Gideon was pointing out the foundling home where he'd lived for so many years, the simple tenement house where he'd first met Harry Kincaid. They even stopped at the candy shop where he had spent the Christmas pennies given to the orphans by the local church. As she sucked on lemon drops, he told her how he used to sneak through a hole in the orphanage's fence and spend his days—as well as most of his nights— watching the glamorous patrons offer gleaming coins to enter such a magical place. He'd vowed that one day he would own such an establishment, and all those coins would be his.

Constance laughed. "And your wish came true," she said.

He was watching her carefully, his gaze curiously guarded. "Most of them."

"Which ones haven't been fulfilled?"

He chose his words carefully before saying, "Let's just say that I discovered that there were other things in life to claim besides wealth and prestige. It took me a long time to learn that lesson."

The intensity of his gaze made her look away.

What was happening to her? She'd prepared herself for this outing by vowing to resist any advances this man might make. But there had been no advances, no stolen kisses, no ribald banter. Instead, he'd thrown her completely off guard by informing her that he no longer wished to beguile her into becoming his mistress.

So what did that mean? Had he suddenly lost interest in her altogether? Did he find her less than desirable? Had the evening at the opera been a sham?

Drat it all, she'd been so determined that she wouldn't be seduced. Now that there was no chance of such a thing, she was bitterly disappointed.

Needing to draw her mind away from such troubling thoughts, she asked, "Where are we going?"

"I thought we'd stop by the theater on Kensington since we're so close."

Constance had not been to Ruby Hall since the day the police had interviewed Gideon about Mary MacClannahan's murder. She and Gideon had been so busy with his other theaters, the local suppliers, and craftsmen that she wasn't even aware of what progress had been made with the building. But as much as she longed to see the changes, she also mourned the fact that her time alone with Gideon had come to an end.

This time the streets they took to the theater were more familiar to her. Enough that she knew she could find her own way home should she need to do so.

Gideon skillfully maneuvered the carriage to the performers' door at the back of the theater. Once there, he alighted, extending a hand to help her.

Constance willingly accepted his offer—even though a carriage block made the intricacies involved in handling her new crinoline much easier. She wanted to touch this man. She wanted him to touch her.

A boy ran forward to take charge of the horse and buggy, but even then, Gideon did not release Constance. He kept her glove-covered fingers twined firmly between his own until the rattling of the vehicle disappeared.

A strange peace lingered in this narrow alley once the buggy had disappeared. There was no evidence of workmen of any kind, only the red brick of the theater's outer walls stretching toward the sky and the cool cobble-stones underfoot.

"Miss Pedigrue?"

"Yes, Mr. Payne."

"I wondered if I might have your permission to conduct an experiment, using you as my subject."

She was immediately on her guard. His posture had grown quite indolent, reminding her that he was a sensual man and probably used to sensual pleasures.

So why didn't he want to seduce her?

What had she done to change his mind?

"What sort of experiment?" Her query was not as steady as she had hoped it would be.

"It is rare that I am able to find someone who is completely removed from my own milieu."

Why did such a phrase cause her breath to hitch?

"I wondered if I might use you as a sort of . . . test patron."

"Test patron?"

"Yes. The workers will finish with their jobs late tonight, and the performers will conduct a dress rehearsal tomorrow, then open their show the following evening. If you are so inclined, I would like to have you come to the final dress rehearsal rather than opening night. Since Ruby Hall has developed a . . . special performance, we shall pretend that you are one of my theater guests, and you shall see a show from start to finish. Then, if you're so inclined, you can offer an honest review of the program. Are you agreeable?"

Of course she was agreeable. Her heart began a slow, pounding beat, her body thrumming with impatience.

Should she admit that she'd been in love with the stage most of her life? Or that of her three sisters, she was the only one who could remember what life had been like before their mother had disappeared? That she could still recall how Louise Pedigrue had displayed a flair for the exotic, the way she could dance and sing and mimic other people's voices?

Once, when Constance was five or six, her mother had sneaked them both into a circuit performance of *A Midsummer Night's Dream*. The play had been held in a stifling tent, and Constance had understood only half the words, but it hadn't mattered. Until last night's opera, she'd longed to see another such production. The thought of attending another so soon was intoxicating.

"I would be delighted to attend the dress rehearsal."

"Good. Shall we say seven o'clock?"

She chuckled softly. "As far as I know, I have no other plans."

Gideon offered her one of his heady grins, then, crooking her arm into his elbow, he escorted her to the rear door.

They stepped into bedlam.

Where once the stage had been a flat, smooth, empty space, now it was crowded with trunks, hatboxes, cages, and crates.

Constance's eyes widened as she took in the colors and scents and people—exotic, unusual people in colorful attire who spoke in loud, energetic voices and waved their arms about as if they needed broad gestures to help communicate.

Gideon was pulling her irretrievably forward, but she barely noticed as she was led past a cage filled with poodles and another one of rabbits.

Eagerly, she wondered what play the theater would be performing to require such animals.

"Gideon?"

"Mmm," he grunted absently, his mind already diverted with business.

"Gideon! I need you to check this costume!" a female voice shouted from somewhere upstage.

"I'll be right there."

Constance waited a beat before asking again, "Gideon, what sort of presentation will take place here?"

He glanced at her in surprise, then bent to peer into a

cage that held a furry black bear cub. "I thought you knew."

She shook her head. "No. I'm quite sure that you didn't mention the title of the work to me."

"That's because there is no title. It's a series of variety acts."

Constance felt the first twinge of unease.

"Variety acts?" She'd never heard of such a thing. Granted, she'd never been to a proper theater, never seen a proper play but . . . "Variety acts?" she asked again, more clearly this time.

Gideon straightened, and once again she was struck by the fact that he knew much more about this whole encounter than she did, and that fact amused him no end. His eyes had grown dark, and his lips had adopted a lazy, sensual grin.

"I don't understand, Gideon."

His smile flashed even wider. "Oh, I think you do," he drawled. "Surely, even in Boston, you've heard of burlesque?"

*Burlesque.*

She'd fallen into the hands of the devil and had been employed in his workshop.

Constance took a step backward, then another. But her hasty retreat caused her to bump into a steamer trunk. A basket that had been balanced on the top wavered and fell, spilling garters and clocked hosiery onto the floor.

No. Oh, no. This couldn't be happening to her. After everything she'd already endured, she couldn't have stumbled into a burlesque theater. It wasn't possible.

But as she stared at Gideon, noted the grin that spread over his features, she knew this was no mistake. This man owned a theater that catered to the lowest form of theatrics. She'd heard what went on in these sorts of shows. Animal tricks, comedy routines, magical acts, singing, dancing, and . . .

And women who took off their clothes.

"I have to get out of this place," she whispered. But even as she tried to dart forward, Gideon placed his hands on either side of her shoulders, effectively trapping her against the trunk.

"What's wrong, Constance?"

She glared at him, wondering why she felt a sting of tears behind her eyes. "You know very well what's wrong, Mr. Payne. I shouldn't be here. No decent woman should—"

"What is decency, Miss Pedigrue? Enlighten me."

She bit her lip, sure that he was mocking her, but his features had adopted a sincere cast. One that wrenched at her heart.

"Decent folk don't engage in such bawdy forms of entertainment," she offered weakly.

"Why not?"

"It isn't done."

"But why?"

She could have stamped her foot in frustration, but to do so would cause her skirts to flatten even more against his thighs, so she resisted the urge.

"Such displays lead to lasciviousness."

"Is that a fact?"

"Yes."

"Who told you such a thing?"

"My father."

"Is this the same man who locked you in his house for twenty years?"

She refused to dignify such a comment with an answer. Even if it was true.

"What else did your father say?"

Since he'd asked, she supposed it wouldn't harm him to hear the truth. "It isn't good to dally in sensuality."

"Is that so?"

"Yes. To do so leads one to the path of temptation."

"What sort of temptation?"

"Temptations of the flesh."

To her horror, he moved a step closer, his hips pressing against hers. "But what if I want to be tempted? What if I want to be tempted every single day?"

Then his head was bending, his lips taking hers in a kiss that seared her soul and sent her senses reeling. His mouth moved against hers, his tongue bidding entrance and sliding between her teeth to stroke the delicate flesh he found beyond.

She shuddered, gripping handfuls of his shirt so that she wouldn't sink to the ground as her limbs became weak and her body began to throb with an aching rhythm. Automatically, she found herself pressing against him, rocking, rubbing, seeking some sort of comfort that she wasn't even aware of needing.

When he broke free, they were both breathing heavily. If it weren't for the faint sound of voices, Constance knew he would have kissed her again and again.

"Was that so terrible?" he rasped, the huskiness of his voice thrilling her.

She could only shake her head.

"Do you think your father would have approved?"

Again, she gestured no.

"But you liked it, didn't you, Constance?"

She was sure that she shouldn't answer such a question. To do so would cause untold problems in the future, but she couldn't seem to help herself. The word "Yes" slipped between her lips, sounding hungry and sensual even to her own ears.

He framed her face in his hands, staring deeply into her eyes. "You should run from me, Constance. You should run from this place." His gaze grew even more intense. "If you don't, I will be severely tempted to show you many more things that your father wouldn't have approved of."

"What sorts of things?"

His brow creased in astonishment. "Passion. Love. Excitement."

*Love.* The word stuck in her head like a burr. How

many times in the past had she told herself that she would have to build a life for herself? One without the benefit of a lover or husband? She was too old to capture anyone's heart—or if she did, such a man was bound to be as elderly and stodgy as Mr. Quiggly who'd tried to kiss her on her departure from Boston.

But here she stood, locked in the embrace of a powerful, sensual man. And he was willing to show her all she had missed over the years. The ecstasy. The joy.

Her hands loosened from their white-knuckle grip on his shirt. Then, without thought to the consequences of her actions, she allowed them to slip beneath the hem of his shirt.

He sucked in a quick breath as she encountered the hardness of his stomach, the moist summer heat of his skin. Bit by bit, she allowed her fingers to fan out so that she could explore further. His ribs, his back, his spine, then his chest again. His nipples.

"You don't know what you're doing, Constance," he whispered hoarsely, and she smiled, a slow, rich smile that made her feel beautiful and powerful.

"I think I do."

"You can't possibly want me to—"

"But I do, Gideon. I'm tired of being good. I want you to show me how to be very, very bad."

Then she was lifting on tiptoes and kissing him, allowing her own mouth the freedom he had displayed on so many occasions. She explored his lips, his cheeks, his jaw. She moved down to suckle his Adam's apple, then dipped lower to nip at his collarbone. Then, when she drew back, she offered him the same look, the same smile Eve must have given Adam when she tempted him with the apple.

"Teach me," she whispered. "Teach me how to be wicked."

# Eighteen

Louise hissed and would have shot through the shadows lingering backstage if Etienne hadn't snagged her arm and held her close.

"Let me go, Etienne," she gasped. "Constance needs me."

He chuckled. "I think she's doing quite well on her own."

Louise shot him a scathing look. "That man is all but attacking her."

"Judging by what we overheard, I'd say Constance could be accused of the same thing."

Louise would have kicked Etienne in the shin for such a remark, but he wisely stepped back.

"Constance is not a little girl, Louise," he reminded her. "She has the right to pursue a man's affections."

"Not that man's. I won't have my daughter married to someone who owns a burlesque house."

He shook his head, making a *tsk*-ing sound with his tongue. "Since when have you become so prudish, my dear? Your own parents once worked in a place like this—as did you."

Louise wilted at the reminder. "Etienne, she's so inexperienced in such manners."

"Perhaps. But you yourself said that Gideon Payne is a good man."

"That doesn't mean I want him seducing my daughter."

Etienne took her shoulders, turning her toward the couple. "If you will look closely, I would wager that the seduction is mutual."

Seeing the ardor of her daughter and the way Gideon reciprocated in equal measure, she was forced to concede. "I suppose you're right," she murmured.

"Gideon! That costume!" a voice shouted, and the couple sprang apart.

It was then that Louise caught her first real glimpse of her daughter's face, and she gasped.

Etienne squeezed her shoulders in reassurance. "They've parted, Louise," he noted needlessly.

She gripped one of his hands. "No, Etienne. It's not their kiss. She looks like . . ." Louise licked her lips, peering at Constance through the gloom and knowing that her first impression had not been mistaken. "She looks like Gideon's late wife."

He stood in the fly gallery, watching the couple from the scenery platform overhead, his fingers curling into the cold iron.

Maura had betrayed him. Damn her! She'd betrayed him a second time.

Striding to the end of the catwalk, he descended the ladder as quickly as he could, then burst outside, where he filled his lungs with the summer heat.

He had waited for her all these years. He had plotted and schemed and prepared. And for what? She had fallen right into Payne's arms again. She'd allowed herself to weaken under his spell. So much so that she had forgotten the man who really loved her—who had loved her since she was a girl.

His fists struck the brick wall in anger, and the pain woke him from the daze he'd been in.

He had to get out of here before someone saw him and began asking questions. But this was not the end of the situation. Maura was his. His!

If he couldn't have her, then by hell he would make sure that Gideon Payne wouldn't, either.

After their aborted embrace, Constance spent most of her time helping the various actors settle into their dressing rooms and collect their things from the crates that had been delivered to the theater. She brewed an inordinate amount of tea and coffee and oversaw the purchase of a bottle or two of liquor. She fed poodles and cuddled rabbits and avoided the bear cage altogether.

By late afternoon, most of the performers had disappeared to prepare for various evening activities, and the theater became still and serene.

"Miss Pedigrue?"

She looked up to find one of Gideon's stage managers regarding her from the doorway to Gideon's office.

"Yes, Mister . . ."

He flashed her a crooked grin, "Lester's my name, but most folks call me Les."

"What can I do for you?"

"Gideon's ready to leave. He asked me to come fetch you."

"Thank you, Les."

As soon as the man disappeared, Constance closed the accounts book that Gideon had asked her to double-check. Gathering her hat and her gloves, she made her way through the lobby to the main doors leading into the auditorium.

Her skirts whispered as she stepped into the coolness to be found there. Ahead of her, the stage loomed out of the artificial darkness, intriguing her with its empty spaces and somehow making her feel infinitely safe.

Seeing no evidence of the man she was supposed to

meet, she walked down the aisle, standing beneath a lamp that offered a meager glow in the cavernous area. Looking out over the empty seats that would soon be crowded with people, she wondered what it would be like to be an actress bowing before her adoring public.

"You like what you see, don't you?"

Constance shivered when Gideon's voice melted out of the shadows. She should have known he was near. She should have sensed him, much as a bird sensed the arrival of a cat. No. That analogy no longer fitted. She was not Gideon's prey. She was a willing participant in his embraces. The mere memory of their earlier kiss filled her with a hunger to experience more. So much more.

Slowly, she turned to face him, feeling the warmth of the gaslights flooding her features. Staring at him, at the way he watched her so expectantly, she wondered what he wanted her to say. That she had grown to love this place—its smells, its energy, its escape? Or that she craved the opportunity to become someone else? Someone he could love?

He moved toward her, his steps slow and measured, each footfall echoing hollowly.

"What is it about the stage that intrigues you, Constance?"

She managed to offer him a negligent shrug. "The whole theater is fascinating. I never saw anything like it in Boston."

Only a few inches separated them now. He reached to cup her cheek, and she wished that she had the courage to lean into the embrace, to encourage him to continue his caress, to draw him closer.

But that wasn't possible. Not now. He must make the first physical overture. He must prove to her that he saw her as a woman in her own right, not the mirror image of his late wife. She could never settle for less.

"What were you used to in Boston?"

He knew. She was sure she'd told him enough for him to surmise the circumstances of her existence there. But he wanted more, so much more—things she didn't know if she could offer him. He wanted her to trust him enough to reveal secrets she had never shared with another living soul. She didn't know if she was ready for such emotional intimacies yet. Even so, she wasn't sure how she could refuse him what he wanted.

"Tell me," he urged, his voice feathering across her skin and causing gooseflesh to pebble her arms.

"My father had a very respectable home," she began, choosing her words with care.

"Respectable?"

The single word was offered so blandly that she found herself oddly encouraged.

"The house was in a good neighborhood, among good people." She bit her lip, wondering if he would think her ungrateful for deciding that such niceties weren't enough.

"You weren't happy."

His remark was not worded as a question.

She moved away from him, knowing that she would not be able to speak if he continued to touch her.

"I should have been. After all, the city teemed with people who had so much less. There was food aplenty on our table. In the winter, we had enough coal."

"Enough," he interrupted, his lips pulling into a frown.

She ignored him. "My father wasn't always stern and forbidding. When my mother left us, he brought us to Boston in the hopes that we would have a better life there. He arranged for tutors and governesses to see to our needs, but he offered us very little of his own love."

When Gideon's brow creased, she hurriedly said, "We were not unhappy. My sisters and I had one another, after all. But oftentimes I wondered what our life would have been like if Mama hadn't disappeared."

"Where did she go?"

*I think my father killed her.*

The words reverberated in her head, but she forced them away. To say them aloud might make them true. So she shrugged and said, "We were never told. One morning, we woke to discover she was gone. Papa told us she had found another husband and other little girls to make her happy."

"You believed him?"

That comment took her by surprise. Had he sensed her hesitation? Still unable to voice her fears, she said, "My father would never lie. He considered such actions beneath him."

"But he wasn't above imprisoning his daughters? He wasn't above beating them?"

Constance sucked in her breath. "I never said—"

"No. You never said your father beat you. But that day in the park, the first day I met you, you instinctively protected yourself as if you were used to such a thing."

She shivered, wondering what else he had managed to surmise about her past. "My father was a strict disciplinarian. When he was displeased, he looked for an outlet."

"You were that outlet?"

She was growing increasingly uncomfortable with this line of questioning. "Patience and Felicity were so small when we moved. Only babies. I suppose that I assumed it was my responsibility to protect them."

"How often did he beat you?"

Constance found herself oddly driven to protect her father. "You mustn't think he was a monster."

"Mustn't I?" He took her by the elbows, refusing to allow her to draw away. "Why do you continue to defend him? The man did his best to mold all of you into the same bitter, joyless form in which he was cast."

She shook her head. "No. He loved us."

"Loved you? Is that how a man shows his love? By denying his daughters contact with the outside world? By teaching them to abandon the simple joys that life can offer?"

"I'm sure he thought that he was helping us."

"How?"

She searched for some logical explanation. "He wanted us to be good. He didn't want us to grow up to be . . ."

"To be like your mother?"

She gazed at him with wide eyes, not wanting to hear the words.

"Was that it, Constance? Was he using you as a means to punish her? Was he so enraged by your mother's abandonment that he felt he should keep his daughters chained to his side?"

"He needed us."

"Why?"

"He was sick, bedridden."

"But he had the money to hire a nurse."

"We were his family."

"You were his slaves!" He shook her slightly. "Be honest, Constance. Be honest with yourself if you can't admit such things to me. Your father wanted to control you. He wanted to ensure that you would never leave him."

"No. If my sisters or I had fallen in love—"

"You were never given the chance. He would never have allowed a man to enter any of your lives. He would never have let you go."

"But—"

"But what? Can't you see? He meant to control you—in every way possible. And he continues to control you now, from beyond the grave."

She forced herself to offer, "That's preposterous."

"Is it?" He forced her to turn, forced her to look out at the empty seats in the house. "Look out there, and tell me that you don't wish you could stand in this very spot, in front of an adoring public, and give a performance that would bring them all to their knees."

"No." But her protest was weak. Telling.

"Why won't you do it?"

"It isn't proper."

"But you told me yourself that such views about women in the theater were outdated and outmoded."

"I—"

"So if that's the case, then what prevents you from pursuing your heart's desire?"

Her heart's desire. Acting?

No. Just as Gideon had told her that his dreams over the years had changed, hers had altered in the last few weeks. She didn't want a career in the theater. She didn't want a life of travel and an adoring public. She wanted Gideon. Only Gideon.

"I don't think—"

"Don't think, Constance. Reach deep inside yourself for the truth. What is it you want? What is it you need?"

She tried to wrench away, but he held her fast. Closing her eyes, she wondered what he would say if she answered his question, if she told him exactly what she dreamed of most.

Him.

She wanted him.

She wanted him to look at her in adoration. She wanted Gideon to love her with all his heart. But if she dared to declare such a thing, he would draw away from her.

"I have no desire to act," she stated firmly, offering half the truth.

"Why?" he growled close to her ear.

She fought for a logical reason. "It isn't seemly."

"Is that your opinion or your father's?"

"My father is dead."

"His body is dead, but he still affects everything you do, everything you say."

"Stop it!" She wrenched free. "Stop talking about me as if I have no will of my own, as if I have no mind of my own."

"Then start using it!" he shouted, causing her to start. "Decide what you want, what you *really* want, then make some effort to attain it."

With that, he abruptly turned, striding from the theater and slamming the door.

Constance stood stunned.

*Decide what you want, what you* really *want, then make some effort to attain it.*

The words reverberated in her head, filling her with anger.

"And what am I supposed to do, Gideon?" she said aloud. "Beg you to love me? Beg you to see me for myself?"

"No. I don't think he'd respond well to such a tactic at all."

Constance whirled, a gasp lodging in her throat. Looking to the spot where the sound had materialized, she tried to pierce the darkness but saw nothing. "Who's there?"

A quick peal of laughter betrayed the identity of her witness. "Come now, Constance. Have you forgotten me so quickly?"

Long before a figure emerged, Constance heard the whisper of fabric against the floor, the rustle of satin. Then, when she saw the glowing tip of a cigar, she knew who had been privy to her outburst.

Penny Whistle.

Heat flooded her cheeks, and Constance thanked heaven above that the stage was dark enough to hide her blush.

Penny stepped into the light, revealing a tiny bonnet set at a rakish angle on her head. She braced one hand on the handle of her parasol and struck a pose that made Constance overtly aware of the flesh exposed by her décolletage.

"So you're smitten with my friend Gideon, hmm?"

Constance tried to offer the woman a look of unconcern, but judging by Penny's giggle, she wasn't successful.

"Don't bother to deny it, my dear. Frankly, I'm surprised that it took this long for you to consider snapping him up. He's quite a catch."

"I wouldn't know."

Penny made a clucking sound. "You don't make a very convincing liar." She drew on her cigar, then smiled widely. "I myself heartily approve of your intentions."

"I have no intentions."

"Then you should." She gestured to the door where Gideon had made his retreat. "It's been ages since I've seen him so . . . alive."

Constance huffed in disbelief. "I've made him angry, that's all."

"Even anger is an improvement over that facade of granite he adopted after Maura died."

Constance tried to maintain an expression of indifference, but actually her heart had begun to pound in a slow, measured beat. "So what are you suggesting I do, Penny? Strut about the stage and take off my clothes? Is that how I should capture his attention?"

Penny took a deep drag of her cigar and studied Constance through the smoke. "Not at all. I think such measures would push him over the edge entirely, and that's something I wouldn't recommend to anyone." She grinned. "I'm merely suggesting that you flirt with the *possibility* of such an adventure."

Constance's brows creased. "I don't understand."

"No, I suppose I'm speaking in riddles." She lowered her cigar and began treading a slow circle around Constance's form, studying her as she went. "Tell me, Constance. How far are you willing to go to get the man you want?"

Constance couldn't answer. She wasn't sure what reassurances were needed of her.

"Would you be willing to tread near the edge of

respectability?" Penny asked softly, her tone rife with temptation. "Would you be willing to tempt Gideon to the brink of disaster?" Constance still had not said a word, but Penny must have read her thoughts, because her smile faded into something rich and mysterious. "Very well. Tell Gideon you've changed your mind, that you've decided to become a performer. I guarantee he won't allow such a thing to happen."

Constance wasn't so sure. "What if he agrees to such a proposal?"

"He won't." Her grin was smug. "I saw the expressions that raced over his features. He's become very possessive of you. I would even go so far as to say he is half in love."

Constance's heart leaped at the words. Then, remembering the heated words they had just exchanged, she shook her head. "No. He's still in love with Maura."

Penny laughed outright. "My dear, he *never* loved Maura Kelly. He was obsessed with her, yes, but his fascination would have worn off within weeks if she hadn't trapped him into remaining married by claiming she was pregnant. After that, Gideon did his best to make the marriage work, but such a feat became very difficult when she began parading her lovers under his nose. If not for the fact that she claimed to have miscarried, I'm sure he would have thrown her out long before she committed suicide."

Penny shook her head. "No, my dear. He might have been intrigued by your resemblance to Maura—he might have even felt the stirrings of the old passions. But what I see in him now is not a mere physical obsession. It runs much deeper." She tapped Constance near her collarbone. "I would even wager his emotions stem straight from the heart."

"Constance!" The outer door squeaked open, and Constance whirled to face the man who had captured her very soul. "Are you coming? Or are you going to find your own way home?"

Home.

With Gideon.

"I'll be right there!" she called, and the door shut again. Constance turned to thank Penny for her advice, but the woman had vanished into the darkness as silently as she'd come.

# Nineteen

I've changed my mind, Gideon. I've decided I'd like to try my hand at the stage."

Gideon hadn't spoken to her since she'd climbed into the carriage, but at her bald pronouncement he fixed her with a withering glare.

"You what?" he asked through a tight jaw.

Although she was quite sure he'd heard her the first time, she repeated, "I would like to perform on the stage."

"Why?"

She huffed in mock indignation. "You were the one who told me I should follow my dreams, and after working with you so closely the last few weeks, I've decided that it would be foolish to balk at the prospect now."

She secretly smiled when it appeared that he was none too happy about her news. Maybe Penny *was* right. Was this the way to make Gideon realize that he cared for her? Not for Maura but for her?

"What sort of an act do you plan to do?"

"A dance."

"Dance," he repeated as if she'd lost her mind.

"Something similar to Penny Whistle's old routine. I'm sure she would teach me if I asked."

His brows drew together, and he regarded her thunderously. "You intend to . . . *strip?*"

"Probably."

Gideon took a deep breath, gripped the reins more firmly, then urged the horse to an even greater speed. "I see."

She wasn't yet sure what he thought of the idea, but at least she'd captured his attention.

"You've given the matter some real thought? Even though twenty minutes ago you were dead set against the idea?"

"Of course I've given the matter some thought—I think that, unconsciously, I've been toying with the prospect since I arrived in New York. This isn't the sort of thing I would conclude willy-nilly."

"Wasn't it you who railed on and on about the depravity of such a practice?"

"Yes." She was forced to grip her hat to keep it from being whipped from her head. "But that was before I thought about the liberating possibilities of such an occupation."

"Liberating? In what way?"

She pretended to study the houses that raced by, knowing that she needed the diversion to keep her features clear of guile and avoid Gideon's too intent interest.

"Since coming to live with you, I have discovered a life such as I never dreamed existed. In these past weeks, I've lived in a house rife with modern contraptions. I've brushed elbows with society mavens and statesmen. I've been dressed in the finest creations I've ever owned, and I've eaten foods that are delicious beyond description. I'm beginning to believe that a woman's reputation doesn't amount to a hill of beans if she's trapped in a meaningless life."

"So what does all that have to do with stripping?"

"Don't you see? I don't want to return to being the mousy spinster I appeared to be when I arrived. I've tasted the freedoms that money and a free-thinking attitude can bring, and I could never be content with what I once had. I want more, so much more."

He was eyeing her suspiciously, and she wondered if she'd applied her reasoning a bit too liberally. Holding her breath, she waited for him to forbid her to join his company. When he did not, her disappointment was nearly overwhelming.

"Do you mind if I think about your little proposal, Constance?"

She felt a tiny twinge of hope. "Not at all. Take all the time you want."

*As long as you admit that you care for me as much as I care for you.*

"Perhaps you should wait until you've witnessed tomorrow's dress rehearsal before you commit yourself to such an outlandish idea," he said tightly.

"I don't think the idea is outlandish at all," she said, making her tone as breezy as possible. "And neither do you. Otherwise, you wouldn't own a burlesque theater."

Gideon brought the carriage to an abrupt halt—and this time, Constance didn't allow him the time to help her alight. Instead, she jumped to the walk and hurried to where Birch held the door open, taking a great deal of enjoyment from the white-knuckle grip Gideon maintained on the reins.

Constance spent less than half the following day amid the clutter at Ruby Hall before Gideon drove her home, informing her that he had some personal business to tend to. It was only as he had ushered her inside, gathered the mail, and was walking out the door again that he offered, "Oh, I forgot to inform you that we are expected at an engagement this evening after the dress rehearsal."

"What sort of engagement?"

"A ball."

She gasped. "We were invited to a ball, and you didn't tell me until now?"

Gideon's features softened ever so slightly as he positioned his hat on his head. "Since the invitation was delivered only this morning, I'm telling you now."

Constance was not reassured by his flippant retort. "You should have told me the moment you decided to attend."

He shrugged. "Why?"

"Because I need time to get ready!"

"It's barely midday. How much more time do you need?"

"More than you've given me." She rushed to the staircase in very real distress. "What should I wear?"

He shrugged. "Whatever you'd like."

"But I've never been to a ball before. I have no idea what is expected."

Gideon's stiff posture eased. Leaving the door ajar, he closed the space between them and stroked her cheek. "You are so beautiful that it won't matter what you do."

His compliment flowed through her body like warm honey, immediately easing her panic.

Beautiful. He'd called her beautiful.

Constance became aware of the silence of the house. Absent were the chatter of Mrs. Potts and Mrs. Merriweather and the thumping footfalls of Birch.

"They have probably gone shopping," Gideon explained, anticipating her query before it could be uttered. "After the gala opening night of Ruby Hall, I've decided to have a reception at the town house. I gave them a list of instructions after breakfast."

The patch of floor at the bottom of the stairs began to feel much more intimate than it should. Light glittered through the stained glass in the door, mottling the hardwood with bits of color.

The two of them were alone. Completely alone.

Despite the need for hasty preparations, Constance felt the urge to linger. Without stepping away from Gideon, she withdrew her bonnet with aching slowness and set it on the hall table. She was utterly conscious of the way Gideon watched her, seeming completely absorbed by the simple activities.

Needing to feel the warmth of his gaze, the intensity of his interest, Constance began on the first glove, unlacing the small metal hooks that held it together from wrist to forearm. When she'd bought the gloves, she'd thought the unusual fasteners to be a clever gimmick. But now there was a certain sensuality about the way she was able to expose the delicate skin bit by bit, and she thought she knew the intentions of their creator.

Gideon was following each movement as if he were entranced—especially when the hooks had been completely unlaced and she tugged the leather from her fingers. His rapt attention filled her with an odd sense of power. A primitive, primal instinct that as a woman she could trap this man with the slightest display of femininity.

Unfortunately, he took that moment to meet her gaze, and she realized that he wasn't the only person who could be enslaved.

"What are you doing, Constance?"

She shrugged with an unconcern that she didn't feel. "I don't know what you mean. It's a rather warm day— so now that we've returned home, I thought I'd be more comfortable without my gloves."

She dropped the glove on the table beside her hat, enjoying the way Gideon watched it plop onto the surface, the tensile leather still retaining the slight shape of her fingers. Then she began unlacing the second one.

Gideon shifted. "I'm pleased that you feel comfortable enough in this house to . . . disrobe."

"I'm hardly disrobing, Gideon."

*Gideon. Not Mr. Payne.*

He began closing the slight distance between them, crowding her. But with the hall table at her side and the wall at her back, she had no avenue of retreat.

As if to underscore that point, Gideon placed his hands on either side of her head, effectively trapping her.

"Aren't you?"

"Aren't I what?" she asked, unable to remember what they'd been talking about. His body was so near that she found any sort of coherent thought difficult.

"Aren't you disrobing?"

"A glove could hardly be compared to removing one's clothes."

"Is that what you think?"

His head was bending toward hers. She couldn't move—she didn't want to move. She wanted to kiss him with a palpable ache.

As his mouth brushed against hers, Constance melted into the embrace, reveling in the way such a small point of contact had the power to rob her of her strength and fill her with a pounding yearning for more. So much more.

Unconsciously, she moved closer, her hands reaching and finding the hard planes of his chest. His shirt was soft against her palms, but she could feel the heat of his body seeping through the cloth, sense the crisp hair matting his chest.

Then there was no time for such simple observations, because he was hauling her close to his body, and his lips had ceased their gentle coaxings. His kiss became fierce and hungry, filling her with a wild abandon.

Her arms swept beneath the hem of his shirt, and she clung to him. Never, in her entire existence, had she experienced such an overwhelming flood of desire. Straining against him, she moaned when his tongue slipped into her mouth, seeking an even more intimate exploration. Following his example, she made her own foray, delighting in the way her efforts caused him to lose his balance and slam her against the wall, his body falling against her own.

Her gasp turned into a moan of pleasure when she felt the hard length of his body and the blatant evidence of his arousal.

Gideon broke off the kiss and tipped his head back, gasping for air. Unable to help herself, Constance drove her fingers through his hair, forcing him to look at her again.

"Don't stop," she whispered.

He buried his face in the crook of her neck, and a flurry of gooseflesh spread over her body as he nibbled at the sensitive skin exposed there.

"Gideon," she sighed, then felt him smile against her.

"I like it when you call me by my name."

She laughed softly, but her mirth was quickly forestalled by Gideon's hand encircling her waist, then slipping up, up, up . . .

"How many layers are you wearing?" he whispered into the shell of her ear.

"Too many."

"I want to feel you."

"I know."

Reaching for her wrist, he placed his lips against the skin she had exposed to him only moments before. When the tip of his tongue traced a feathery trail up to her forearm, her knees lost their strength altogether, and she sagged against him.

"Tonight," he whispered. "After the ball."

She nodded, knowing that she was agreeing to make love with this man. "You are stealing my very soul," she whispered.

"Not your soul. Just your will to resist."

"I should tell you to stay away from me."

"Yes. You should."

"But I don't want to."

"I don't want you to, either."

Then he was scooping her into his arms and carrying her up the staircase, kissing her the entire way to her room before depositing her on the bed. Leaning close, he took a shuddering breath.

"Tonight," he said firmly, but the reminder was more for his sake than hers.

"Yes. After the ball."

He moved away from her then, backing out the door and closing it reluctantly.

Smiling to herself, Constance hugged her arms around her waist to contain the urge to shout in triumph and utter joy. This man made her feel so alive, so precious, so . . .

Needed.

And she hadn't felt needed in a very long time.

Potts giggled from behind the half-closed door to the dining room, and Merriweather slapped a hand over her friend's mouth.

"Shh. They'll hear you."

Potts shook her head and dislodged Merriweather's cautioning grip. "Those two wouldn't hear a cannon blast at this point."

Merriweather grinned in delight. "You could be right."

"Oh, Roberta," Potts exclaimed, grasping her friend's hands. "Isn't it wonderful? I was so hoping that Miss Pedigrue could help Mr. Payne find the joy in life again."

Merriweather's eyes twinkled. "I know what you mean. I've been doing everything in my power to throw the two of them together."

"And we must continue to do so."

Merriweather nodded in complete agreement. "Those two need each other."

"There's been enough unhappiness in both their lives."

"Agreed."

"So what should we do now to help them?"

Merriweather offered Potts a sly smile. "Not a thing. Somehow, I sense that nature will take its course as long as we help to keep outside distractions to a minimum."

"Quite right."

"Now off to the kitchen—both of us—or we're likely to disturb the love birds."

Potts snickered. "Somehow, I sense that Mr. Payne will not be rising at his usual time in the morning."

"You never know, Potts. He isn't aware that we know what has occurred, and being the gentleman he is, I'm sure he would wish to spare Miss Pedigrue any embarrassment."

"You're so right," Potts agreed as she slid open the door, then gasped when she discovered Birch had suddenly reappeared from nowhere and was looming in the opening.

He didn't speak, he merely held out his hand, one bony finger pointing in the direction of the kitchen.

Knowing they were being silently chastened for their eavesdropping, Potts and Merriweather hurried to resume their chores.

Since hearing of the prospect of a ball, Constance had been on tenterhooks. More than ever, she knew that she needed to look her best that evening. She needed to prove to Gideon that she could be more than his assistant. She could be his . . .

*Wife?*

The thought shook her to her toes, but she knew she didn't dare hope for such a relationship with Gideon. The best she could wish for would be a place as his companion. A very close, intimate companion.

As soon as Gideon left the town house, she approached Birch with a note and somehow made him understand that she needed him to deliver a message to Penny Whistle. In less than a half hour, the woman appeared at her doorstep—just as she'd known Penny would.

"I need to look as beautiful as possible," Constance stated bluntly. But at that, Penny had merely laughed and waved the comment away.

"My dear, you will be as beautiful as you already are!"

The day had been spent primping and preening. Penny had tried a dozen hairstyles before deciding upon one, then had chosen every article of clothing for the evening ahead, the China silk underthings, the impossibly tight lacing of Constance's corset, and her own best burgundy ball gown.

"The dress is from Paris, my dear, from a new upstart designer by the name of Worth. Frankly, I think the man is a genius. He knows just how to make a woman feel like a goddess."

And Penny hadn't lied. When she descended the staircase to meet her escort, Constance blessed every uncomfortable hour of preparation, every pinched seam of the gown, every yard of its voluminous skirt. The flare of raw desire that ignited in Gideon's eyes was more than enough to repay her for her efforts.

Gideon stopped her at the bottom of the staircase, reaching to adjust the bow of her cape, his fingers lingering there as if he wished to part the cover-up and discover what delights she had hidden beneath. But even though Constance longed to have him see the expanse of bare flesh left exposed by the daring cut of her gown, she decided to save that moment for the theater—perhaps even the ball.

"You'll put the empty theater seats to shame, Constance. Moreover, I won't be able to concentrate on the rehearsal," Gideon murmured as he pressed a kiss to the spot below her ear.

The simple caress caused a shiver to slip down her spine and pool low in her belly.

"Your performers will capture your attention, I'm sure. Especially once your actresses begin to divest themselves of their clothing."

Her tone was so disapproving that he winced and offered, "You obviously don't understand the strength of your own charms."

Since the servants had gathered in the cool shadows of the corridor to watch their departure, Gideon nodded in their direction, then drew Constance outside. "Come along, my dear. If we're to go to the theater, we'd best leave now. Before I change my mind."

With that, he drew her into the evening air. As if she were visiting royalty, he attended to her every need, helping her into the carriage, adjusting the wick to the tiny lamp mounted inside, and covering her skirts with a light rug lest the breeze bespeckle the fabric with dust.

His solicitousness had the effect of a strong wine on her spirits, causing her heart to swell with some unnamable emotion.

No, not unnamable. She knew very well what she was feeling for this man. And for the first time, she allowed herself to admit the truth to herself. She loved Gideon Payne, heart and soul, mind and body. And if this was all he could ever give her, if Maura had irretrievably scarred his heart, Constance would do her best to make him happy.

"You're very quiet," Gideon commented.

"I'm just enjoying myself," she said, offering him a coy smile that caused his eyes to narrow.

"I would think you'd be a bit . . . uncomfortable at the idea of watching a burlesque performance—especially since you profess to be considering such a profession for yourself."

Constance had been so wrapped up in readying herself for this night, she'd forgotten she'd threatened to become a stripper herself.

"What could possibly cause me to be uncomfortable?" she countered. "As you have pointed out to me time and time again, my upbringing has been far too stuffy. It's time I opened myself up to the joys to be found in life.

After all, in only a few hours you've promised to introduce me to the pleasures of the flesh. How can a mere variety show compare to that?"

He sucked in his breath at her reminder, obviously startled by her boldness.

"I had expected you to change your mind about the . . . culmination to tonight's activities."

"And why would I do that?"

It was obvious that Gideon was ready to offer her more than a dozen reasons, but the carriage drew to a halt in front of Ruby Hall, and Constance gasped in pleasure.

Every lamp had been lit for their arrival, and the theater gleamed in the evening light like a precious abalone shell as the exterior took on the luster of the setting sun. A garnet carpet had been rolled down the front staircase, and a line of livery-clad ushers waited to show them inside.

"Gideon!" Constance gasped in delight. "All this for a dress rehearsal?"

"I wanted you to capture the whole effect of the evening. Especially since I would not ask you to come during a performance when most of the audience will be filled with men."

That thought filled her with a sense of wicked fun that she had never experienced before. To think that she was about to witness a performance that no woman—no decent woman—would deign to attend was thrilling rather than dismaying.

As Gideon helped her step to the jewel-colored runner, she surprised herself even more as she realized that she really didn't care if someone witnessed her entrance to Ruby Hall. This was the adventure of a lifetime.

Once they were inside the theater, one of the ushers offered to take her wrap, but Constance demurred, citing a nonexistent draft. Without pause, she allowed Gideon to lead her up the circling staircase where Mr. Bentley and Willoby had forced her introduction to this man.

Then Gideon led her up another, smaller staircase and down a lamplit hall to his private box.

She gasped when she entered the tiny cubicle. Where the box at the Crystal Palace had been ornate, this retreat from the realities of the world was like something from a pasha's paradise.

Exotic silks and satins draped the opening looking onto the stage. A swooning couch lay to one side, a rich garnet and gold settee to the other. And in the middle was a small table lit with candles and glittering with the finest China and silver.

"I thought we would dine while you watched the show," Gideon said, pulling out a chair that faced the stage.

Without being told, Constance realized that this was the mysterious errand that had occupied Gideon's time throughout the afternoon.

"Oh, Gideon," she sighed, at a loss for a more adequate way to describe her delight.

As she settled into her seat and arranged her skirts, Gideon cupped her shoulders with his hands, lingering behind her.

Whatever servants or employees had helped to arrange the meal were discreetly absent, and Constance trembled, realizing that she and Gideon were completely alone in this hedonistic hideaway.

"This is what I am," Gideon murmured, so softly she almost didn't catch the words. "I will never be a proper, blue-blooded gentleman. I have neither the desire nor the training for such a role."

Her eyes grew heavy as the warmth of his hands and the potency of his declaration filled her with longing.

"I am just a man, Constance. For too long, I've lived in a wasteland of my own choosing. But you've made me think, made me remember, made me alive again. It's only fair that I warn you, I have no morals that will save you from the person I've become."

No morals? How could he claim such a thing? In

Constance's opinion, this man, this heart-scarred, battle-weary man, was the most honorable creature she had ever known.

Reaching for one of the hands resting so heavily on her shoulder, she tipped her head, grazing his knuckles with her lips.

"You are everything to me," she whispered, but as a fanfare of music signaled the beginning of the theatrical performance, she doubted Gideon heard her. Even so, she knew there was more than enough time for such declarations. She and Gideon had all night.

And with a little luck, they would have a lifetime.

He stood in the shadows of the park, his eyes trained toward the Ruby Palace, his heart slowly breaking into thousands of tiny pieces.

*Maura?* he silently whispered, already knowing that he'd lost her to Gideon Payne. The moment she'd stepped from the carriage, she'd glanced up at the man, so briefly that any other person might not have noticed the light that entered her eyes.

Love.

She was in love with Gideon Payne.

Just as she'd once been in love with *him*.

A sob rose in his throat, bursting free and causing a flock of birds nearby to scatter. Stunned, he turned and stumbled toward the pond before someone could be attracted to the noise.

*Why, Maura? Why?* he inwardly wailed. He'd done everything he could to show his devotion. He'd punished those who had wronged her and prepared the way for her triumphant return to the stage. But she hadn't even noticed. Not once had she tried to talk to him alone or thank him for his efforts.

*Damn her!* he thought, his hands balling into fists. *Damn her to hell and back!* She couldn't do this to him. Not now. Not after everything he'd done!

He began to run, flailing at the trees and shrubs that

tried to hold back his progress. But then he stumbled, a horrible thought streaking through his brain.

Surely she still didn't blame him for that night so long ago when Gideon Payne had caught them and he'd run into the darkness in an effort to preserve his identity. She loved him. She would never be so petty.

No. The whole situation was his fault. His puny attempts to prove his devotion weren't enough, that was all. He would have to find a better way to win her heart.

Even if he had to kill Gideon Payne to do it.

# Twenty

If Constance had been asked what she had seen at the theater, she would not have been able to describe a thing. From the instant the lights had dimmed, her attention had been drawn completely to the man at her side.

Amidst the noises of bawdy songs, barking dogs, and comic banter, she and Gideon had shared a meal rife with sensuality. The simplest tasks took on entirely new significance as Gideon offered her portions of food from his plate or held ripe red berries to her lips.

She could not even clearly recall that bumping, rollicking music used by the strippers, because at the close of their meal she and Gideon had retired to the swooning couch, where he had eloquently proved how the mere touching of hands, the caress of his lips to her hair, the whisper of his breath against her nape were far more powerful than any artificial enticements to be found in a burlesque hall.

Indeed, the performance was barely halfway through its course when he'd touched the ribbon to her cape, and she'd known that she was about to surrender that final barrier—as well as the rest of her inhibitions. If not for the sudden crash of a sand-filled counterweight dropping from the fly system, which caused one of the curtains to tip drunkenly from its moorings, she was quite certain that she would have surrendered herself to Gideon there and then.

But as the confusion from the stage interrupted their idyll, Gideon grasped her hand and pulled her upright. "Come along. Since I am honor bound to make an appearance at this blasted ball, let's introduce ourselves to the business associates I'm expected to meet, then make our hasty getaway."

Constance had barely had the time to breathe—let alone think—as she found herself spirited away from the theater.

The ball proved to be a glittering, extravagant affair. As Constance stepped into the opulent foyer of the town house, she was completely dazzled by hundreds of candles, sparkling jewels, exotic flowers, and beautiful men and women dressed in their best finery.

Despite her buoyant mood and her potent awareness of the man at her side, Constance felt completely out of place. What was she doing at such an event? She didn't belong in this world any more than she belonged in a chicken coop. Her entire childhood and tutelage up to this point had never prepared her for such a blatant introduction into the crème de la crème of society.

She hung back a little, clutching her cape to her throat.

Sensing her unease, Gideon drew her out of the path of incoming guests and leaned low to ask, "What's wrong?"

Constance knew that her pride should prevent her from answering, but she looked up at him, desperate for some means of escape. Finding him watching her with utmost tenderness, she admitted, "I don't belong here."

"Why not?"

She huffed at the way he'd missed such a simple point. "I'm not from this sort of people."

"What does that mean?"

"It means I was raised by a miserly old grouch who never prepared me for such a sumptuous affair!" The moment the words were free, she bit her lip in consternation, old lessons racing through her brain in a litany of reminders.

*One shouldn't speak ill of the dead . . .*
*Honor thy father . . .*
*Remember your place . . .*
*Refrain from putting on airs . . .*
*Be true to your family . . .*

Gideon's arm wound about her waist, and she willingly leaned into that support.

"You're upset over nothing," he murmured. "These people are no different from you. They are all nouveau riche, having made their fortunes in much the same manner I have. You are from the same roots."

"No. No, I'm not. This is not the sort of world to which I was ever taught to become accustomed."

"You don't have to be 'accustomed' to it. You merely have to enjoy it."

"But how can I? How can I possibly endure the evening knowing that my every word, my every move, will be watched and evaluated and criticized?"

"No one will care a fig about who you are or what you do. Even if they did, what do you care?" When she gazed up at him with troubled eyes, he reiterated, "What do you care of other people's opinions?"

"I—"

He closed her mouth with a nudge of his finger under her chin. "Life is too short to spend worrying what people think, Constance—and if your father taught you otherwise, no wonder he died a lonely, mean old man."

"But—"

"Enjoy yourself. I promise you, no one will notice what fork you use at dinner or the extent of your vocabulary. You're shortchanging them all if you think that people will judge you by such niceties instead of what's here"—he tapped her forehead—"and what's here"—he tapped the spot over her heart. "Open yourself up to the pleasures that are available, and learn from them. Then make your decisions about whether or not you 'belong' here."

With that, he drew her inexorably closer to a line of maids who waited to take their wraps. Sucking a steadying breath into her lungs, Constance unhooked her cape, then allowed Gideon to lift it from her shoulders.

This time, however, it was his turn to offer a hissing inhalation. Glancing at the mirror on the wall in the parlor behind the maids, she watched his eyes flame, then felt his hands, warm through the soft cotton of his gloves, settle on her bare shoulders.

"What in hell are you wearing?"

She wasn't sure if she should be frightened or pleased by his reaction, but after staring into the reflection of his passionate gaze, she began to sway toward pleasure.

"It's a ball gown. You told me to wear what I wished, so I borrowed a ball gown from Penny."

"Yes," he drawled, his voice a caress against her taut nerves. "But I wish you'd worn all of it."

She laughed softly, then watched in astonishment as his eyes narrowed at the sound. His fingers curled more tightly into her shoulders, and for the oddest reason she felt the urge to flirt with this man. This dangerous, enigmatic man.

"I *am* wearing all of it."

In the mirror's depths, she was able to see the way his eyes fell to her bare shoulders. Her décolletage was low—far lower than she would have ever dreamed herself capable of enduring. Except for a tiny gold necklace with the dangling jet beads that he'd given her at the opera, her body was unadorned until reaching the cotton netting of the bertha draped over each breast. Below that, the bodice of her gown had been stretched over a corset drawn as tight as she could bear. The violet color enhanced the creamy whiteness of her skin, and the huge belled skirt made her waist seem incredibly tiny and fragile. Even Constance didn't recognize herself in the mirror. She looked so glamorous, so sophisticated, so unlike the woman who had bundled her cat in a basket and traveled to New York.

How had she changed so much in such a short amount of time?

Her forehead creased in a frown, but she wasn't given the opportunity to pursue the thought since Gideon was taking her elbow and leading her to the staircase.

"I think it's time we surrounded ourselves with people," he said pointedly.

Constance pretended ignorance. "But why?"

"So I don't ravish you on the spot."

"You once promised to seduce me."

"Somehow, I think that your gown was meant to turn the tables on me. Tell me, Constance, have you decided to employ your own methods of seduction?"

She smiled at him coyly, snapping her fan open and peering at him over the top of the staves. "Perhaps I have."

"Well, it's too late. I am already your prisoner."

By the time she'd absorbed the sincerity of his statement, they had reached the top of the second floor. There the host and hostess, Claudia and Rupert Raines, were waiting to receive them.

Deciding that Gideon's advice to enjoy the evening had its merits, Constance found herself adopting a role that she really didn't own. The dress, the atmosphere, the man at her side all made it possible for her to believe that she was someone from this glittering society world.

The evenings spent reenacting dramas with her sisters in their attic bedrooms swam over her, and she drew upon all those times she'd played a countess, a princess, an actress of repute. From there, it was quite easy for her to extend her mitted hand for the host to kiss, then offer a ladylike squeeze to her hostess's fingers. She murmured polite "how do you do's," informed several women where she'd purchased her dress, and remarked on the beauty of the home that surrounded them.

Finally, she and Gideon had run the gamut of the receiving line. Taking his hand, she tugged him resolutely to the stairs and the third-floor ballroom. After her recent success, she was eager to experience her first ball.

He followed her with an indulgent expression, but she ignored his reaction as she caught sight of the swirling figures on the dance floor and the multitude of gaily dressed guests. Around her the air was heady with the scent of a myriad mingled perfumes, the delicacies arrayed on the banquet table, and the musky odor of flowers and candles.

"Oh, my," she breathed.

Then she had no opportunity to breathe at all, because Gideon had wrapped his arm around her waist and whirled her onto the dance floor.

At first, Constance struggled to remember how to waltz. Her only real practice had been the bumping and bumblings she and her sisters had attempted while watching a neighbor's party through a bedroom window. But Gideon's steps were slow and sure until she followed suit. Then he began to whirl her around and around until her head was swimming.

When the music stopped, Constance fought to catch her breath. She was so intent upon opening her fan and fluttering it in front of her face that she didn't notice the stillness that had swept over the room, or the way her companion grew still. It was only when his fingertips dug into her side that she looked up at Gideon and noted that his features had turned to granite.

"What's wrong?"

When he didn't answer, she followed his line of sight to the tall, regal man who had just entered the room and stood staring at Constance as if he'd seen a ghost.

Grimacing, she supposed that the stranger was yet another theater admirer of Maura Kelly.

Ignoring the man, she fanned her flushed cheeks, then grew conscious that the stranger wasn't the only person staring. Most of the room was watching the exchange with avid fascination, their gazes equally divided among Constance, Gideon, and the stranger.

Constance peered at Gideon, intent upon asking him for an explanation, but when she noted the pallor that had flooded his cheeks, she hesitated.

A murmur from the interested onlookers signaled to Constance that the stranger was moving toward her, and she automatically stiffened, sensing that she was about to be plunged into a drama that she didn't understand.

"Come with me, Constance. I feel the need for some air."

Gideon's grip on her arm was nearly painful as he led her through the French doors to the terrace beyond. But if he'd thought to avoid the stranger so easily, he was doomed to be disappointed, Constance thought as she caught a glimpse of the man trailing behind them.

Gideon must have been aware of the man's arrival as well, because he made his way to the far corner of the terrace, as far from prying eyes as possible. Then he turned and confronted the man with a hard stare.

"Payne," the stranger murmured in greeting. The candlelight glinted on the waves of blond hair surrounding his face, and Constance admitted that at any other time she might have considered him attractive.

If Gideon wasn't at her side to pale the man in comparison.

"Hayes."

"Won't you introduce me to your companion?"

Constance noted the way Gideon's jaw clenched, but he finally murmured, "Constance, this gentleman is an old childhood acquaintance, Luther Hayes. Luther, I would like you to meet my fiancée, Constance Pedigrue."

Constance stared at him, about to blurt, "Your *what?*" But one look at his fierce expression persuaded her to continue with the ruse.

Luther? Where had she heard that name before?

Lifting her hand, she allowed Luther to kiss her

knuckles—which he did with the same reverence he might show a queen. Extricating herself, Constance wound her hands around Gideon's elbow, convinced that if he intended to thrust her into a role of his choosing, she could not pass up the opportunity to act as if she really were his wife-to-be.

"Dearest, I'm not sure I remember what you've told me about Mr. Hayes. I think the name is familiar, but I'm not sure how. Surely your reticence was an oversight."

Gideon's cheek flinched slightly at the endearment, and he laid his hand over hers as a warning.

"Not really. I hadn't thought of him until this moment."

"Then you were never close?"

"No." The word was implacable. Dangerous. "Not for some time."

Constance flashed Luther a dazzling smile. "You must not make yourself a stranger, Mr. Hayes. If the two of you are friends, you must feel free to visit our home."

Luther was staring at her, his gaze intense. "My absence has always been at the request of Gideon here."

"Oh, really?"

When neither man responded or made any attempt to satisfy her burning curiosity, she fought the urge to stamp her foot in impatience.

"Come now, gentlemen. Perhaps you should let me in on your secret. It's obvious that the two of you feel a certain amount of ... tension at this impromptu meeting."

There was a beat of uncomfortable silence before Luther volunteered, "I fear that you are the source of our ... discomfort, Miss Pedigrue."

"Oh?"

"Yes. You bear a striking resemblance to a woman we both knew."

Maura again. Why did the woman's ghost constantly intrude?

"It's uncanny, really, how much you look like her."

She frowned. "I've seen a picture of Maura Kelly, and I don't think the likeness is all that accurate."

"It's accurate enough to make my heart stop." Her brows rose at the unseemly retort. "You see, Maura and I shared a fondness," Luther continued, almost defiantly.

"You were her lover," Gideon growled under his breath. "Then you were the reason for her death."

Luther glared at him. "On my honor, I never—"

"You were found in her bed!"

"Dammit, that wasn't me!"

"I saw you. I saw you try to scramble over the balcony." Gideon wrenched free of Constance's grasp. "Dammit, you let her leap from a window in order to follow you!"

Luther lunged toward Gideon, knocking him to the ground, then landed on his supine form and began pummeling him with blows.

The noise drew the attention of a couple standing near the doorway. The woman screamed in horror, and guests pushed their way outside to see the source of the ruckus.

Turning to a knot of men who had just appeared, Constance ordered, "Don't just stand there. Separate them!"

A half-dozen burly guests pulled them apart.

Luther lunged, attempting to grab Gideon by the throat, but then, as if realizing that his instincts had caused him to make a spectacle of himself, he forced himself to relax, straighten, and grow calm.

Furious at the scene that had been thrust upon him, Gideon ignored him. Tugging at his vest, he took Constance's arm and drew her to him.

"I think we should leave."

"Yes," she readily agreed. "That would be best for all concerned."

Allowing him to usher her from the room, she offered her hasty farewells to the host and hostess, informed them that Gideon hadn't been "feeling well" lately and that fact had been responsible for his unseemly behavior. Then she followed him into the cool night air.

"My cape," she gasped as the carriage and driver magically appeared.

"Leave it. Our hostess will have it delivered tomorrow."

Not wanting to return to the scene of the spectacle, Constance surrendered to his commands and stepped into the close confines of the carriage. As soon as he'd taken his seat beside her and rapped the roof of the conveyance, the horses leaped into motion, and they were barreling down the crowded nighttime streets.

"Is it really necessary to make our escape so precipitously?" Constance asked as she grasped the leather handhold bolted near the window.

"Yes," Gideon growled. Then, obviously relenting, he said, "No, I suppose not." Rapping on the ceiling again, he signaled the driver to slow their flight.

Cool air streamed through the window, and Constance shuddered. She still wasn't used to having her shoulders bared to the evening breeze.

Seeing her predicament, Gideon shrugged from his jacket and wrapped it around her torso.

"Perhaps we should have sent the driver for the cape."

Imagining the prying eyes that followed their every move from the time Luther had thrown Gideon to the floor, she shook her head. "No, I think a swift retreat was the best option." Then, remembering the debacle that had preceded their flight, she rounded on him. "What on earth possessed that man to behave that way?"

Gideon avoided her gaze. "Call it a return to our original breeding."

"What is that supposed to mean?" When he refused to answer, she tartly said, "I think I deserve an explanation at the very least."

"You aren't my mother, Constance."

"No," she retorted. "I'm your *fiancée*."

At that reminder, he did have enough grace to look away, his lips twitching. "Sorry."

"I should hope you'd be thinking of a better apology than that. I can only wonder what sort of gossip will be flying around that ballroom tonight."

He offered her a dark look. "I told you once before that you shouldn't worry yourself about what other people think."

"Perhaps not, but I believe you owe me the courtesy of a more detailed explanation."

"About what?"

"About you, Luther . . . and Maura."

"Where have they gone, Etienne?" Louise asked when her bodyguard returned to the ballroom.

Only yesterday Louise had received an invitation from Claudia Raines—who had doubted the actress would appear but had put such an influential performer on her list nonetheless.

The moment she'd read the engraved card, Louise had known she would attend the party. Not because she was particularly fond of balls but because she knew Gideon would be included in such a gathering and she'd hoped to talk to Constance.

Unfortunately, she and Etienne had arrived a trifle late because of traffic. By the time they'd made their way to the third floor, Gideon had already been dancing with Constance. Then that awful brawl began, and her daughter disappeared.

"According to the maid who gathers the wraps, they left abruptly. Constance didn't even bother to collect her cape."

Louise sighed in disappointment. She would have to wait for another opportunity for a "chance" meeting. But when?

When Etienne didn't speak again, she turned to study his features, then grew immediately concerned.

"I managed to draw Luther Hayes into the Raines's study under the guise of calming him. After several glasses of brandy, he was quite free with his thoughts—even with a total stranger."

Louise gripped his arm, sensing she was not going to like what she was about to hear.

"He explained to me that Gideon has always believed that Maura and he were lovers. But he swore time and time again that he never slept with the woman."

"Then who was Maura with that night?" Louise asked, remembering the tale of Maura's suicide that had raced through the theatrical grapevine.

"Luther said he saw her once with a very distinctive man. Luther burst into her dressing room to congratulate her on a particularly stunning performance and caught her kissing someone else."

"Well, Etienne? What did he say this man looked like?"

Etienne glanced at the people who cluttered the ballroom and bunched together to gossip about the evening's events.

"I think we'd better go," he said abruptly, pulling her toward the door.

"But why?"

"If the description I heard belongs to the man I've begun to suspect, Gideon must be warned."

"Tonight?"

"Yes. Tonight. And we'll take Luther with us to prove our point."

# Twenty-One

The tiny lamp in the corner of the carriage cast most of Gideon's features in shadow, but Constance was still able to discern the gravity of his expression and the forceful thrust of his gaze.

"Do you really want to know about Maura and me? About how I came to this point?"

Buried inside the question was a warning that she was about to tread on dangerous ground.

Constance hesitated, knowing that if she pursued this line of inquiry, she'd live to rue the day she had forced Gideon to confide in her. After all, he was a man who guarded his past and his privacy with a fierceness that bordered on being an obsession. Such confidences would come at a dear price.

But she had to know. She had to delve into this man's soul to discover what made him so fierce, so protective, so devoted to a solitary life.

"Yes, Gideon. I really want to know."

The carriage was drawing to a stop in front of the town house, and Gideon helped her to alight.

"Come with me."

He led her into the house, up the staircase, then into

the east wing. Reaching the double doors and the end of the corridor, he took one of the tapers from a sconce and ushered her inside.

Constance waited in tense silence as he lit the nubs of beeswax that remained in the candelabrum inside. With each guttering flame, another portion of the room was revealed to her.

So this was the Gold Room.

It was obvious that some effort had been made to repair the chamber, but there was no disguising the smells of mold and decay, the chill of the draft seeping through the still-broken window, the scorch marks on the walls and surrounding Maura's portrait.

*Maura's portrait.*

Constance moved toward the painting as if a spell pulled her closer. She'd lied to Luther when she said that she'd seen a picture of Maura, and now that she was face to face with the oil and canvas version of the actress, she shivered at the uncanny resemblance. Constance could have been looking into a mirror.

"She was very beautiful," Gideon commented softly, and she whirled, a tiny corner of her wondering if that meant that he thought Constance was beautiful, too.

"You must have loved her a great deal."

"I was obsessed with her." Gideon fixed his gaze on Constance. "There is a difference."

So Penny had been right in her assumptions.

"You married her," Constance said pointedly.

One of his shoulders shifted in a dismissive gesture. "At the time, I thought it was the best thing to do. She was besieged by admirers on every side—including Luther Hayes. In their eyes I saw my own desires."

She shivered as the room was flooded with the haunting remains of a primal passion.

Gideon drew his jacket from Constance's shoulders and dropped it on the ground. "She had a way about her." His knuckles stroked her collarbone, then skimmed her neck. "She drew men to her like bees to a sweet field of buttercups."

Constance was afraid to breathe, afraid to remind this man that she wasn't Maura. That she would never be Maura.

"She swore to me that all those men were an annoyance. She swore that I was the love of her life." His hand cupped her cheek, then she gasped as he turned her in his arms and wrapped his arm around her neck and chest, forcing her to stare at the painting. "Look at her, Constance. Those eyes speak volumes. In their depths everything a man has ever wanted, ever dreamed of possessing, can be found."

He leaned closer, his voice growing harsh as he spoke next to her ear.

"She told me she loved me—and those sweet, smiling eyes made me believe her. She told me I was the only man she could ever love. She begged me to make a public claim on her, and I willingly agreed, knowing that only a wedding ceremony and a band on her finger would convince her fans that she wasn't free to accept their attentions."

His arm shifted, wrapping around her neck in a loose choke hold, and Constance shivered. For the first time since meeting him, Gideon was frightening her. She doubted that he was even aware of his own actions or the way her head arched against him in an effort to maintain her ability to breathe.

"We were married in May. A big church ceremony. I remember that she chose lilacs for her bouquet— lilacs . . ." He uttered a short laugh, but Constance was at a loss about what he found amusing until he bent to sniff her perfume. Lilac water. Then he bent even closer to whisper, "She even had the audacity to wear white."

Constance gripped his wrists, trying to alleviate his hold.

"She wasn't a virgin when I took her that night—even

though she tried her best to convince me she was." He was moving closer to the painting, taking Constance with him. "But I told myself I didn't care. I decided that the past didn't matter as long as I was her only future. But within weeks, I knew our marriage was doomed. That was when Maura informed me that she was pregnant."

He stopped, staring up at the portrait with a mixture of anger and reluctance. "She was very clever, playing the one trump card she knew I could not resist. Less than a month later she . . . conveniently went to bed, claiming a miscarriage. But I had my doubts there had ever been a child in the first place."

The tone of his voice dropped to a harsh whisper. "Then I returned three days early from a business trip. I'd decided that it didn't matter if the baby hadn't really existed. Maura was finally open to the idea of becoming a mother. That was all that mattered."

He paused, his eyes taking on a far-off gleam. "I'd paid a florist forty dollars to gather the last of the lilacs to be found in the city, and my arms were heaped with them as I crept upstairs and opened the door . . ."

Tears were streaming down Constance's cheeks. Not from the way he held her, not from the way he believed her to be a mirror image of his dead wife, but because she knew how the story would end.

Abruptly, he released her, then raked his fingers through his hair in a bid for calm. "They were in bed together. My wife and Luther Hayes."

"You'd known him before then?"

"Known him?" His bark of laughter was bitter. "He was my oldest and best friend. I grew up with him. Until the Kincaids took me in, he was the closest thing I'd ever had to a brother. Later we even entered the same business and helped each other to succeed."

Constance shuddered, realizing now the depth of his feelings of betrayal.

"He didn't even have the decency to face me. He dodged to the balcony and galloped into the darkness. Maura was so distraught, she ran after him, begging him to come back. When he didn't, she climbed onto the railing, screaming to me that she would die before she endured another of my embraces. Then she jumped."

Constance wrapped her arms around her body, chilled to the bone. Not by the draft, or even by the story, but by the anguish that cloaked Gideon's features. She had grown so used to his unflappable calm, his driving intensity, his potent anger, but she couldn't reconcile herself to the horrible emotions that gripped him now.

He sank into a nearby chair and rubbed his face with his hands, obviously regretting that he'd told her anything at all.

Knowing that she could not allow him to retreat into his emotional shell, she rushed toward him, then caressed his cheek, his hair.

He started as if she'd burned him and attempted to rise, but she pushed him down, wrapped her arms around his neck, and drew his face against her breasts.

"It's all in the past, Gideon," she whispered.

He resisted her for a few seconds, then held her tightly. "Is it?"

"Of course it is. In time, when you're calmer, you'll find a way to confront Luther for his perfidy—tonight has already set those wheels in motion."

"And then?"

"Then the healing will begin."

He lifted his head, some of the fierceness returning to his gaze. "You make the whole situation sound so simple."

"No. Nothing about this whole mess is simple. But there are only so many options available to you—although I would refrain from brawling in public in the future."

"You would?"

She heard his soft laughter, and her muscles eased

their tight grip. "Mmm. That would be my recommendation."

He stood, his body sliding against the slick taffeta of her gown and creating a delicious friction that no longer had anything to do with past regrets and tragedies.

"What else would you suggest?"

"That you put Maura in her place."

"What place?"

"The past."

He grimaced, and she framed his face in her hands.

"I am not Maura," she stated bluntly. "The resemblance might be . . . uncanny. But I am not Maura."

He didn't immediately answer, and a tiny part of her died, a tiny part of her soul that had hoped he would readily admit such a thing himself.

This time it was Gideon who tipped her head up to his inspection. "Who are you, then?" She frowned in confusion, but he continued, "How did you come into my life? What force brought you to me?" He grimaced. "In the beginning, I even entertained the notion that Luther might have sent you as some sort of twisted jest."

"What?" she gasped.

"But I knew all along that such deceit wasn't possible. Not from you."

His thumb stroked her bottom lip, and he whispered, "What do you want of me, Constance?"

"Want?"

"You must want something. Otherwise, why would you stay here when I have done everything in my power to frighten you away?"

She shyly placed her hand on his chest. "Perhaps you weren't listening when I informed you that I can be very pig-headed."

"I was listening."

"Then I suppose you've noticed the result of such a character flaw. The more I'm pushed away, the closer I long to be."

As if understanding her tacit wish, he tightened his

grip, bringing her lips flush against his own. "You should run from this place, Constance."

"I believe you've offered that advice before." Her fingers delved into his hair. "My answer has not changed. I have nowhere that I would rather be."

Then she was drawing his head to hers, bringing his lips closer and closer until only a hairsbreadth separated them.

"Are you to be my saving grace, Constance?"

"No," she whispered. "I believe that you are to be mine."

Then there was no more time for talk, no inclination. The kiss he offered her was hungry and filled with passion, and she had no will to refuse him. Indeed, standing on tiptoe, she deepened the caress, needing to feel him so close to her, so warm, so vibrant, that there could be no doubt that he was kissing *her*, not a ghost.

It had been a simple enough matter for him to draw the servants away from the town house. By arranging an errand that needed their immediate attention, he was able to slip into the empty house and wait.

He heard the pair of them enter and climb the staircase. Clinging to the shadows in the corridor, he'd even managed to hear Gideon relate the events of Maura's supposed suicide.

But she hadn't died. She was standing right in front of the man, and he was too stupid to realize she was drawing him into her trap.

*Just as she drew me into her little game.*

His jaw clenched, and he reached into his pocket, withdrawing the heavy knife that he had sharpened to a razor's edge. He blinked against the sudden sting of tears in his eyes.

*Why, Maura? Why? Why didn't you love me as much as you claimed?*

Swiping at the moisture that plunged down his cheek,

he cursed himself for being a fool. He should have known that Maura could never love anyone but herself.

Backing deeper into the corner, he waited, his breath hitching in his throat, his heart pounding. Tonight he would demand his own brand of satisfaction for her lies.

Gideon swept Constance into his arms, marveling at how right she felt against him.

"I love you, Constance," he whispered as he carried her toward the door.

Her eyes became luminous and wide with wonder. "What?" she breathed.

"You heard me," he said, louder this time. "I love you—more than life itself. And if you'll have me, I want you by my side until the day I die."

Her fingers tangled in his hair. "As your mistress?"

"As my mistress, my companion, my confidante, and my wife."

She gasped in disbelief, hugging him so tightly that he barely managed to navigate the hall. Knowing he had to kiss her again, love her, hold her, he kicked open the door to the Peach Room and settled her on the bed. Then he stretched on top of her, delighting in the sweetness of her body and the rich emotion shining from her eyes.

"You really want to marry me?" she whispered.

"If you'll have me."

"Oh, yes!" she exclaimed, throwing her arms around his neck. "Yes, yes, yes!"

Then he was kissing her in an attempt to satisfy his craving for this woman. She had brought him back to life and filled him with such joy that he wondered what he had ever done to deserve her.

His hand swept down her body, settling over one breast, and he chuckled in delight at her gasp of pure pleasure.

"What are you doing?" she murmured, her eyes half closed.

"I'm making love to you. Any objections?"

Her head rolled from side to side. "None at all."

Then she was pulling his lips to hers, making his heart beat thunderously and his . . .

Thunder?

Distracted, he lifted his head and cocked it toward the source of the noise. Judging by the ruckus, someone was threatening to pound the front door in.

"Birch will get it," Constance reassured him, but after another mind-drugging kiss, it became obvious that they were alone in the house.

"Maybe they'll go away," Constance offered ruefully.

Gideon sighed in defeat. "I am beginning to wonder if we will ever be able to consummate our relationship without some sort of interruption." Rolling from the bed, he offered a teasing "Don't move until I get back."

Once in the corridor, he marched down the staircase and wrenched the door open. When he saw Luther Hayes on the other side of the threshold as well as another pair of shadowy figures, he growled, "What the hell?"

At that moment, a woman stepped into the light, and he immediately recognized the features of Louise Chevalier, an actress with whom he'd once been close friends.

"Don't shut us out, Gideon," she warned. "We've come here on a very important errand."

"Nothing is so important that you have to rouse me at this time of the night, Louise."

She didn't respond to his blatant warning. Instead, she pushed past him and made her way into the foyer.

"I'm afraid you're wrong, Gideon. What I have to say concerns us all. You, me, and my daughter Constance."

Constance heard the muted footfalls in the corridor and smiled in secret satisfaction. Gideon hadn't waited long at all to rid himself of the pesky visitor and return.

Stretching her arms over her head, she closed her eyes and waited for the faint, betraying squeak of the door.

"Back so soon?" she teased.

There was a moment of silence, then a rasping voice that she did not recognize answered, "I have been here all along."

Her lashes sprang open, and she gasped when she found Birch leaning toward her. Immediately, she discounted the evidence of her own eyes. Birch couldn't speak. Mrs. Potts had told Constance that he was deaf and dumb.

"You look surprised, my dear."

The words were clear and undistorted, and Constance instinctively shrank backward, rolling to the floor and placing the bed between them.

"What are you doing in my room?" she demanded.

Her haughty tones had no evident effect. Birch circled the bed—and too late she realized he'd cut off her only real avenue for escape.

"Damn you, Maura," he snarled. "Did you honestly think that I wouldn't mind that you took up your relationship with Gideon from the very spot you left it?"

She shook her head. "Birch? Maura is dead. I'm . . ."

"Shut up! I won't listen to any more of your lies. You thought you could fool me—that you could fool us all. But I knew you better than that. I knew that you hadn't really died that night. You staged that suicide quite cleverly, but I was well aware that you hadn't actually killed yourself."

Constance searched for something to say, but, staring into Birch's wild eyes, she detected a hint of madness that she had never seen before.

"Birch, you're mistaken. My name is—"

"Stop it!" He lunged forward, grasping her wrist with one hand and brandishing a knife with the other. "I won't listen to you. Not anymore. You promised you loved me. You promised you would never leave me. You promised that if we were ever separated, you would come back to me. But you *lied!*"

"Constance?"

The call came from below, and Constance instinctively screamed, "Gideon, help me!"

It had been a mistake to be so bold, she realized as Birch hauled her tightly against him, then began to carry her bodily from the room.

"Constance!"

*Please hurry, Gideon. Please hurry!* she prayed silently, not daring to utter the words aloud. It took all her strength to wriggle and buck and kick her tormenter. Even so, her efforts had no real effect. Birch was far too large and strong.

He dragged her into the Gold Room, then kicked at the planks that covered the window leading onto the balcony. Instantly, Constance knew what he meant to do, and she doubled her efforts.

"You finally understand me, don't you, Maura? I won't let you whore with him again. This time your death will not be staged."

The boards fell away, and he lifted her high, allowing her feet to dangle over the railing.

"This time we'll meet in the eternities, my beloved," he whispered as his grip began to loosen.

Constance searched wildly for a way to save herself. As if in slow motion, she saw Gideon burst into the room, then Luther, then another pair of figures. Then there was no time to think at all as she felt herself slipping, slipping.

Wildly, she flailed her arms in front of her, knowing that her only chance for survival would be to catch hold of the iron railing. Otherwise, she would tumble fifteen feet to the stone pavement below.

Birch turned ever so slightly as Gideon shouted some sort of warning, and in that instant she knew she had been offered her best avenue at escape. Holding her breath, she let go of Birch's hands, even as her own fingers groped wildly, then caught around the scrollwork at the bottom of the balcony.

For several minutes, she hung there, unable to see what was happening in the bedroom but hearing the scuffling noises of a fight, what sounded like a pistol shot, then a howl of pain. A body tumbled headlong over the side, and she squeezed her eyes shut, unable to watch, praying with all her might that it hadn't been Gideon who had plunged to his death.

Then she felt several strong hands lifting her, carrying her, and setting her on the floor. As Constance struggled against the faintness that swirled around her, she thought she was drawn close to a woman's form. She caught a hint of perfume that was so familiar her heart ached at the scent.

"Mama?" she whispered, her eyes flickering.

As her gaze focused, she realized she must be dead because she recognized the face that hovered over hers. She knew that sweet smile and the love that shone from the woman's eyes.

"Mama?" Constance said again, unable to fathom what was happening to her. The hands that touched her cheek were real, oh, so real. As were the tears that dripped from the woman's eyes.

"Yes, baby. I'm here. I'm finally here."

Constance frowned in confusion, then started, staring into the gloom of the Gold Room. She saw Luther Hayes standing in one corner, a still-smoking pistol in his outstretched hand. Another tall, dark-haired gentleman approached and reached down to stroke her mother's hair.

But Gideon. Where was—

"Here, Constance."

As if he'd heard her thoughts, Gideon called to her. Immediately, she found the place where he leaned against the far wall, clutching his hand to the bright streak of blood appearing on his sleeve.

"You're hurt!" she exclaimed. Ignoring the blackness that threatened to envelop her, she rose to her feet and staggered toward him.

"Just a scratch," he assured her.

Not satisfied with his own analysis of the situation, she lifted his hand away, then shuddered in relief when she discovered that the wound was long but not deep.

"What happened, Gideon?"

He drew her close to him, and she clutched at the lean muscles of his waist in order to reassure herself that he was alive.

"It appears your mother was at the ball tonight. She saw the fight between Luther and me."

Constance gazed at her mother in disbelief. "You were there?"

Louise clasped her hands together and looked to the stranger beside her for guidance.

"Tell her, Louise," the man said as he helped her to her feet.

"I've been searching for all of you girls for years," she said, her expression begging Constance to understand. "Ever since your father stole you away from me."

"Papa . . . stole us?" Constance frowned. "But he told us that you'd found another man to love. Another family."

Louise's distress was real. "I know. I discovered that point after I spoke to Felicity and Patience."

"You've *spoken* to them?"

"Yes. You see, I only found you a few weeks before your father died." She shrugged helplessly. "I was the one who changed his will. I'd missed so much of your lives that I wanted to grant you all a special wish."

Constance digested the information, knowing now why she had thought it strange that her father had seemed to have altered his will so abruptly. He hadn't changed the document at all, nor had Patience. This woman had.

"I meant to approach you earlier," Louise hurried to explain. "I had even planned to bump into you at the ball." Her lip quivered. "I had no idea that you would recognize me."

"I-I always thought . . . I mean that . . . I was sure . . . Papa had killed you," Constance admitted slowly, the words strangled with her own tears.

Louise began to cry openly. "Oh, no. No. Constance, he was too much of a coward, don't you see? That's why he spirited all of you away."

"But how did you come to be . . ." Constance looked to Gideon.

When she could not continue, Gideon explained. "Etienne, Louise's bodyguard, had a chat with Luther after our tussle. He swore to Etienne that he had never bedded Maura but that he had seen her kissing an extremely tall man with blond hair."

"Birch," Constance breathed.

Gideon eyed his longtime nemesis with real regret. "I've wronged you horribly these past few years."

Luther sighed. "Not without cause. I never should have allowed Maura to tempt me. If she would have had me, I probably *would* have become her lover. That's why I never bothered to deny your accusations. I was never formally charged by the police, but even so, I thought it would be best to move away from New York, forget what had happened, and allow time to cool your temper."

Luther's grin was rueful. "When I received Claudia's invitation to attend her ball, I made the trip in hope of meeting with you. You must understand my shock when I walked into the ballroom and saw a woman I thought was Maura dancing in your arms."

"We were able to persuade him to come with us this evening to warn you," Louise inserted. "Although we had no proof that Gideon's butler was Maura's one-time lover, we thought it best to apprise Gideon of the situation, since he and I are former business acquaintances."

"I'm so glad you did," Constance said with a shaky laugh. Then she hugged Gideon tightly as she realized what could have happened if Birch had tiptoed into her bedroom as the two of them were kissing. She could almost see the blade arcing into Gideon's back.

"Birch, is he—"

"Dead," Gideon said as he stroked her back. "He won't harm anyone ever again."

# Twenty-Two

It was well after midnight when Louise was able to satisfy the police officer who had been interviewing her.

Since the police had been summoned to the house, the household members had been sequestered from one another while an examination of the events could be made. Through it all, Louise had done her best to remain strong, but, separated from Etienne's strength and concerned about her daughter, she'd soon grown impatient with the officers and had refused to answer anything more until she could assure herself that Constance had not succumbed to her ordeal.

Not willing to anger a woman who had a good many friends in high places, the policeman had finally released her, and Louise had gone in search of her daughter whom she'd been told was alone in Gideon's study.

Louise's hands rested on the latch of the pocket door. Yet, as much as she longed to throw them wide, she froze.

So much had occurred since she had located her estranged husband and her children. She could scarcely believe how her efforts to reunite with her daughters had caused them all to be led through such a gamut of adventures and dangers. Louise had been incredibly fortunate so far. Although her younger children had grown to accept her and welcome her in their lives, could Louise dare to dream that this bizarre, lifelong drama would end in complete happiness?

"Go on, *cherie*. Don't hesitate now that all your dreams are within reach."

Twisting, she saw that Etienne had joined her in the corridor and waited in the shadows, one shoulder propped against the wall.

"She thought he'd killed me, Etienne," she whispered achingly, her whole being suffused with guilt at the torment her daughter must have endured.

"And, as usual, you are blaming yourself, *ma petite.*" Etienne pushed himself away from the paneling in mock disappointment. "Don't you see, my love. She doesn't blame you. None of this was your doing."

"But I—"

He placed a finger on her lips. "You are guilty of nothing but love, my sweet. Your daughters know this, and I know this. So why can't you free yourself of the past?"

*The past.*

Was this ordeal actually over? Had she really managed to survive Alexander Pedigrue's treachery? Were she and her daughters really about to embark upon a bright, shining future filled with promise?

"It's over," Etienne whispered, reading her thoughts. Bending, he kissed her gently on the lips. "Go to your daughter. Tell her all those things you've wanted to say for years. Explain to her how one man's hatred nearly destroyed all of you. Then bury the past and move forward toward all the things that wait for you. Your daughters, your career . . ." His lips slid into a hopeful smile. "And me."

Rising on tiptoe, Louise threw her arms around Etienne's neck and hugged him close.

"I don't deserve you," she said, her eyes blinking against a rush of tears.

"Shhh. It is I who have been offered a gift beyond price," he said, rocking her, holding her, making her even more grateful that she had found a man who loved her so completely that he had buried his own needs for years on her behalf.

"You and I have a marriage to plan," she whispered next to his ear.

He grew so still that her heart fluttered in alarm until he replied gruffly, "I had begun to believe that you would change your mind."

"Etienne, no," she vehemently protested, then caught the teasing light in his eyes. Laughing softly to herself, she pressed her lips to his in a gentle kiss. "Perhaps we should elope. Tomorrow."

"And miss having all your daughters as witnesses?"

"They would understand."

"But I would not dream of asking such a thing of you. Marriages are for families. Yours. Mine. And one day soon . . . ours."

She blushed, and he chuckled in delight. "I've passed my fortieth birthday, Etienne. To contemplate another child would be . . ."

"Madness?" he supplied, but, reading the tension bracketing his lips, she knew he was offering her a way to refuse gracefully.

"No, my love. To contemplate another child would be heaven on earth."

Constance turned at the low rumble of the pocket panels spreading wide. Her heart leaped, thinking that Gideon had come for her, but it wasn't he who stood in the threshold, it was a stranger.

No. Not a stranger.

Her mother.

"Mama?" she whispered, the word foreign on her lips.

She saw Louise's lip tremble at the title, but her mother did not approach. "I wanted to make sure you were well. I've been worried sick about you for . . . years."

Louise's voice broke on the last word, and, needing the comfort that had been denied her for so long, Constance ran into her mother's arms.

"Oh, Mama," she sobbed, inundated with memories as the sweet scent of Louise's perfume enveloped her, soothed her.

Louise's arms wrapped around Constance's shoulders. "I love you, little one," she whispered. "And I'm here. I will always be here for you."

Constance shuddered at the endearment she had not heard since childhood. Drawing her mother to the leather-tufted settee, she settled against Louise's side, resting her head in the all-too-familiar crook of her mother's shoulder. She began to sob for the little girl she'd been and the woman she would have become. And through it all, Louise rocked her, whispering maternal words of love and comfort that were as old as time itself.

Finally, as the tears began to ease, Constance drew back and wiped the moisture from her own cheeks, then Louise's. "Oh, Mama, how I've missed you," she sighed with infinite joy. "From now on, we must always be close."

This time, it was Louise who wept and Constance who comforted. But as she held her mother close, she knew that this night, this moment, this bond with the woman who had given her life was one of the most perfect things she would ever know.

Dawn was breaking when Gideon closed the door behind the last police officer, Etienne, Louise, and Luther. In the interim, a good deal of explaining had occurred, and the stories had been told and retold to Potts and Merriweather, the police, and even a host of reporters.

As the lock clicked in place, the foyer was filled with a blessed silence.

Gideon rubbed his brow, sensing the woman who approached him from the direction of his study. "Potts and Merriweather—"

"I sent them to bed hours ago."

"Thank heavens." He held out his arm, and she willingly fell into place by his side as he headed for the stairs. For several minutes, they were surrounded in silence before he said, "I don't know what to say, Constance. After all you've been through, you'll probably be wanting to live with your mother from now on."

Constance resisted the urge to offer a tart response. Live with her mother, indeed. Did he think her feelings for him were so shallow that she would run at the first hint of trouble?

Instead, calming herself, she asked, "Is that what you want?"

They had reached the landing, and Gideon took her hands, looking down at them. "Right now, I think that your own wishes are more important than mine," he stated simply.

The warmth and desire that Constance had experienced in his arms only hours before kindled low in her body.

"Does that mean that you would be willing to have me stay?"

He looked at her then, his expression unguarded— and she was humbled by the blatant love and adoration she saw reflected there.

"If I were to have one wish," he said slowly, "it would be that you would remain with me. Now and for all time. As my wife."

Unable to hold her emotions in check any longer, she threw her arms around his neck and hugged him close. "I'd hoped you would give me such an answer."

He locked her against his body with a powerful embrace. "How could you ever doubt such a thing?"

She buried her face against his neck. "So much has happened in the last few hours that I wasn't sure if I'd dreamed your proposal." Lifting her head, she framed his face with her palms. "I wasn't sure if I'd imagined your passion."

He growled low in his throat. "Never doubt either of those things, Constance. I love you with a depth of emotion that I have never experienced before. You manage to bedevil me and bewitch me all at once." His smile was warm. "And I wouldn't have it any other way."

Sighing, she brushed her lips over his, thrilling at the immediate response she garnered.

"I love you, too, Gideon Payne."

"Heart and soul?"

"Heart and soul."

"And if I were to suggest that you join me in my bed tonight—just to sleep—would you object?"

"Not at all." She stepped free of him, taking his hand and pulling him down the corridor. "But I think we'll be doing much more than sleeping."

His eyes sparked with sudden desire. "Really?"

"Yes. Because I don't intend to wait another minute for your lovemaking."

As the words slipped free, she was being lifted in his arms. Gideon eliminated the last few yards to his room, then slammed the door shut with his foot.

"I hope you don't plan to change your mind," he said as he set her down and began to fumble with the fasteners of her gown.

"There's not much chance of that," she assured him breathlessly as she reached for his own buttons.

Soon they were laughing at the layers and layers that separated them, and their own impatience made the task of undressing that much more difficult. But in time Constance stood proudly in front of her husband-to-be, her bare skin gleaming in the glow of the lantern that Potts must have lit earlier that evening.

"You are so beautiful," Gideon breathed as he lowered her onto the bed. "But no one else will ever see you like this. I will never allow you on the stage."

She grinned into his neck, her fingers digging into the resilient flesh of his spine.

"I will agree to such a condition, if you make the same promise to me—that no other woman will ever see you without your clothes."

"Such an easy promise to make," he murmured, his hands stroking her sides, her shoulders, then moving to cup her breasts.

Constance's eyes fluttered shut as she was struck with a bolt of pure passion. "Such an easy promise to keep," she whispered in return.

Within seconds, the time for talking had passed. There was only this moment and the sensations that raged between them. Finally, Constance was allowed to explore the hard planes of Gideon's body, to taste the skin of his throat, his chest, his nipples.

Consumed with a hunger like she had never known before, she rolled him onto his back and studied him with her eyes and her fingertips. With each loving stroke, her pulse thrummed more insistently and her body ached with desire. Inch by inch, she allowed her caresses to slip lower and lower until she held that part of him that waited for her possession.

Gideon hissed, pushing her onto her back and stretching her arms overhead. "Much more of that, and I won't be able to wait."

"Why on earth would you want to wait?" she asked coyly.

His lips took hers, tasting, sucking, searching—and she willingly returned each gesture in full measure, praying that Gideon would not delay much longer. Her body was on fire, and an insistent yearning to be possessed by him could no longer be denied.

When he settled over her body, she whimpered in

delight, willingly parting her legs, tipping her hips until his manhood probed against her most sensitive flesh.

Then he was moving against her, gently at first, but his movements becoming more insistent when she urged him on with kittenish moans of pleasure. Finally, after drawing away for a fraction of a moment, he thrust completely into her body, and she cried out in a heady measure of pleasure and pain.

"Have I hurt you?" he rasped.

"No, no," she whimpered, her body instinctively bucking against him. "Please don't stop. Please, please don't stop."

Her urgings must have released him from the last of his doubts, because he began to arch against her. Somehow, he knew just what to do, how to coax and caress and dominate in order to bring her to a pinnacle of pleasure.

Constance gripped the bedclothes beneath her, praying that their union could continue forever, but still driving toward some nameless, unknown goal. Within her, muscles she hadn't even known existed began to quiver, then burst into a spasmodic, pleasurable release she had never dreamed could occur. Crying out, she surrendered to the sensations, feeling her mind spin out of control.

Vaguely, she became aware of Gideon's body trembling above her. Her lashes fluttered open, and she saw that he, too, was straining for his own release. With a cry, he stiffened completely, and she felt a warmth spread deep within her body.

For several long moments, he lay above her, his weight supported by his arms. When at long last he opened his eyes to stare down at her, she offered him a slow, delicious smile.

"That was wonderful," she drawled, her body completely drained of energy but still filled with a rush of gratification.

Gideon's answering grin was filled with a sheepish sense of self-congratulation. "Are you sure?" he asked.

"Mmm-hmm."

Rolling away, he drew her against his side, kissing the top of her head. "It's only a prelude to what's to come in our life together."

"I hope so."

His arms tightened, and he pressed a lingering kiss against her temple. "I know so," he whispered roughly. "Because in that moment Birch attempted to throw you off the balcony, I knew that my life would be meaningless without you."

She blinked at the tears that sprang to the surface.

"Never doubt that I love *you*, Constance Pedigrue," he continued, his voice thick with emotion. "You are my soul-mate. My one true love. You are not a pale imitation of Maura. *She* was a counterfeit copy of *you*."

Tears slid down Constance's cheeks as she bent over Gideon, kissing him as if she had never done so before—reverently, confidently.

After so many years without love, she had found all she craved here in this man's arms. Never again would she feel lonely or lost or ill prepared. Gideon Payne loved her.

And that was all she had ever needed to make her feel complete.

# Epilogue

*Canada*
*1860*

Constance studied the contents of the crowded tea table with a critical eye but was unable to find fault with the elaborate refreshments. The service at the Gray Mist Inn was invariably impeccable—a fact she'd discovered while sharing the honeymoon suite with her husband for the past three days.

She smiled in secret delight, tugging at the hem of the tablecloth to smooth a tiny wrinkle from the delicate linen. Who would have supposed after Constance's first encounter with Gideon Payne that they would one day share a honeymoon suite anywhere, let alone in the secluded seacoast resort town in New Eddington, Canada?

The month-long vacation had been an anniversary gift from Gideon. Constance's dreams for an elaborate family wedding had been thwarted when Constance's younger sister, Felicity, had been unable to travel because of morning sickness. And since Patience had herself been a new bride, Constance had surrendered her hope to have her sisters present, so that her life as Gideon's wife would begin as quickly as the law would allow.

She had no regrets for her hasty nuptials or for the

simple ceremony with only her mother, Etienne, Penny, Potts, and Merriweather in attendance. But she had always thought that the Pedigrue sisters should gather as soon as possible in order to celebrate a grand reunion with their mother.

Unfortunately, once Felicity's pregnancy had advanced enough to let her travel, Patience had found herself with child. Then Louise's hectic performance schedule had taken her to London, Rome, and Paris.

But finally—*finally*—the long-awaited meeting was about to take place. In an effort that had remained a surprise until mere weeks ago, Gideon had contacted his fellow brothers-in-law. Logan Campbell, Felicity's husband, had secured the entire third floor of the exclusive Gray Mist Inn—an almost impossible task, since reservations for the four suites on that level were made years in advance. But calling upon the favors of friends and fellow abolition sympathizers, he'd managed to secure the coveted accommodations.

In the meantime, Garrick Dalton, Patience's husband, had dispatched one of his ships to bring their mother home from Europe with the greatest possible speed. And Gideon had organized a dozen entertainments—from a private ladies' tea party to the appearance of a renowned opera singer.

Nothing could be more perfect.

A soft knock caused Constance's heart to rap against her ribs in excitement. Gideon had disappeared nearly an hour earlier—no doubt scouting the possibilities for expanding his theatrical empire into Canada. Therefore, the summons could only be from one of the Pedigrue women.

Rushing to the door, Constance threw open the panels to discover Felicity standing in the hall, her arms already opened for an expected embrace.

"Constance!"

In an instant, Felicity and Constance were holding

each other close, their words of greeting tumbling over one another in an effort to say everything at once.

When at long last they separated, Constance eyed her sister with great care. In the past year, the two of them had been in constant contact by post. Constance had heard the hair-raising details of Felicity's adventures in the West—being quarantined in a bordello, falling in love with a member of the Underground Railroad, and making a daring escape to Canada. But even after such trials and the birth of a child, Felicity looked radiant.

"I know, I know, I'm not wearing my woolen underwear," Felicity said impudently, referring to the last piece of advice Constance had given her before Felicity had journeyed to St. Joseph. "Frankly, I've grown fond of having other, kinder fabrics next to my skin."

"So have I," Constance confessed, laughing at her own foolishness on that day long ago when she'd advised her sister to wear her woolens, despite the weather.

Constance didn't bother to close the door, since the entire floor of the inn would soon house family. She drew Felicity toward the table set for tea. "Where's the baby?" she asked as she gestured to a chair.

"Louis is with his father at the moment. Logan volunteered to take him for the afternoon so that our party would be uninterrupted." Felicity's eyes twinkled mischievously. "Somehow, I have a feeling that the spontaneous gesture was a bit of an excuse to show the boy to your husband. The offer was made the moment he recognized Gideon from the wedding portrait you sent." Felicity took her seat, adding, "Don't be surprised if he starts giving Gideon ideas about beginning a family of your own."

Constance merely smiled, not about to rise to the bait—especially since she and Gideon were expecting a bundle of their own soon after Christmas. But no matter how much she might long to blurt the news out early, Constance didn't intend to announce anything until Louise and Patience were present as well.

A muffled thumping noise came from the hall, along with a muffled "Blast!"

Recognizing Patience's voice, Constance hurried back to the still-open door. Patience, who was struggling to carry a huge cake decorated with some indistinguishable lumps of frosting, sighed in relief when she saw her sister.

"Help me," she sighed in earnest supplication.

Since Patience had never been known for her patience when tasks went awry, Constance rushed to take the dessert.

"I told you not to bring anything, Patience."

"I know, but Emaline insisted on making something for the tea as a surprise," she said, speaking of her husband's little sister, Emaline, who had once been Patience's pupil. "However, I think you should use caution before tasting the concoction, since this is her first attempt at making a cake and the whole thing has been packed in a box in her cabin since we left New England. I just hope—"

The rest of her warning was lost when Patience caught sight of Felicity sitting at the table. She rushed to hug their "little" sister, then sank into a seat. "I'm positively famished. I hope Mother hasn't been delayed. Traveling in one of Garrick's ships always makes me hungry."

Since marrying Garrick Dalton, Patience had been on nearly a dozen sea voyages, and she'd written all sorts of letters describing her fabulous adventures. At first, the trips had been quite short—a day's journey to Boston or Nantucket. Since Emaline had been shipwrecked as a young child and had developed an aversion to ships, Garrick had been loath to captain a vessel again. But as Emaline's confidence had grown beneath Patience's tutelage, the trips had become longer and more elaborate. Constance had grown quite fond of receiving envelopes with exotic addresses or packages with foreign surprises.

Constance set the cake on the last spare bit of space on

the table, then frowned. "Don't tell me you didn't bring your little boy, Patience."

"Garrick has him. When he saw your husbands on the portico—"

"I sense a conspiracy," Felicity murmured, dipping a finger into one of the blobs of frosting on Emaline's cake. "I've never known men to be too obliging about watching children unless they have some sort of ulterior motive."

Patience shrugged. "Garrick informed me that this was a *ladies'* tea, and men—including little boys—were not allowed. Of course, Emaline argued that she wasn't included in such a category, but Garrick further clarified that only the 'Pedigrue Women,' as he calls us, were invited. He also mentioned something about a surprise . . ."

The last word trailed invitingly into the ensuing expectancy.

"What sort of surprise?" Constance immediately questioned, causing both of her sisters to laugh.

"I do believe that Constance has shed her stuffiness since marrying a man who owns a burlesque house, Patience," Felicity pronounced archly.

Constance huffed in indignation. "I have never been . . . *stuffy* in any way."

Felicity licked her finger, then coughed and grabbed the glass of cool ice water next to her plate.

Patience offered her younger sister an "I told you so" look before saying to Constance, "You have always been completely insufferable." She adopted a sing-song tone and began to mimic the instructions Constance had once offered by rote, "Felicity and Patience, you must never fidget in church . . ."

". . . run in public . . ." Felicity added.

". . . scuff your shoes . . ."

". . . use slang . . ."

". . . speak above a murmur . . ."

". . . forget your handkerchief . . ."

". . . or be in any way common!" both women finished together.

Constance frowned at her sisters in mock disdain—even though everything they said was true. She'd always been a stickler for society's mores.

Until Gideon Payne had taught her that such notions could be incredibly limiting.

"And always, *always* wear your long woolens," a voice said from the door.

The women at the table looked up in surprise. Louise Chevalier Pedigrue Renoir had joined them.

"As I recall, that was the phrase you always associated with Constance whenever you spoke of her to me," Louise said, amusement sparkling from her eyes and her arms opening wide to embrace her girls as they ran to greet her.

"Finally, I have you all together," Louise whispered as she hugged them as a group, then held each daughter again, one at a time.

Constance's throat tightened with sentimental tears as Felicity, Patience, and Louise made their way to the table—all of them talking at once in order to catch up on the latest news.

"Come along, Constance. We need to hear all about your work as Gideon's assistant," Patience prompted at the first lull in conversation.

As they settled into their seats, Constance began to pour tea. Of them all, she didn't try to speak yet. She was much more interested in listening to all the news her mother and sisters had brought with them. Tales of the wilds of the Canadian frontier, exotic seaports, and the glamour of Europe. And with each report, she found herself studying her family, noting all of the changes that had occurred since she'd seen them last.

Felicity, impulsive, irrepressible Felicity, had become a woman since she and Constance had parted. She positively beamed with energy, her eyes alight with happiness and love—as well as a certain serenity that Constance had never seen in Felicity's features before.

Patience was still vivacious and spontaneous, but she'd developed a sense of confidence that she'd never displayed before. As she spoke of her husband, her sister-in-law, and her son, her features filled with pride and unabashed devotion.

And Louise . . .

When Constance had bid good-bye to Louise soon after wedding Gideon, Louise had still seemed unsure of her place in her daughters' lives. Yet, after months of correspondence with her "girls," she was secure in their love and comfortable in her role as their mother.

So much had changed, Constance realized with a rush of emotion. Alexander Pedigrue had done everything in his power to punish them all. He'd denied Louise the opportunity to see her daughters grow, then had done his best to punish his children for the "sins" of their mother. He'd taught Constance to ignore her own passionate nature, caused Patience to fear a man's domination, and made Felicity deny her flair for adventure.

But, one by one, the Pedigrue sisters had foiled his plans. They had survived the severity of his moods, the limitations of his rules, and the joylessness of his existence. Then, through the intervention of a mother, whom they had been told had abandoned them, each woman had found a life beyond her wildest imaginings, a husband, a home, and children.

Settling into her own chair, Constance placed a hand to her stomach. Instinctively, she knew that this moment would always linger in her memory as one of the happiest and most rewarding.

"I have a pair of wonderful surprises for you, my sweets," Louise proclaimed, interrupting Constance's reverie.

She jumped to her feet and hurried to the door that remained ajar. Ducking outside, she returned, carrying a simple rosewood case.

Constance exchanged glances with her sisters. What could their mother have brought that could add any more pleasure to this reunion?

"As you well know, I have had a contingent of lawyers contesting your father's will," Louise said as she set the case on the table.

Taking a small key from her pocket, she opened the box and sighed as she pondered the contents. "I have mixed news, I am afraid. The courts have overturned Alexander's will." Louise's lips twitched in obvious amusement. "My lawyers were able to prove quite easily that his treatment of his daughters demonstrated an incipient . . . madness, if you will."

Felicity gasped. "You had them declare Papa mentally unbalanced?"

Louise's smile became positively sly. "I'm afraid so."

Patience clapped in delight, commenting, "Father is probably spinning in his grave right now."

"It serves him right," Constance mumbled, then shrugged when the others stared at her for speaking ill of the dead—something she wouldn't have dreamed of doing before meeting Gideon Payne.

"Brava, sister," Felicity said, lifting her teacup in salute.

"In any event," Louise interrupted, bringing the conversation back to the matter at hand, "the courts have decided to honor a will Alexander drafted long before he abducted you." A hardness entered her tone as she took a bundle of legal papers from the box. "In that will, Alexander left everything to me with implicit instructions that his estate be divided equally among my surviving heirs."

Constance stared at her mother, bemused. She and her sisters had all failed to live up to the exacting requirements their father had stipulated. Not one of them had been awarded the yearly pittance he'd offered as an inheritance.

As for herself, Constance had never regretted the loss—and she was sure her sisters hadn't either. Even so, there was a sense of poetic justice to the overturning of his will. Constance, her sisters, and their mother had managed to thwart Alexander Pedigrue's machinations, including, it would seem, his last decree for their futures.

"Do you mean to tell us," Felicity said slowly, "that we are about to share Papa's estate?"

"His *entire* estate?" Patience clarified, her own eyes wide. "The *entire* Pedigrue fortune."

"Ye-es . . ." Louise said, drawing the word out, ". . . and no."

At the hesitant disclaimer, Constance stared at the legal documents as if they held the answers to the universe.

Louise took a deep breath. "You see, the wording was very explicit, and my lawyers were unable to change one small detail that your father insisted upon." She propped the papers against the teapot in the center of the table. "Your father insisted that his estate be divided among all *my* surviving heirs."

Constance darted a questioning look at Felicity and Patience, but they seemed as confused as she by their mother's statement.

"I was never much good at explaining such things in words," Louise muttered. "Etienne," she called toward the door. "Why don't you bring my girls their second surprise?" Clasping her hands together, Louise offered all of them a nervous smile and said, "I picked up a little something for you all in Paris while we were visiting Etienne's family, and I hope you aren't disappointed."

Etienne poked his head inside the room—and for the first time since meeting her mother's strong, indomitable bodyguard, Constance thought the man appeared slightly ill at ease. But then again, Etienne didn't strike her as the sort of gentleman who frequented ladies' tea parties for anything other than professional reasons.

"You're sure?" he inquired, his tone so doting, so unlike a bodyguard, that Constance lifted her napkin to her lips to hide a smile.

"Yes, *cheri*. I think now is the perfect time for such a presentation."

He swung the door wide, exposing a huge basket and revealing that he had not been waiting alone in the hall. Behind him stood Gideon and Logan—who stood holding tiny Louis in the crook of his arm. To one side stood Garrick with baby Thomas, the massive Dalton family sheepdog, Oscar, and Emaline, who hopped from foot to foot in obvious excitement.

"This must be a special surprise indeed to have gathered such an audience," Patience commented wryly.

"Etienne and I think so," Louise said. "And we hope all of you will, too." She touched Constance's arm. "My dear, will you please do the honor?"

Not sure what "honor" she was meant to perform, Constance stood and moved toward Etienne and the basket. As she drew closer, her brow furrowed. A porcelain doll had been placed in a nest of silk and lace.

A doll? What an odd choice of gift for three grown daughters. The toy must have been incredibly expensive for her mother to buy only *one* doll for all three . . .

Constance gasped.

The doll had moved.

"Mother?" she whispered in disbelief, turning to Louise for confirmation.

Louise nodded, her eyes brimming with sudden tears.

"Oh, Mama." Constance tentatively reached into the basket, sliding her hands beneath the warm, very real, unmistakably feminine baby.

Immediately, the infant wriggled, sighed, then offered an irritated grunt at being disturbed.

Biting her lip to keep from blurting a response that might startle the babe even more, Constance lifted the bundle clear of the basket, holding it gently against her body. The baby stretched, yawned, then opened one eye.

Two. Brilliant blue eyes that were nearly identical to Louise's.

Constance turned so that her sisters could see what she held.

"If my instincts are serving me properly, I believe we have just been informed that we will be sharing our newfound fortune with a little sister," she said, the words nearly reverent as Constance looked down at the tiny pink face with its brilliant blue eyes.

Pushing the bonnet aside, Constance caught a glimpse of apricot-colored fuzz. She would have red hair. Just like Patience's.

Constance held out a finger for the baby to grasp. Such long, delicate hands. Just like Felicity's.

Then she smiled, tracing a stubborn little chin.

*Just like mine.*

"Etienne and I have named her Hope," Louise offered, her voice husky with unshed tears.

Etienne set the basket on the floor and moved to take his wife's hand. His tender gesture allowed her to contain her emotions and continue.

"After searching for my three girls for so long, I'd begun to despair of ever being truly happy again. But Etienne convinced me that somehow, some way, love would work its magic and we would find one another one day."

Louise kissed Etienne's hand, and Constance was sure her stepfather blushed.

When we were finally reunited as a family, I thought my happiness complete . . ." This time, it was Louise's turn to blush. "Until I discovered that Etienne and I weren't quite in our dotage."

Soft laughter accompanied her statement.

"To my immense gratitude and delight," Louise continued, "God has seen fit to grant me another opportunity to see not only my own child grow but two fine grand—"

"Three," Constance blurted, then felt a heat rise in her

own cheeks. Catching Gideon's grin, she explained, "Come Christmas, you will have three grandchildren to spoil."

The room dissolved into chaos as everyone began to talk at once. All plans for a "ladies'" tea party were forgotten as the men raided the refreshments and the women took charge of the babies.

At one point, when Felicity demanded a turn at holding Hope, Constance stepped back so that she could watch the ever-changing scene—one that was far more satisfying than any drama because it was real.

"Happy?" Gideon murmured, cupping her shoulders and drawing her to him, her spine resting against his chest.

"Immeasurably," she replied, her voice low and meant for his ears alone.

"Love me?" he asked, using the familiar prompt to a ritual begun the day they were married.

"More than ever."

"Are you certain you aren't disappointed?"

"About what?"

"Sharing your inheritance."

She waved aside that silly notion. "As far as I'm concerned, the money will be kept in trust for our own heirs."

Gideon's arms wrapped around her waist, and his hands rested tenderly upon the slight swell hidden beneath the gathers of her skirts.

"I'm sure Erastus will be very grateful."

Constance frowned. "We are not naming our child Erastus."

"Rufus?"

"No."

"Maitlin?"

"Never."

"But Maitlin is a wonderful name. It's a strong name for a boy."

"Not one of mine," she retorted. "Besides, our child will be a girl, and I will not have our daughter—"

"Son."

"Daughter," she repeated, "named after a fabric supplier."

"We could receive an extra discount on all our velvet curtains for the new theater in Chicago."

"I don't care."

"Then what name have you chosen?"

In the past, when Gideon had teased her with his impossible collection of names, she had refused to play his game. But this time, quite seriously, she responded, "I would like to name her Joy."

Gideon did not immediately respond, and when she looked up at him, it was to find his eyes rich with love and gratitude. "I would like that very much."

He bent to kiss her cheek, then whispered in her ear, "You and the child you carry have made my own joy complete."

"As have you, love," Constance whispered, her voice trembling with emotion. "As have you . . ."